THE PROMISE OF PAIN

THE PROMISE OF PAIN

DAVID PENNY

THE THOMAS BERRINGTON
HISTORICAL MYSTERIES

The Red Hill

Moorish Spain, 1482. English surgeon Thomas Berrington is asked to investigate a series of brutal murders in the palace of al-Hamra in Granada.

Breaker of Bones

Summoned to Cordoba to heal a Spanish prince, Thomas Berrington and his companion, the eunuch Jorge, pursue a killer who re-makes his victims with his own crazed logic.

The Sin Eater

In Granada Helena, the concubine who once shared Thomas Berrington's bed, is carrying his child, while Thomas tracks a killer exacting revenge on evil men.

The Incubus

A mysterious killer stalks the alleys of Ronda. Thomas Berrington, Jorge and Lubna race to identify the culprit before more victims have their breath stolen.

The Inquisitor

In a Sevilla on the edge of chaos death stalks the streets. Thomas Berrington and his companions tread a dangerous path between the Inquisition, the royal palace, and a killer.

The Fortunate Dead

As a Spanish army gathers outside the walls of Malaga, Thomas Berrington hunts down a killer who threatens more than just strangers.

The Promise of Pain

When revenge is not enough. Thomas Berrington flees to the high mountains, only to be drawn back by those he left behind.

PLACE NAMES

For many of the Spanish cities and towns which lay beyond the boundary of Andalusia the current Spanish name has been used, except where the town had a significant Moorish past, such as Cordoba and Seville.

I have conducted research on the naming of places within Andalusia but have taken a few liberties to make the names easier to pronounce for a modern day audience. Where I have been unable to find reference to the Moorish name of a place I have made one up.

---

al-Andalus: Andalusia
al-Basharāt: the Alpujarra region south of the Sierra Nevada
al-Mariyya: Almeria
Gharnatah: Granada
Ixbilya: Sevilla
Malaka: Malaga
Qurtuba: Cordoba
Sholayr: Sierra Nevada mountains

SPAIN 1488

THE ALPUJARRA REGION, ANDALUCIA

CHAPTER ONE

When Thomas Berrington woke tears had frozen his eyes shut. It was not the first time such had happened since he came to the high Sholayr, and he was sure it would not be the last. He lifted his hands and laid the palms across his eyes, waiting for their meagre warmth to melt the ice, broken tears tracking down his face as the ice gave up its reluctant hold. He had woken to find himself still alive, unsure if that was for the good or not.

The half-ruined hut he had made his home for the last ten days offered little shelter. The roof was intact at one end only. A crumbling chimney at the other offered a place to make a fire, as long as you didn't mind getting wet when it rained or snowed. Thomas thought he might make a fire today, but hadn't the day before, or on any of the other days he had been there. He might hunt today but had not the day before. He had gone to sleep hungry, the pain in his belly a familiar companion. Cold and hunger and constant pain had ceased to concern him. He almost welcomed it for the numbness it brought, which washed away memory.

As he waited for sight to return an internal image lit a trail through his mind—of his wife Lubna lying in a court-

1

yard, and he jerked his head as if movement could repel it. The last remnant of ice snapped from his lids and he opened his eyes to discover a grey pre-dawn, sunrise still some way off. He leaned into a corner of the wall and tried to think of nothing. Failed as memories crowded in, stalking his waking hours as well as his dreams. However far he ran, however high he climbed, he knew there could be no escape. Lubna was dead ... stolen from him. No, not stolen. He had abandoned her at the moment she needed him most. She died because of his failure.

He stood with a jerk, angry at himself, and walked outside, averting his gaze from what hung from the stoutest rafter.

Round-headed pines whispered a soft song in response to the wind. Snow and ice crackled beneath his bare feet. On the mountain far to the east, the first promise of coming day caught against snow-capped peaks, painting them blood red. When Thomas looked down the slope, past shattered rocks, he saw a lone figure climbing toward him. He knew who it was. He had always known who it was, for the man had been tracking him for days.

Thomas perched on a rounded rock and waited.

He had stopped trying to escape his pursuer, though knew if he had wanted he could have eluded him, never to be found. The decision to allow himself to be caught puzzled him. It augured redemption, and he was sure redemption was not what he sought. He welcomed pain as his due, as all he deserved. He waited, watching the figure climb the stone-shattered slope. Let him come. Let the world beyond these cold peaks find him, for all the good it would do.

Jorge Olmos stepped onto the narrow ledge which fronted the hut, breathing hard. "By all the Gods, Thomas, but you're a hard man to find."

Thomas stared at him, saying nothing.

"And it's good to see you too, Jorge. Thank you for coming to rescue me."

Thomas turned his gaze away. Retreating shadows cut the valleys and ridges that tumbled to where the sea lay, grey and misted. He studied the play of light and dark, holding the words he wanted to say inside. He tried to think of nothing, tried not to think of love and loss and friendship, but he knew it would make no difference to Jorge. It never had.

"Do you have any food? I'm starving. I set out hours ago and haven't eaten since yesterday morning." He dropped the sack he carried on his back, a self-built monstrosity of sailcloth and rope that looked heavy. "I have a little bread in here. It's stale but you don't look as if you'll care." Jorge cocked his head. "Have you eaten anything at all the last six months?"

"I'm still here, aren't I?" Thomas hadn't meant to speak, but Jorge could always sneak past his defences. He had loved the man once. Loved him like his own brother … but no, he wouldn't let his mind go there. Any love he might once have felt had been scourged from his soul.

"I'll light a fire, shall I? You're sure you have no food?"

Thomas shook his head, making no move from his seat. He watched as Jorge lugged the pack inside—though inside was barely a concept for what remained of the hut—and pulled at the ties until he could reach inside.

"I like what you've done to the place." Jorge tugged at the noose hanging from the rafter, setting it swinging. "Do you plan on using this?" He glanced up to where sky showed instead of a roof. "It might not be such a good idea, you know. You're more likely to bring the whole place down on top of you." He gave a half smile. "No doubt kill yourself, one way or another. Belia sends her love, by the way. Will too. Amal would if she could talk."

"You're making up for it, I see," Thomas said. "The same

as always. Why did you come?" He stared at the noose, which continued to swing softly, calling to him. It had been calling to him for over a month as he trekked higher and higher into the flanks of the mighty Sholayr. At every place he stopped, if he could, he tied the noose as a reminder that if this life became too much to bear, there was a solution to his pain. So far he had managed to ignore its call, but wondered how much longer he might do so.

"Why do you think I came?" said Jorge. He had found a stack of wood piled beside the fireplace and knelt to arrange twigs above a handful of dry grass and shavings. He looked around, rose, and checked in the few places remaining in what was left of the hut until he found a flint. He knelt once more and sparked the shavings, blew until a flame appeared. He waited, adding larger pieces of wood as the fire caught. There had been a chimney once, but now only the upper part remained. Smoke rose to be tugged away by a rising wind as the day came awake around them.

"If I knew why you were here I wouldn't have had to ask," Thomas said.

"You've grown stupid then, have you? I suppose it had to happen one day. All that thinking has worn your brain out. I told you it was dangerous."

Thomas half turned despite himself. He watched as Jorge drew out a quarter loaf of dark Spanish bread and laid it on a flat stone beside the fireplace. Despite the broken roof and walls Thomas had turned the ruin into some kind of home. He was surprised how it had become so.

Jorge fed the fire with more sticks, before tearing lumps of bread off and spearing them with a sliver of wood to toast into edible submission.

Thomas almost smiled at the domestic mundanity as Jorge sprinkled oil and herbs on the bread. The aroma made his mouth water, before he managed to shut his thoughts down and set his expression. He knew it had been a mistake to allow Jorge to catch up with him, but he had begun to believe it was that or use the noose.

Thomas wondered when the decision to choose life over death had come, or if it even had. Ever since he had walked away from Malaka, almost every moment of every day had been filled with an aching emptiness. His sleep, when he managed to find any, was shattered by dreams that only made the pain worse. He had lost people before. People close to him. But those losses were nothing compared to the void left by Lubna. Not even the theft of Eleanor, snatched from him when they both had little more than seventeen years, had affected him in this way, though at the time he believed her loss would remain with him forever. Now he hadn't thought of Eleanor in years, her image only conjured in weak comparison.

Lubna had been his wife. She had carried their child when her life was stolen, and Thomas had not been there to save her.

He wondered where Jorge had learned to cook. Had he learned to cook? He was making a reasonable show of knowing what he was doing, the sight even stranger than the thoughts Thomas harboured. The breeze brought a scent of warm bread to him and sparked a painful cramp in his stomach, which had not tasted food in ... He tried to remember when last he ate, and couldn't.

"How fares Belia?"

Jorge looked up, as if surprised he wasn't alone.

"She is well."

"And..." Thomas's voice drifted away, his mind doing the same. He pictured Will, his body loose as he lay against Lubna, and his chest hitched. He wiped at fresh tears and breathed deep. "And Will?"

"He misses you, of course. As does Amal."

"Amal doesn't even know who I am."

"Will talks to her of you. Not everything he says is true, but most is."

"She is too young to understand."

"How can we know for sure? She smiles when he tells his tales, so I think she does. She is proud of her father. You need to come home, Thomas."

"Why? There is nothing there for me anymore."

"There is Will, and there is Amal. And there are others who love you. Belia and me, and Olaf."

"Except you are here. Why have you abandoned them?"

"Usaden is their protection. A better protection than I could ever offer."

"He is there and Lubna is not. You were meant to take her to safety and Usaden was meant to protect her."

Jorge fed more wood on the fire, even though there was nothing left to cook. Thomas watched his breath come hard, his body stiffen with anger, and knew he had gone too far. Knew he would no doubt do the same again. Lubna's death wasn't Usaden's fault, or Jorge's. It was his.

"Is Olaf back on the hill?"

Jorge nodded. He made a show of checking the bread, as if it was some fine banquet he had prepared.

Thomas turned away to the endless vista of hills, the sky distant and cloudless as the day took relentless hold. He forgot about Jorge as he sank back into his own misery. To one side the peaks of the Sholayr sparked white with snow. It had fallen here a few days before, and Thomas had wondered if the cold might steal what little spark of life remained in him. But he had been unlucky and woken the next day. Morning after morning came, an unending tide of pain with nothing to offer but more of the same.

He had no recollection of how many days or weeks or months had passed since Malaka fell, taking the life of Lubna with it. He recalled that when Abbot Mandana and his son Pedro Guerrero—a secret he hadn't known of until

6

that day— stormed the Alkhazabah, it had been summer. Now it was late winter, so not a year, but close to half a year. And still there was no lessening of the ice gripping his heart. He didn't think there ever would be. The pain was his punishment. It was all he deserved. It hadn't been Jorge's fault, or Usaden's, or Olaf's or anyone else's. It had been Thomas who killed her. Thomas who abandoned Lubna to follow a quest for justice that once burned so bright within him. It had been a fruitless quest. He had thwarted a plot to steal Malaka's gold, and in doing so lost the person who mattered most to him. Even then, Fernando, king of Spain, had stolen away more than half the riches of the richest city in the land. Now it would be used to continue the fight against Thomas's beloved al-Andalus—the fight against a way of life he had made his own. Except his life was now forfeit, for there was nothing left for him to live for.

Except Will. And Amal.

Jorge was right. Thomas's children needed a father. But was Thomas the man for that job, or would Jorge not make a better replacement?

The man came, bringing the scent of toasted bread. He pushed Thomas aside so he could sit on the same rock, even though there were others nearby. He handed a lump of warm bread to Thomas and said, "Eat."

Thomas stared at the bread and his stomach cramped. He thought he might try some in a moment.

"How can I eat? I accepted joy into my life and then destroyed it. I may never eat again."

"Don't act like an idiot." Jorge spoke with his mouth full. "Or a victim."

"What am I if not a victim? I had a wife, a son, a daughter about to be born. Instead she had to be ripped from her dead mother's belly. I loosened the ties on my heart and allowed joy to enter, only to have it dashed away." He looked at the bread again and knew Jorge was right but was unwilling to give up his cloak of misery yet. He took a bite, saliva flooding his mouth, and was sure he groaned.

"Will and Amal need you."

Was that enough? Thomas tore another bite from the bread. It was tough, tasteless, but he could recall no better meal since he had walked out from Malaka half a year before. He had been filled with rage that day, but somewhere over the days between he had lost it. He had no wish to find it again, for the rage seemed to be a part of someone else, someone he had once been and was no more.

"Who killed her?" Thomas asked.

"Don't think on it."

"I can think of nothing else. I need to know. Who struck the blow? And Yusuf—the last hope for al-Andalus —who struck him down?" He glanced at Jorge, surprised at his placid face, surprised he was not also angry. "Usaden was there. He might have told me, but if he did I have forgotten."

"It wasn't Mandana," Jorge said

"Do you speak of it between you?"

"Now and then, of course we do. Usaden feels a measure of responsibility. He's a good man."

Thomas nodded but said nothing, waiting.

"Mandana ignored the small gathering in the courtyard and went in search of riches. It was why he was there. Another group of soldiers came, led by someone Usaden didn't know, not then. But you would have."

"You make no sense." Thomas ate more of the bread, each mouthful spreading a sneaking warmth through his body.

"Usaden said they were led by a young man. Tall and handsome. He said it was the handsome nature that

8

confused him. Only later when he considered it more deeply did it come to him. He said it wasn't Mandana who struck the blow that killed Lubna, but this other man."

Thomas steeled himself to think back to his time in Malaka: the day a tall man, a handsome man, had come to the Infirmary carrying his already dead wife in his arms. How he had raged, blaming Thomas and Lubna for not being able to save her. And another day, when chaos reigned. The day Lubna died. He had made efforts to expunge it from his mind but failed. Of course he had failed. Forgetting that day would mean forgetting Lubna.

Mandana had come to the Alkhazabah with soldiers, but had he been their leader? It was a long time ago and much of that day had slipped from Thomas's memory—but the other man had been with Mandana, close to him outside the fortress walls.

"You are thinking," said Jorge. "I can see it on your face. What is it?"

"Yes, I know the man. His name is Pedro Guerrero." Thomas's chest shuddered when he breathed in. "He hates me, hated Lubna, because he blamed us both for the death of his wife."

"You make no sense."

"One of us must have told you. It was before the Spanish came, before we moved into the city. Guerrero claimed he had been out in a small boat, his pregnant wife waiting on the beach. She was attacked by some men. Violated. Left for dead. He saw it all, he said, but accepts no blame to himself, even though he left her there on her own." Thomas shook his head. "I believe he was spying on the city's defences for the Spanish."

"I think I remember you telling us," said Jorge.

"We managed to save the child," Thomas said, "but he blamed us for that as well. He should have killed me, because it was mostly my work that day, but he was a coward and took the life of the woman I loved. Tried to take the child she carried as well." Thomas looked up. "I came here to find him, but I let myself sink into my own misery. That stops today."

"He could be anywhere in Spain," said Jorge.

"I don't care where he is—there is nowhere far enough to escape my justice."

CHAPTER TWO

It wasn't Jorge but his tasteless bread that made Thomas find his boots and lead them away from the ruined house. Unfed, his hunger had grown quiet. Now, teased by the merest scrap of food, it rose like a wild beast, demanding more.

"Where are we going?" Jorge ran to catch up. "All my things are back there. We're not going home, are we?"

"All your things?" Thomas said. "Is there anything you care about leaving behind?"

"Only you."

Thomas shook his head. "I want you to show me where you got the bread. I assume they have other food as well?"

"Have you got money?" asked Jorge.

"No, but you will have, won't you?"

Thomas was aware he must have eaten at some point because he was still alive, but he had no recollection of doing so. He had no recollection of much since leaving Malaka with fire in his heart—a fire which had cooled and then died, like his heart had died. Hate, like love, was an emotion he no longer had the energy to maintain. Despair had become his friend. Day after day he awoke disappointed to discover his body had refused to let go its tenuous hold on life, but still unwilling to end it himself.

"The village is a day away," said Jorge. "I expect I can loan you enough so we can go there and eat food cooked for us and sleep in soft beds with beautiful women." He started down the slope and picked up a track that led south and west—a track Thomas hadn't even known was there.

"You already have a beautiful woman," he said.

"A man can never have too many beautiful women."

"Even a man lacking balls?" The comment was unfair, but Thomas knew he had lost what little social graces he might once have possessed, and there had been few enough of those to start with.

Jorge grinned. "Oh, most women find that an advantage, once they get used to the idea. There are many women, both young and old, who consider me handsome."

"Blind women?"

"Possibly." Jorge smiled, his features seeming to glow. "Ah, Thomas, the women of the harem. I thought I had witnessed beauty before, but I was wrong." He turned to look at Thomas. "I have you to thank for my blessed life." He reached out and touched Thomas's arm—a brief contact, come and gone in a moment.

The touch of Jorge's finger sparked a warmth in Thomas that spread through him. "I unmanned you—that is nothing to thank me for."

"Oh, but it is. You saved me. What life was there for a boy on the streets of Qurtuba? I would have ended up servicing men, or joining the army or the church, and you know I am no fighter, and certainly no believer in God. I would have died young. You both saved my life and gave me an honourable profession to which my skills—the few I possess—are perfectly suited."

"What brings you here then, chasing me?"

Jorge smiled. "Love, of course."

Thomas would have made a dismissive sound, but just then they crossed a low ridge and he saw the village Jorge was taking them to appear far in the distance. It was a long way off as yet, but a destination all the same, and Thomas had not had a destination for months. He wondered if it was a good idea to accept one now.

Good idea or not, as the day progressed the village grew closer. The goat track they followed widened. Cultivated fields appeared to either side, almost vertical, each small patch of carefully nurtured ground barely a foot wide, but still capable of growing a crop. Thomas saw peas and beans, turnips, olives, almonds, mulberry and sugar cane. The track became more distinct, leading to an isolated farmhouse where goats grazed on the hillside behind. There was no-one to be seen, but a curl of smoke rose from the chimney. The track ran close to the door, and as they approached a black-and-grey dog came running out, barking wildly.

Jorge leaped backwards, but Thomas stayed where he was. He took in the look of the dog and held out a hand.

"Kill it!" said Jorge.

"It's not going to hurt us."

"You, maybe. Dogs hate me."

"I wonder why that is." Thomas went on one knee. The dog continued its constant barking, but its tail began to wag from side to side. "He's more afraid of us than we are of him."

"Speak for yourself," said Jorge.

Thomas stood and moved to one side, but the dog stayed where it was in front of the door.

"He's protecting the house," Thomas said.

"He's welcome to it."

Thomas glanced at the sky. The day was growing late. "Perhaps we can buy some food from whoever lives here."

"I can buy some food, you mean," said Jorge.

As Thomas approached the dog's snarls increasing, but when he came within touching distance the sound faded into a rumbling growl. Thomas reached out and touched its head, knowing it wouldn't bite him, though how he knew he couldn't say for sure. He had owned dogs when he was a boy in Lemster but never since, and he wondered why not. He liked them. And it seemed they must like him because the dog turned its head and licked his hand.

"Kin!" A voice called from within and in an instant the dog turned and trotted inside. There came the sound of conversation and then a man appeared in the doorway, a pitchfork in his hand. "What are you here for? There's only me and my wife, nobody here you want."

Thomas wondered who the man thought they were. "We want to buy a little food, if you have some to spare."

"Food?" The man looked Thomas up and down, then applied the same inspection to Jorge. "You look hungry, yes. Your companion not so much."

"But I have the money," said Jorge. He smiled, and Thomas saw a softening of the farmer's features. The dog he had called Kin came and stood beside him, waiting.

The farmer looked beyond Thomas and Jorge, searching for something.

"You're not them, are you."

"Not who?"

"Doesn't matter, only that you're not them." He turned and shouted to someone inside. "Tell Luis he can come out of the cellar, then go see if there's enough food for two more." He turned back and addressed Jorge. "No payment necessary. We help each other out in these parts." He looked at them for a while before coming to the decision Jorge was the one he needed to talk with. "Are you lost?" He glanced at Thomas. "You friend looks ill."

"He's been better," said Jorge. "He grieves for his wife."

14

"Sorry to hear that." The words were still addressed to Jorge, as if Thomas wasn't there. "Recent?"

Thomas turned away and walked to the edge of the flat land where the house perched. He stared down at the distant village and wondered if they could reach it before nightfall. The ground looked rough, but there was a twisting path that descended to a wider track. If he possessed a little more enthusiasm he would have started down. Instead he stood, waiting to be told what to do. The conversation between the farmer and Jorge washed past him without recognition. He was thinking of Lubna again, as if Jorge's presence had breached the dam in his mind to release a flood. Thomas was fighting not to let it sweep him away.

He jerked when a hand touched his shoulder, surprised when he turned to see two other people standing beside the farmer. The first was a woman of the same age, not so much younger than Thomas himself. Both were thin, and he worried they were taking food from their mouths. The third figure was a man close to twenty years, taller than his father—if that's who he was—but with the good fortune to have inherited his mother's looks. A handsome young man, broad-shouldered, with intelligent eyes.

"This is Pedro and Elvira," said Jorge, introducing them. "And their son Luis."

"What were you doing in the cellar?" Thomas directed the question at Luis, and saw his mother tense.

"They say we're welcome to share their meal," said Jorge, as if Thomas hadn't spoken. "And we can sleep in the barn. There's a place above the goats that's dry and warmer than the hillside."

Thomas nodded, losing interest—he was trying to work out why he felt so detached from events around him, suspecting he had avoided human company for too long and could no longer bother even with the merest civility.

He took a breath and tried to show interest, but suspected the effort failed.

Only after they had eaten broth, and a stew of goat, potatoes and some sort of green vegetable did Thomas begin to discover his manners. He asked about farming the land, curious how someone could forge a living from such inauspicious material. Pedro appeared pleased at the questions and proceeded on a long and detailed explanation of water management—which here, unlike most of the rest of Spain, consisted of how to divert too much water away rather than having too little. He then launched into a theory of terracing that Thomas allowed to wash across him. Jorge leaned toward Elvira, as always attracted to females before males, and she responded as women always did when Jorge turned his charm on them. Thomas was aware of Luis observing him, but the young man said little, only adding information when prompted by his father.

Sweet, dark wine was brought to the table and drunk.

Going outside was a shock after the warmth inside the house, and Thomas drew his robe close around himself. Pedro and Elvira remained inside while Luis showed them the platform in the barn. Fenced goats beneath filled the air with their stink. Jorge climbed the ladder, but Thomas went outside to breathe clearer air and stood where he had before, staring down into the darkness where an occasional yellow glow of lamplight marked where the village lay. He heard Luis join him and smiled.

"They send me to the cellar when strangers come," said Luis, finally answering the question Thomas had put.

"They don't like strangers, do they?"

"Not in these parts, not this past half year. I tell them we must fight but they send me to hide. Every time they send me to hide in the cellar."

"Away from the strangers?"

"Have you fought?" said Luis. "Your friend is big, but

soft. You're not soft, are you? You have fought. You've been a soldier of some kind."

"Of some kind, yes."

"I thought so. You wouldn't hide in a cellar."

"Sometimes hiding is the sensible decision. You can't fight everyone, not if there are too many." He glanced at Luis. "Who are they?"

"You're right, there are too many of them. A dozen the last time they came. Soldiers."

"Why do you hide and not your parents?"

"They're old."

Thomas almost laughed, would have if the sensation had not been so unfamiliar. "Your father is younger than I am, your mother a couple of years younger again, isn't she?"

"She likes your friend," said Luis.

"Everyone likes Jorge. Women especially."

"The soldiers only take men of fighting age, those older than fourteen and younger than forty—sometimes less if they are not strong. They want men who can fight."

"Why?"

"How would I know that? I hide when they come."

The dog, Kin, came out and stood between them. Thomas wanted to stroke its head but didn't because it was Luis's dog, but when he made no move Thomas dropped his hand to the hard, ridged skull and rested it there. The dog was tall, so he didn't have to reach far.

"He likes you," said Luis.

"Dogs know people better than other people do. He knows I like him. I had dogs like Kin when I was a boy. Hunting dogs. I wager he can chase down a hare."

Luis chuckled. "Oh, he can do that. Where are you from? Not around here."

"Gharnatah."

This time Luis laughed. "No, you're not."

"I am now. Before that, a long time before, I lived in England."

"Where is England?"

"A long way north. Cold. Wet. Not somewhere you want to go."

"Where are you and Jorge going?" asked Luis. "Are you going back to Gharnatah? Can I come with you?" His head moved, but if he was trying to look at the land his father owned the night was too dark. "There are two people I would not wish to leave behind, but they would come—I know they would."

"You father wouldn't leave this land."

"Not them," said Luis.

Thomas smiled, wondering why he did so—suspicious of the hint of happiness. "A girl?"

"Yes, a girl, and another. Dana carries–" Luis cut himself off. Thomas knew what he had been about to say, but made no mention of it.

"I'm going to bed," he said.

"I hope the goats let you sleep."

"I don't sleep much anymore."

CHAPTER THREE

Thomas let his eyes track along the hillside, colourless in the pre-dawn light. Tatters of mist hung where a stream carried snow-melt from the peaks of the Sholayr. The village lay nestled where two streams combined, not quite a river but on the way to becoming one. The flat land around the houses had been tilled to grow crops, a process Thomas now knew more about than he wanted after Pedro's instruction over their meal. On the hillsides grew olives, almonds, oranges, lemons and limes. It was a good place to live, isolated from the war that was destroying Thomas's beloved al-Andalus—insular to some but welcoming of others. They would be suspicious of strangers.

Kin padded from the barn where he had slept—where he probably slept every night—and came to Thomas, who wondered if Will would like a dog. And, because he had thought of Will, he tried to think of Amal too, but no image came—only one of Lubna when she was younger, when she had come to his house as a servant. He had liked her then, loved her before long, but she had not shared his bed until two years after she first lived under his roof. He had slept with her sister then, the beautiful Helena who was now held captive by Muhammed, Sultan of Gharnatah.

Thomas shook his head, trying to dislodge the memories and failing. The sound of a hacking cough from behind was a welcome distraction, and he turned to see Pedro bring up an impressive gobbet and spit to one side. The farmer raised a hand in greeting, turned, and walked around the side of the house to start work. It seemed as if another meal would not be on offer, so Thomas went to wake Jorge. He was still asleep, lying on his back with one arm across his face. Thomas watched him, sensing a swelling of emotion he directed away from his conscious mind. He knew this man better than any other in the world, liked him better than anyone now that Lubna was gone. And yes, loved him, though not in the way he knew Jorge had occasionally loved other men. The man was incapable of restraint, unable to comprehend that such a thing as restraint made sense in a world descending into chaos. Almost certainly he was right, Thomas thought. Maybe a man had to pursue whatever pleasures he could, seek happiness wherever and whenever he could find it in the time left to him. Except Thomas couldn't believe he would ever feel pleasure again. And without pleasure, without friendship and love, what was the point of life at all? He could never be like the miserable priests who considered God enough.

Thomas knelt and shook Jorge, continued to shake him as he turned over with a curse.

"Go away, it's the middle of the night."

"It's not. Time to leave these good people and start to take care of ourselves."

"I have been taking care of myself, unlike you." Jorge sat up, scratched at his head which now grew a fine head of hair. "Gods, I need to piss." He went to the edge of the platform and descended the ladder.

Thomas left him for a minute to finish, though Jorge would not have cared had he watched.

"Do we really have to go? I like Elvira."

"She's married, and her husband looks like he could tear you limb from limb without drawing sweat."

Jorge smiled. "I wasn't planning on telling him. But no mind, there'll be women in the village."

"Is there a woman in this life you don't like?" Thomas asked.

Jorge glanced at him. "Good question. I believe not, and life is none the worse for it."

"What does Belia think of your infidelities?"

"We have an arrangement. She knows she can do whatever she wishes and allows me the same. We know we are meant to be together."

"And does she lie with other men?"

"No. But she can." Jorge smiled. "She has told me she would lie with you. You offer her something I cannot."

Thomas waited, but Jorge was clearly not going to mention what it was he possessed that Belia might find attractive. Thomas knew in any case. It had been raised before by Jorge, but not by Belia. Thomas still possessed his balls. He was capable of setting a seed in a woman's belly. He knew Belia loved Will, and Amal too now, as much as if they were her own. Except they were not. Jorge had told him she would like a child of her own.

"If she asks me I will do it," Thomas said, and Jorge frowned, not aware of what thoughts ran through Thomas's mind, and then it appeared to come to him.

"Why the change of mind?"

"I have no-one to be faithful to anymore."

"Not even your pretty queen?"

"You know that my relationship with Isabel is not of that nature."

"But she would like it to be, wouldn't she? As would you."

"Don't judge all men by your own standards." There was no emotion in Thomas's voice. He didn't blame Jorge —he didn't think, or feel, anything anymore. All that remained was the pain that racked his mind and body, pain he welcomed as something to mask the greater pain threatening to engulf him.

"I'm hungry," Jorge said.

"We're both hungry, but we'll eat soon enough if we leave now."

But it was an hour before they started down the twisting path. Elvira had put out bread and cheese, much to Jorge's delight, and Luis wanted to come with them, but was told he had work to do.

"We don't need to go to the village now," said Jorge. He patted his belly as if sated.

"I thought it was you who wanted to go there. To meet these beautiful women. Besides, I'm curious about the soldiers Luis told me about."

"Come back to Gharnatah with me and forget all about this place. You don't belong here."

"I don't belong anywhere," Thomas said. "This will be a distraction. Something to pass a little time until I decide what I'm going to do with the rest of my life." Even as he spoke, the prospect of enduring more of the pain that ruled his every moment brought a sense of despair, and he wondered if he could ever be healed, or if he even wanted to be.

They passed an old man tilling a field with an azada, his

22

movement rhythmic, energy-conserving. He looked up and watched them pass, leaning on the long wooden handle. He said nothing and then, when they had passed, began to work again. Thomas thought he had the look of someone who could work all day long.

The village was no more than a half-mile distant when they passed a track that led away to the left. Thomas slowed, turned aside, not yet ready for the chaos of meeting more strangers. The track led to a clearing surrounded by the cliffs of a small quarry. A wooden hut sat near the path, but the quarry appeared to be no longer worked. The broken rock face had weathered to a faded brown.

"Why are we here?" asked Jorge.

"Curiosity."

Jorge shook his head, and Thomas knew he was right. There wasn't much here to be curious about, but he went to the hut and tried the door. Locked with a padlock that was easy enough to pick if he could be bothered. He peered through a gap in the planks but saw little. Barrels stacked one on another, some picks and iron rods and heavy mallets—the tools of trade for a quarryman. He turned away and followed Jorge, who had returned to the main track. Thomas had closed half the distance when Jorge turned and ran toward him.

"Men are coming!" Jorge tugged at Thomas's sleeve. "Hide!"

"There are men everywhere, why should we hide?"

"No, there are not. I was going to tell you, but it didn't seem the right time." Jorge pulled Thomas around behind the hut and sat with his back to the wooden wall, which creaked against his weight.

Thomas continued to stand, staring at him. He walked to the side of the hut and looked into the quarry. He could hear horses now, more than a few but no more than a score, he judged. Then voices. He stepped back so he was almost hidden by the hut, just in time as two men rode into the quarry and stopped. Their heads turned, scanning the empty clearing, then tugged at their reins and trotted away again.

Thomas sat beside Jorge. "What were you going to tell me?"

"The last two weeks when I was following you, every town and village I passed through was full of women, but no men."

"Heaven for you, I would imagine."

Jorge ignored the comment. "I asked where their menfolk were, but they wouldn't tell me. They were afraid of me. Me. Women afraid of me!" He shook his head at the unpredictability of the world. "Some places chased me away."

Thomas stood and offered his hand to Jorge, pulled him to his feet. "This is a strange country. It's like nowhere else I've been in Spain or al-Andalus. I don't even know who rules here."

"I can tell you who rules," said Jorge. "Nobody."

They reached the main track and stopped. The horsemen they had heard were at the village. A clutch of women confronted them, but the soldiers simply rode past, knocking two to the ground. Thomas watched the scuffle, his hands twitching with the need to do something. But what? He knew he no longer possessed the strength he once had ... but did the skill remain? It might be enough.

Before he could come to a decision the men re-appeared. They stopped, and their leader argued with one of the women. For a moment Thomas thought he was going to get off his horse and hit her, but instead he turned and rode away toward the quarry.

Thomas grabbed Jorge and dragged him back to the hut, crouching beside him, but nobody entered a second time, and once the sound of the horses had faded they came out again. All but one of the village women had disappeared. She stood in the sun, shading her eyes. Thomas turned and looked in the same direction, up the hill. The group of soldiers—he counted and came up with sixteen—had reached the farmhouse. The sound of clashing steel came clearly through the air, but the distance was too great to make out any details of what was happening.

Thomas started back the way they had come.

"There are too many," said Jorge.

"Pedro and his wife offered us hospitality. I won't leave them at the mercy of those men."

Jorge looked toward the village. "I should go this way to see if there's anyone who can help. At least see if they have weapons."

Thomas looked at him for a long moment before nodding. "All right, but I'm going to the farmhouse." He left Jorge standing at the entrance to the quarry and began to climb. He started at a run, but before he had gone far his lungs burned and his legs had turned to water. He slowed, plodding up the slope, knowing he was going to be too late.

CHAPTER FOUR

Thomas could do nothing, still too far away when the soldiers gathered themselves at the edge of the hillside readying to leave. One man lifted in his saddle and stared down toward the village. Thomas threw himself to one side, trying to burrow into the ground. He was afraid, a new emotion for him, and one he didn't welcome. The fear had come with the pain, and he wanted both gone.

The soldiers turned east and rode out, in no hurry. Thomas tried to see if Pedro or Luis were with them, but if they were he failed to make either out. The reason, when he reached the narrow plateau, was clear. Pedro lay on his back, arms spread, eyes wide and staring unseeing at the cloudless sky.

Thomas knelt beside him, even though he was clearly dead, and felt for a pulse in his neck. Nothing. He looked around but there was no sign of Elvira or Luis.

He found Elvira inside. He had more than half expected her to be violated, because as Jorge had said she was a handsome woman, but her clothes were intact, her limbs arranged more neatly than her husband's, a small puncture wound over her heart the only damage done her. But it was enough. Thomas closed her eyes as he had done for Pedro and began to search the small space. Someone had mentioned a cellar and it took him a while to find it, and when he did cellar was an exaggeration. There was a space below a small wooden door barely wide enough for Thomas to push his head and shoulders through. Beyond this there was enough room for one man to hide, if he was flexible enough to curl his legs to his chest. The space was empty, with no sign anyone had hidden there or been discovered and dragged out. Thomas explored the other rooms. A small bedroom contained a marital bed that would never be used again. Another, smaller room had a horse-hair mattress on the floor and a small table. Above the table was a narrow set of shelves holding notebooks and drawing materials. The table faced the single window so that light fell across it. A sheet of paper lay on the surface, the start of a sketch only half completed. Thomas turned it as a familiarity came to him, and discovered he was looking at his own face. Except the face he saw was gaunt, lacking any trace of humanity. He reached for one of the other notebooks, sure that Luis, who must have drawn the sketch, lacked in skill and had made a poor job of it. But what he saw made him realise how much he had changed, for Luis drew well.

The first book contained drawings of Pedro and Elvira, another of a girl and boy, both captured at various ages as they grew up. Thomas flicked through the pages, finding other people, drawings of animals, birds, trees. Each shone with a remarkable clarity and Thomas knew Luis had captured his true essence.

He stopped, flicked back, because there were a series of sketches different to the others. These were of the youth, older now, close to Luis's age or near enough. He was good-looking, smiling. Further on the young woman was captured, and Thomas let his breath go in a sigh and sat.

There were six sketches of her. The first showed her facing out from the paper with a challenge on her face. Three sheets further on the same challenge remained, but now Thomas saw why the expression was there. She posed naked, hands in her lap to cover her sex, her perfect breasts displayed. Whoever the girl was, she was both beautiful and wanton.

Thomas looked along the shelves. There were more notebooks, but he was reluctant to take them down. He closed the one he held, uneasy after looking at the images. The book had been in plain sight, available for Luis's parents to see if they chose to leaf through it. Thomas was sure they must have—almost any parent would. Had they approved of their son sketching a naked girl? Did they know the girl? Almost certainly.

Thomas rose and walked from the room. It was none of his business, and irrelevant to the task he had to carry out.

He went outside and searched for what he knew would be there, found an azada and took it to the vegetable plot beside the house where the soil was already loose. By the time Jorge arrived Thomas had removed his shirt and sweat streaked his chest and belly, but the hole was almost deep enough.

"Where are Elvira and Luis?" Asked Jorge, who would have seen Pedro. He stood beside the house in the shade, as if not wanting to get too close to the grave or see Pedro's body again.

"Elvira's inside," Thomas said. "There's no sign of Luis. I'm nearly finished here, but I'll need help with the bodies. I've no idea what God they followed, but if they're in the ground by sunset that should do."

Jorge looked away, not meeting Thomas's eyes. "I can't. I would help if I could, but I can't. I'm sorry, Thomas."

"Then why did you come here? What did you expect to find?" Thomas began to dig again. The ground was harder now, and he was starting to think four feet would have to be deep enough.

"What about the dog?"

"Run away, I expect. Or with Luis, hiding out somewhere."

"Luis isn't hiding," said Jorge. "He's been taken."

Thomas stopped digging again. He looked at the hole and decided it would do. He tossed the azada out and climbed after it.

"And how do you know that?"

"Jamila told me."

"Who's Jamila?"

"The woman in the village," said Jorge. "She's their leader. Only until the men return, she said, but I can tell she doesn't expect that to happen."

"What did she tell you?"

Jorge pushed away from the wall and looked into the freshly dug grave. He dragged air deep into his lungs, let it go. "All right, I'll help, and then we go to the village and Jamila can tell you everything she knows." Jorge stared at Thomas. "I think you'll want to hear what she has to say."

Thomas ignored Jorge and went inside the house. Elvira was light enough for him to lift by himself, and he carried her outside cradled in his arms and around to the newly dug grave. He knelt and lay her softly on the ground beside the hole. Pedro was heavier. Thomas took his shoulders, Jorge his feet, stumbling as he tried to help without actually looking at the body.

Thomas slid into the grave and eased Pedro to the base. He pushed him onto his side, then reached for Elvira and repeated the operation until they lay face to face. It seemed appropriate.

"Do you know any words?" he asked, once he had climbed out.

"Many, but none that will help here. I never gave much

29

attention to religion when I was a boy, and none at all since. I don't like the priests from either side."

Thomas nodded, agreeing with the sentiment, but it didn't seem right to simply push the earth back over the two of them without saying something. He searched far back in his mind and began to speak aloud. It didn't take long.

"What was that?" asked Jorge.

"English," said Thomas.

"It's an ugly language, isn't it."

"Probably the way I spoke it. It's been a while." He looked around, half expecting to see Luis coming down the hillside from where he might have watched the burial of his parents, but there was nothing. Thomas picked up the azada and began to push earth over the bodies, mounding it where there was too much.

"Will this Jamila know what God they followed?" he asked Jorge when they were finished.

"She might. She said they came down to the village now and again to buy supplies or sell animals. She told me Luis went down there more often. He was keen on one of the girls."

Thomas thought of the sketch but said nothing. It was none of his business, nor Jorge's, even though Jorge would no doubt understand what had gone on between the two better than he would himself. He turned away, a sour taste in his mouth.

The day had softened toward evening by the time they entered the village. A small party came out to greet them, or repel them. Six women, three with swords too heavy for them, the others with sickles and pikes. A pack of almost feral dogs barked and growled, bouncing on their front legs.

"We haven't come to fight you." Thomas stopped at a safe distance. "And you know Jorge."

One woman came forward, dragging the sword beside her, the tip digging into the dirt.

"That is good. So you can go on your way and leave us in peace."

"I bring news."

"We don't welcome news here. Whenever news comes it is always bad for us." She waved the hand not gripping the sword. She was younger than most of the others, and Thomas suspected Jorge would find her attractive. He assumed this was Jamila, the leader.

"We come from the farmhouse." Thomas half turned and pointed. "Pedro and Elvira have been murdered."

He watched the woman wince but suspected she must have already known. The soldiers would have been visible from here.

"I buried them, but I don't know what God they followed, if they followed one at all. I said some words, but they may have been the wrong ones."

"They will have been good enough. Are you a priest? You don't look like a priest. Are you sure you didn't kill them yourself?"

"Where is Luis?" A young woman stepped from the small group, and Thomas felt a shock of recognition run through him. She was the girl Luis had drawn. Despite the skill of the sketch, she was even more beautiful in real life. Paper and charcoal could not capture the glow of her skin, or the spark of mischief in her eyes.

"He wasn't there," Thomas said.

"And Kin?"

"Gone too. They might be hiding out."

The girl shook her head. "No—he's been taken. No doubt they killed Kin and he's lying dead somewhere up there."

"Who?" Thomas said, his question addressed to Jamila, who glanced at Jorge.

"I take it you told him nothing," she said

"I thought it would be better coming from you."

"Of course you did."

Thomas liked her. She was firm, determined, and unlike most women she had not fallen for Jorge's charm, looking deeper than the surface. Oh, Jorge had depths, Thomas knew, but they were only ever revealed to those he truly loved. All else was surface vanity and pleasure.

"You are right—you are no danger to us, even less if you turn and leave now." The woman made no move as Thomas closed the distance between them, then she dragged the sword in front of her. "That's close enough."

The dogs came snarling around his feet but Thomas ignored them.

"Who were the men who came here, the soldiers? They killed them, didn't they?'"

Jamila nodded. Her eyes tracked Thomas up and down and he knew what she saw—a tall man, too thin, hair long and matted, beard the same. Dressed in ragged clothes that had gone unwashed for too long. Far too long.

Thomas waited as she considered her response, knowing that to push too hard would result in being rebuffed, even if he might prefer that option.

Finally, she took a step backward. "You don't look like trouble. And if you gave them a Christian burial then you deserve a few answers." She started to turn away, then stopped. "Are you hungry?"

"Jorge will be."

"It's you who looks like he needs food. We can offer you something to eat and a place to sleep tonight if you want. There are plenty of places to sleep." She turned and walked away, dragging the sword that was too heavy for her behind. Thomas twitched with the need to take the burden from her but managed to restrain himself, knowing she wouldn't welcome help.

The other women drifted away now their protective presence was no longer required. A young man stepped from between two houses, a sword held in his strong hand. Thomas recognised him from Luis's sketchbook.

"Send them away," he said to Jamila. "We don't want strangers here. How do we know they're not scouts?"

"They are not those you fear. Why are you showing yourself? If they are who you say then others may be watching, waiting for you to appear." She slapped the young man across the face, but he was not finished yet.

He came toward Thomas, dismissing Jorge as no danger. The sword came up.

"You're not welcome here. Turn around, or die where you stand."

Thomas stared at him, at the show of bravado, the sword cutting through the air offering no danger—unless it was to the youth.

He stepped close and saw the young man wanted to move back but couldn't lose face. Instead, he made the mistake of taking Thomas for someone weak, and attacked. It was not a killing blow, and Thomas suspected the youth would have pulled the strike before it landed, but in case he didn't he reached out and snatched the blade from the air. A twist, a reversal, and the sword lay in his own hand.

Now the youth did step back.

Thomas tossed the sword in the air, caught the blade and held the hilt out to him.

"Jamila is right, we are not who you fear. Here, take it."

The youth hesitated, perhaps believing it some trick but unable to see what it might be. After a while he gripped the hilt.

"Put it away," Thomas said, and the youth sheathed the sword. "Is she your mother?" He nodded to where Jamila stood watching the outcome of the confrontation, and the youth nodded. Thomas walked toward her as she turned and passed between two houses. Whatever was happening here was none of his business, but his curiosity had been sparked, and he would need some answers before he could put things from his mind. Someone was dead, and he would know the why of it.

CHAPTER FIVE

The village was small, houses scattered randomly so there were no streets, only spaces through which people moved. Apart from the young man with the sword, the only other males were children playing in the dust. The youth followed at a distance, trying to look dangerous but only partly succeeding. Despite the lack of any formal layout there was what passed for a central square, except it was oval. There were no places of trade, but Jamila led them to a house and motioned them to wait outside. The young man went into the house with her. After a moment he returned carrying a low table and set it down. The woman came out with cushions and dropped them to the ground.

"Sit."

Thomas watched the young man return to stand in the doorway, where he might believe shadows hid him from someone with less keen eyesight, and even less keen instincts.

Jamila folded her legs and sat on a cushion across the table, and after a moment Thomas did the same. Jorge was already reclining on two cushions as if he belonged there.

"When I saw you coming down the hillside I thought

you might have been scouts left behind by the others," said Jamila. "They have done it before, raided then come back within hours. Aban has almost been caught more than once."

"Aban is the boy?" Thomas said, and when she nodded said, "Your son?"

Another nod.

"And the girl is your daughter?"

This time there came a shake of the head. "Dana is the daughter of a friend of mine. She died, so I suppose Dana is as good as my daughter now, even if she does continue to live in her mother's house. She and Luis were to be married. At least, Dana thought they were. I'm not so sure what Luis thought."

"Might he have run away to escape the prospect, if what you say is true?"

"No—he's been taken. That is what they do, the soldiers. They scour the land for men of a certain age, men like Luis and Aban who can be made to fight for them."

"You know this for certain?" Thomas glanced up as Dana emerged from the house carrying a clay pot and cups. Aban followed with a platter of fruit, nuts and meat. He set it in the centre so they could all reach it, and then both sat close together. Thomas made a mental note to ask Jorge later what he thought their relationship might be, because Dana appeared far too accepting of Luis's fate.

Jamila reached out and poured dark wine into two cups and set them before Thomas and Jorge. "You are welcome to our meagre fare. I apologise for our lack of welcome, but you know the reason for it." She poured wine for herself and drained the cup before refilling it.

"Did you really think we were scouts for the soldiers?" Thomas asked.

"You are not them, I know that now, and everyone will

be grateful for what you did for Pedro and Elvira. But you are strangers all the same. Where have you come from?"

Thomas pointed in a random direction, not knowing if it was the right one or not.

"There is nothing there," she said.

"Then that is where I have come from. Nowhere."

The woman's lips thinned in the hint of a smile. "A man of mystery. Where have you been all my life?"

"That, too, is a mystery." Thomas was rewarded with the full smile. He wondered why he was acting as he was with this woman, but she sparked an unfamiliar pleasure in him he believed had been lost forever. "Why do you keep your son out of sight of strangers? Is it the same reason Luis had a hiding place?"

"I do not need protecting, mother," said Aban.

"Oh, he is so brave. Until the next time they come." Jamila returned her gaze to Thomas, Jorge dismissed. "Luis is young and strong. A farmer, so of course he is strong. They will have taken him, no doubt of it."

"The same men who killed Pedro and Elvira? You need to explain to me what is happening here if I am to avenge them. Those men came to this village first and then left. Did they kill anyone here?"

"Of course not."

"Yet they killed Pedro and Elvira, and kidnapped Luis."

"They must have tried to fight them. It was a foolish thing to do. The soldiers punish any hint of resistance, however small. We learned long ago to do as they say."

Thomas stared at her. A handsome woman. Not young, but not old. He glanced at Dana—young, beautiful, a temptation to any man.

"Why do they leave the women alone? I know how soldiers are. They take what they want, who they want."

"Not here. They steal food, but nobody touches us. I think they have been told not to. They take the men and leave the women. If you try to avenge Pedro and Elvira you will be taken too." She tilted her head and examined Thomas. "If you fight, they will kill you. They are hard men."

"Why did they take Luis? Is that what happened to your man?"

Jamila lowered her gaze and Thomas saw the memory still pained her.

"Have all your men been taken?"

"Apart from those who fought and died, and those too old to fight. There is only one left now, and Ibrahim is sick. Soon there will be none." She raised her gaze once more. "Unless you choose to stay. You will have to hide with Aban when the soldiers come, but there will be compensations."

"I want to fight," said Aban, his attention finally turning from Dana.

"No." Jamila continued to stare at Thomas while she spoke. "You look like a man who has fought. Talk to my son, tell him being brave isn't enough. Tell him how men die screaming. He has no idea. No idea at all."

"Why would he listen to me?" Thomas said.

"He doesn't listen to me, so likely not."

"I hide when you tell me to, don't I?" said Aban

"And argue about it all the time. Talk to him." Jamila let her breath go and rose to her feet. "I have to take food to Ibrahim. Stay here and tell my son why he can't fight these men." She shook her head. "He should know better now Luis has been taken, but the young are headstrong and don't listen to sense."

After she was gone Thomas turned to Aban.

"You think your mother is wrong, don't you?"

Aban wouldn't meet Thomas's eyes. Instead he looked toward Jorge, perhaps sensing he would receive a less stern judgement from him.

"Tell me, what do you think would happen if these men come to the village and you try to fight them? Are you capable of fighting a dozen trained soldiers? Is that what you think?"

Aban shook his head. He reached out a hand and Dana took it, making Thomas frown. There was something strange going on he didn't understand. Luis had been kidnapped and the girl he had drawn naked appeared barely concerned, and now she was holding Aban's hand.

"Somebody has to do something," said Aban.

"But not you. If there were twenty men here willing to fight, then I might encourage it. But one man? One untrained boy?"

"I'm not a boy." Aban's gaze turned away from Dana. "And I can fight. I can fight you now if you want. And kill you."

Thomas returned Aban's stare, meeting the challenge he saw there. He didn't like the boy much, but he would prefer him not to die without reason.

"Go fetch two swords and kill me then," he said. "We will fight here in the clearing, before your mother gets back. You can show her my dead body to prove your worth."

"No," said Dana. She shifted closer to Aban, but he released her hand and went into the house.

"Don't hurt him," said Jorge. "It is pride, nothing more."

"I'm not going to hurt him," Thomas said.

Aban emerged with two swords, neither of them well-made, neither of them particularly sharp, which Thomas judged fortunate. Aban strode to the middle of the clearing and turned to face the table. Thomas knew what had to be done. He shook his head and rose, aware of how weak his body was, hoping his instincts remained as strong as they had once been.

Aban slashed at him as soon as he was close enough, and Thomas sent the boy's sword spinning to the ground.

"Pick it up," he commanded. "Next time don't look at my weapon. Look into my eyes—they will tell you all you need to know."

Aban attacked again, and again. Each time Thomas disarmed him on the first thrust. After the tenth time a sharp voice stopped Aban in mid-swing.

"What are you doing! He is our guest."

Thomas was glad of the interruption. Disarming Aban had been easy, but he was painfully aware of how weak he had allowed himself to become.

"I'm teaching him," he said. "A man needs to know how to wield a sword, in case he ever needs the skill."

"I told you to talk to him, not kill him." Jamila stood with clenched fists on her hips, her face set stern. "I was going to offer you a bed for the night, but now…" She shook her head. "I think it better if you leave."

"They can stay in my house," said Dana, walking to join them. She took Aban's free hand and stood beside him.

"Your house is empty," said Jamila.

"Then there is enough room for them. They can have a bed each if they want. Let them stay. Thomas can teach Aban how to fight again tomorrow."

"I don't want him to fight," said Jamila.

"Sometimes there is no choice," Thomas said. "Better to know how to fight and never need to than be forced to fight and not know how. I cannot teach him enough in the time available but I can show him how to learn."

Jamila shook her head and looked away. "I would rather he doesn't know."

"I have to, mother," said Aban. "Thomas is right. I thought…" Aban searched for some truth. "I thought I could fight him and win." He glanced at Thomas. "I would not have killed you."

"I am glad to hear it."

"How long will it take to train him?" asked Jamila. The four of them stood on the dry ground, Jorge still at the table. Thomas found it difficult to believe anyone else lived in the village, even though he had seen them. He wondered if eyes were watching their encounter.

"Too long. I can show him how to learn, but I don't have time to teach him everything he needs to know." Thomas thought of Usaden, the Gomeres mercenary who was training his son and doing a far better job than he had ever managed himself. There were times he wondered if being too close to someone meant you couldn't help them as much as a stranger. Relationships, and love, got in the way. He knew that was what had happened here between Jamila and Aban. She loved him too much to put him in danger, but in protecting him the youth had failed to learn enough to keep himself alive. Thomas knew it wasn't his responsibility, and cursed the sense of duty he felt to people who were strangers to him.

"How long can you stay?" asked Jamila, and Thomas shook his head at the look of hope in her eyes.

"A few days, perhaps. I was on a quest and allowed myself to lose sight of my goal." He turned and walked away, waving a hand for Aban to follow him. Best to start his training now, he thought. Before more soldiers came.

CHAPTER SIX

"Do you think she expects me to go to her?" asked Jorge. He and Thomas shared a bed barely big enough to accommodate them both. They were in Dana's house, which was meant to be empty, but Dana too was somewhere, presumably in the room she used to sleep in before she lived with Jamila.

"She's barely a woman. Why would she want you to go to her?"

"Women do," said Jorge, as if it was the most natural thing in the world, and perhaps for him it was. There were times Thomas wondered what it must be like to be Jorge, but could barely comprehend it.

"Aban is in love with her," Thomas said.

"And she with him, I judge."

"What about the drawing Luis made of her?" Thomas said into the shadowed dark.

Jorge rolled onto his side to face Thomas. "What drawing?"

"Ah. I thought I'd told you about the book."

"What book? What drawing?"

"There was a sketchbook in Luis's room. He's a talented artist."

"*What* drawing?"

A light showed in the open doorway and Dana appeared, a candle held high. She had changed into a nightdress, the shape of her body showing clearly through the thin cotton which also revealed a small swell to her belly that had not been in the sketch.

"I heard you talking. Do you need anything?"

"Nothing, thank you," Thomas said.

"I am only next door if you do." She smiled, hesitated a moment, then moved away.

Thomas waited until he heard the door of her room close.

"There was a drawing of Dana in Luis's sketchbook," Thomas said. "She was naked when he did it. The drawing, that is. It was good. Realistic."

"When were you going to tell me this?" Jorge's voice was low so he didn't disturb Dana again.

"Why would I tell you about it at all? It was intimate. Private. It's none of your business, nor mine."

"Except you're telling me about it now, and you saw it and I didn't."

"You saw the same thing but for real just now. That nightdress hid nothing." Thomas glanced at Jorge. "Do you think that was an invitation? Perhaps you should go to her."

"It's not me she wants. The invitation was for you. And yes, it was an invitation. Trust me, I know such things."

"Why?"

"Why should you trust me? You know the answer to that. Because in matters of the heart and loins I am an expert."

"Why would she want me? I'm old enough to be her father. Her grandfather even."

"She recognises you as a man who can offer protection."

"And Aban and Luis?"

"Ah, yes. Aban and Luis. Even had you not told me of the drawing, I already knew."

"I'm glad somebody does. What is it you know?"

"They are all three young, but not so young they cannot follow their desires. And it seems to me that Dana's desire was to be with both of them."

"Playing one against the other?"

"No. Playing with both of them. All three of them together. Dana is manipulative, and I suspect the arrangement was at her instigation."

Thomas made a noise and Jorge laughed softly.

"Don't tell me such a thing has never occurred to you?"

Thomas said nothing. He rolled over so he was facing away from Jorge, his mind considering what had been told him.

"It would partly explain why she isn't as upset as you would expect about Luis being taken."

"Oh, she's upset," said Jorge, "but she's hiding it. I'm surprised Aban isn't sharing her bed, unless it's because she hoped you would be. Those two will be closer now Luis is gone."

"I wonder which of them is the father?" Thomas said.

"Father?"

"Didn't you notice the signs? Three or four months, I would say. Dana carries a child ... but which of those two is the father?"

Thomas woke in the deep of night and knew he wouldn't sleep again. He slid from the narrow bed and made his way outside. The wind that had tugged at the streets all through the day was still. He walked to the edge of the village, where the land fell away to a river, hidden but not silent. Frogs called to each other, and Thomas considered hunting a few down. The right kind made good eating, and he thought of the lectures he had given Jorge over the years about how a man could live off the land if he knew how—a man cut free to roam as he wished, attached to nothing. He had been that man once, when he was barely a man at all. It was a barren way to live.

Is that what I want again, he wondered? He had fled to these high hills with a fire inside him, but he had allowed it to fade into embers and then grow as cold as the snow that topped the Sholayr. He had tried to stop thinking of Lubna but knew there would never be a single moment he didn't.

"I miss you, Lubna," he said into the night. "I love you still."

A chill passed through him and he sensed something close without seeing it.

"Is that you, my love?" He looked around. There was nothing visible, but Thomas sensed a presence. "Are you still with me? Are you here?"

It seemed something moved inside him, through him, and the chill turned to a warmth.

Thomas shook his head. He didn't believe in God, nor any kind of afterlife. When you were dead you were dead. There was nothing beyond that final moment. It was why he had once believed a man had to live his life as best he could. To make a difference, so that when he was gone there might be memories to be nurtured by others.

Once again he felt a presence, a familiarity he believed had been lost forever.

Yes, Thomas ... make a difference...

Thomas jerked sharply and turned all the way around, but he was alone. He had heard the voice clearly, as if Lubna stood at his side. It was *her* voice. Could be no other. And he wondered if his mind had slipped at last, its final hold on reality breaking loose. Except the voice had been so real.

"No, I don't believe!" Thomas shouted the words into the night, answered only by the barking of the village dogs. He waited, half expecting some answer from beyond the grave, but nothing came. Only a presence lodged within him that had not been there before.

When he returned to the room Jorge was sprawled across the entire bed, his breath coming in soft snores, and Thomas turned away. He wondered what Dana would do if he entered her room. Would she make room for him? Welcome him? He shook his head, knowing it would never happen. He could never lie with another woman. He had sworn it.

"Do you believe in ghosts?"

Thomas and Jorge sat at a table, eating last night's bread and drinking water drawn from the town well. Dana had set their meal out, such as it was, and disappeared, no doubt back to Jamila's house and Aban.

"Ghosts?" said Jorge.

"Yes, ghosts. Do you believe such things exist?"

"What, did you see the farmer and his wife?"

"Of course not."

"It's just that the question isn't like you. But then you're not like you anymore, are you?"

"No, I expect you're right. Are you going to answer me?"

Jorge was silent for a moment. A long moment, unusual for him, and Thomas took the time to think about what he might be able to offer the people of this town, wondered if he could remember any of the skills he had once possessed.

"Lubna?" said Jorge at last.

This time it was Thomas who remained silent.

"Did you see her?" asked Jorge.

"Heard."

"She always was a voice of reason."

"More than likely, even if it was only a figment of my own imagination."

"She was always the more sensible. Was it good advice?"

Thomas nodded.

"So," said Jorge, "this voice you heard, do you think it was her?"

"How could it be? She's dead. We burned her body. If there is such thing as a soul hers will be with her God."

"Which did she love more," said Jorge, "her God or you?"

Thomas jerked his head, because he heard the voice again, as clear and firm as if Lubna sat next to him. Three words, but they were all that was necessary.

You, of course.

Lubna had always been sparse with her advice, as if she suspected Thomas rarely took it.

Jorge must have seen something on Thomas's face because he looked around the room, searching for something that wasn't there. "What are you going to do?"

"Whatever feels right."

When they entered the small square Jamila and Aban were arguing, but stopped when Jamila caught sight of Thomas. She tapped Aban on the shoulder and pushed him toward the house. For a moment he looked as if he wanted to continue the argument, then Dana appeared in the doorway and he went toward her.

"Does he know she carries Luis's child?" Thomas asked.

"Or his. She told me she doesn't know whose it is."

Jamila smiled, surprising Thomas. "She claims it belongs to both of them." The smile faded. "Only one of them now."

"Luis may still be alive. I'm going to try and find out, if I can."

"Why?"

"Because it serves my purpose for coming here as well as anything else."

"You are talking of your wife, aren't you?" said Jamila. "Jorge told me. Told me how she died. I am sorry you had to suffer in such a way."

Thomas shook his head, unwilling to discuss it.

"Jorge also told me you are a physician. Would you examine Dana? There are others here as well who would benefit from your skill."

"You must have women here who can attend to such things. It's not appropriate for a man my age to examine a girl like Dana."

"I will be with you. Besides, a physician is excused normal conduct, isn't he?"

"Who are the others?"

"Ibrahim is an old man. I suspect there is little you can do for him, but there is also a friend of mine who has a pain in her side that doesn't heal."

"I have nothing with me. No instruments, no drugs or herbs."

"You are better than anything else we have. Will you look at them or not?"

Thomas stared across the dry square. Already the day was growing hot, and dust swirls rose in spirals where the wind curled around the side of buildings.

"I will look, but can make no promises."

"That will be enough. Who do you want to start with? Dana?"

"No, the woman with the pain in her side."

Thomas felt naked as Jamila led him to a house on the

edge of town. He missed his leather satchel, his herbs, the tools of his trade. But he had his fingers, his eyes and his ears, as well as knowledge acquired over thirty years.

The woman was in her forties, narrow-faced with a pinched mouth, but that might have been from the pain she was suffering. Her house sat above a steep slope that fell away to a distant valley floor where a river ran, only partly visible between dense tree growth. Thomas realised he must have stood nearby in the night when Lubna spoke to him.

"I will need her to lift her top," Thomas said. "Perhaps you will help."

It took a moment before Jamila could persuade the woman, and when she did she wrapped her hands across her small breasts. Thomas remained where he was, but his eyes tracked her side. She was even thinner without her clothing, and he knew life in the town must be hard. A multi-coloured bruise marked her side, and it was clear to him what had happened.

"How did you injure yourself? Did your husband hit you?"

"My husband has been taken, like all the other men—except this one's son." There was a sharpness to her voice and Thomas wondered how many others felt the same way about Aban's continued presence.

"A fall, then?" He moved closer. "I need to touch your side."

The woman drew away and Thomas straightened.

"He is here to help," said Jamila. "You must allow it."

"He is a stranger."

"All the more reason he can examine you. He will be gone soon and nobody need ever know."

The woman turned her head to one side, as if not seeing Thomas would make it not real.

He touched her, lightly at first, feeling for what he

suspected, finding a sharpness beneath the surface. When he pressed harder the woman cried out.

"You have broken a rib. When did you fall?"

"I tripped a while ago when I was tending my fields," she said. "I thought nothing of it, but then the pain grew worse."

"I'll see if I can find something for that, but I need to bandage you tightly. You must leave the bandage on for a week at least, two if you can bear it. There will be pain at first but then it will improve."

Still she wouldn't look at him. "Do what you must. I can bear pain. Life is pain, is it not?"

When it was done, and Jamila led him from the house on their way to see the old man, Thomas asked, "Where can I find poppy? And sativa, if you have it nearby."

"We are too high here for those to grow. You may find a little poppy on the slopes beyond the river, but more likely you will need to go as far as Pampaneira."

"This Pampaneira is a town? How far is it?"

"It's large enough for what you need. The journey will take half a day, no more, and I will come to show you the way."

CHAPTER SEVEN

Thomas could do nothing for the old man, Ibrahim. He suffered from age, bad eyes, and a heart that stuttered on the edge of failure. There was also a hard lump in his side next to his liver. His hands were stained permanently from working in the quarry, a tale he told as he was examined. Thomas suspected the constant contact with black powder had affected Ibrahim's health. He had seen it before, the contamination slow and insidious. Few men who worked with the powder lived as long as Ibrahim.

"How many years have you?" Thomas sat on a stool beside the man, who rested on cushions in the corner of his house.

"Three score and seventeen." The man laughed, like it was a joke on the fates. "Not so bad, eh? More than my allotted time, and some." He looked up and met Thomas's eyes. "I expect I will not see three score and eighteen though. Tell me true, physician."

Thomas had never been one to soften such news, even less so now than he was, and he nodded. "No, you will not. You have months left to you, if not weeks."

"It is as I thought."

"I can prepare something for the pain. You do have pain, don't you?"

"All the time."

"And something to keep you going a little longer, perhaps."

"I do not fear death. My life has been good, and Allah will find a place for me where I can run again like I did as a youth." The man attempted to stand, but Thomas put a hand on his chest to hold him down.

"Stay where you are."

"There is something I need to tell you." Ibrahim tried to rise again, and this time Thomas helped until he stood, swaying. "It is outside town, but you might find a use for what is stored there."

"How far outside?"

"There is a stone hut in the quarry where I used to work. I built it with my own hands, quarry and hut both. Use what is held there if you wish, but if you cannot it must be disposed of in a safe manner." He looked Thomas up and down. "You strike me as a man who can do that."

"I know what you speak of. Is the hut locked?"

Ibrahim gave a laugh that turned to a cough, all the answer Thomas needed.

"Rest, I'll go and take a look."

"Can you do anything for him?" Jamila walked beside Thomas as they crossed the small square, her presence almost familiar.

"If I can get the right herbs. I might find something in this town you mentioned—I'll go after I've seen Dana."

They had reached Jamila's house when Aban came running from beyond the village. "They're back!"

Jamila reacted at once, pushing him in front of her. "You know where to go. Hide, now."

"I want to fight."

"Do as I say!"

Thomas turned and strode to the last of the houses. On the crest of the ridge six men sat on horseback. They stopped a moment to survey the village, then started down the slope, not in any rush. Thomas melted into a shadow and watched them come. Soldiers with leather jerkins and hard faces. He moved backward out of sight then ran to the square. Aban was gone, but Jamila remained outside.

"Jorge and I need weapons." He considered trying to get to the hut Ibrahim had told him of but knew there wasn't enough time to prepare an ambush.

"Go join Aban," said Jamila. "They won't take the women, but they'll kill you both if you try to resist."

"Or take us," Thomas said.

"No, you are too old, and you look sick. Jorge they might, but not you. They only take the young. You they will kill."

"Where are your weapons?" Thomas asked a second time.

Jamila took his arm and led him to a small room far in the back of the house. She stopped at a doorway, as if reluctant to enter. Thomas went into the room. Four swords hung across nails hammered into loose plaster, and he recognised those Aban had brought for their fight. There was a shield with an ornate emblem that meant nothing to him, and an axe he recognised as belonging to a Northman, a memory coming to him of Olaf Torvaldsson swinging just such an axe as he brought chaos and death to the Spanish. Thomas knew the axe was not for him, but one of the swords was finely made, well-balanced and light, and he took that. He picked another for Jorge, hoping he might remember how to use it, also taking the shield for him.

Jamila was waiting along the narrow corridor.

"These belonged to your husband?"

She offered a nod. "He fought bravely, but there were too many."

"You saw them take him?"

Jamila gave another nod but said nothing. Thomas wondered what it must have been like for her to watch her husband dragged away.

"I don't understand why they take strong men who might rebel. What keeps them from killing their captors and coming home?"

"The threat against the families they leave behind. Especially the sons." Jamila turned and walked toward the front of the house. "They take the young boys to control the men. They took two of my sons, both younger than Aban. Biorn would not have put them in danger."

"Biorn is your husband?"

Jamila nodded. "A good husband and good father both, and a good farmer. Not all Northmen are warriors, despite what people think."

As they came out of the house Jorge stood in the sun, waiting for them.

"They are almost here." He glanced at the weapons in Thomas's hands, the shield, and shook his head. "There are six men."

Thomas shrugged and held out the shield. "Stay indoors with Aban if you want, but I would like you at my side. There is no need for you to fight, I will do it all. Just look threatening, if you can."

Jorge sighed and took the shield. He pushed his arm through the straps and tested it for weight, then held his hand out for a sword.

Jamila gripped Thomas's arm. "They will kill you. I don't want to watch another man die."

"They can try. Ask Jorge whether I am an easy man to kill." He shook off her hand, unsure whether his boast still held true. He knew he had grown weak over the months he had lived in the mountains.

Jorge followed and stood beside him. "Do you have a plan of any kind?"

"Of course I have a plan."

"Is it one you intend to share?"

"We wait here until they arrive, then ask them to leave."

"That is a plan?"

"The start of one. When they refuse and attack us, I will kill them."

Jorge laughed. "If I didn't know you as I do, I'd think you had a better plan and are keeping it from me. What shall I do?"

"Try not to get yourself killed. That will be enough."

A young girl came running as fast as her skinny legs would allow. She skidded to a halt in front of Thomas, as if knowing who he was and why he was there.

"They're at the edge of town," she said, then was gone.

Thomas waited.

The men came into the square on horseback, not expecting trouble, their swords sheathed. They were talking, laughing. They must know there were no men left here, but still they had come.

A movement to one side caught Thomas's attention and he gave a brief glance. Aban knelt on the roof-ridge of his house, a Moorish bow already strung and drawn half taut. Thomas wondered if he knew how to use it but was sympathetic. At Aban's age he would have been unable to stand aside if men threatened his family.

The soldiers stopped laughing and slowed. There appeared to be no leader, only one who was a little braver —or more aggressive—than the others. He said something to his companions then urged his horse into a canter. His sword came from its sheath and he leaned forward, readying a thrust.

Thomas waited until the last moment then stepped to one side. He lifted his own sword and allowed the man's speed to do the work. His blade slid smoothly through the leather jerkin and into flesh beneath. The sword was jerked from Thomas's grasp, but he had expected such. He stepped back and took Jorge's as two others came forward. They were slower, more careful.

"You might like to stand by the house," he said to Jorge, then turned to meet the new attack.

The men left a decent space between them, but they should have dismounted. To reach Thomas they were forced to bend almost out of the saddle, and he hobbled the first horse, which stumbled to spill its rider. Thomas finished him with a single thrust. When he turned the other man had seen sense and was riding around the edge of the square back to his companions. Aban's arrow took him in the shoulder. The man managed to remain in the saddle but his sword arm hung useless at his side.

Four men now.

Thomas walked toward them.

He frowned, aware something was different, and it took a moment to recognise what it was. He was used to battle, used to killing. Ever since when, at thirteen years of age, he had witnessed the chaos of Castillon where his father died. Fighting had always taken him in a certain way. It closed down his humanity, filled him with a searing cold that left no room for fear or mercy. Now, standing in a sun-filled square in a village barely worthy of the name, he was surprised to find the cold no longer present. Instead, heat seared his fingertips, and a fire nestled in his chest and belly. He shook his head. Different, that was all, and there were men to kill.

Only three remained capable of making any kind of attack, and Thomas saw that might not happen as they discussed their next move between themselves. He saw one wanted to run, the other two unsure. What they saw was a single man. No doubt they had confronted single men before and triumphed—but Thomas was sure they had never met a man like him. He wondered if he was still that man.

He considered letting them ride away, then decided he needed answers to the many questions he had, so he ran at the soldier who wanted to leave the most. The man jerked his horse sideways, hoofs skidding on the dry dust, but he was too late. Thomas leapt, hitting him hard on his side and tumbling them both to the ground. He was on his feet in an instant, leaving the man stunned, ready to meet a fresh attack, but none came. Instead, Aban loosed more arrows, one after the other. None hit their target, but the remaining men turned and fled. Thomas watched as the winded man rose to one knee, then hit him hard on the side of the head. By the time he got back to the house, dragging the man behind him, the fire had left his body. He was winded, aware of how weak he had become.

"I need somewhere to tie him up so I can question him," he said to Jamila, who had come to stand outside and watch.

"I will take you to an empty house. Are you going to kill him when you have what you want?"

"It depends if I believe him or not."

She stared at the man, who was starting to regain his wits. Thomas knew he should have hit him harder, another sign of his weakness.

"If you don't kill him," said Jamila, "can I?"

CHAPTER EIGHT

Thomas glanced to where Jorge stood, as far away as he could get short of leaving the room.

"You don't have to stay if you prefer not to witness this."

Aban had secured the captured man, his relish at doing so clear. The soldier's arms stretched above his head, a rope binding his wrists pulled tight over a beam. His feet had been left free, but he had to stand on tip-toe to relieve the pain in his arms. A shaft of sunlight came through a window and fell directly on him. Sweat beaded his face, more from pain and fear than the heat.

"A year ago you would never have treated a man this way," said Jorge.

"A year ago I was married with a wife expecting our first child. Men change."

"That is more than clear. I will stay. Someone has to provide a civilising influence."

Thomas saw concern on his friend's face and wondered if he had really changed so much. He assumed he had, but didn't see it himself. Yes, he had changed, of course he had, but not in the way Jorge meant. His emotions had closed down, for to allow them full rein would send him howling at the moon, but he still considered himself a good man. Except, in this moment, he needed answers and was impatient for them.

He stepped closer to the prisoner. A man of medium height, thin to the point of emaciation, his cheekbones harsh on a face that reflected Moorish heritage.

"This can go easy for you or hard. Which is entirely up to you."

"I have done nothing." The man spoke Arabic, because that is what Thomas had used, but it was a bastard variant native to these mountains.

"You came here for plunder. For men of fighting age." Thomas reached out and tugged at the rope angled over the beam. The man cried out as his feet left the ground.

"Make it easy for me! I was following orders, nothing more. I will tell you whatever you want to know."

"Fetch a chair," Thomas said to Aban, who stood in the corner watching, his face impassive but a manic brightness in his eyes. The boy hesitated, then turned and left the small room which was all the building consisted of. It stank of animals, and their dried droppings littered the floor.

Thomas stood in front of the man. He said nothing, waiting, staring into his eyes as if he might see into his soul. He glanced briefly to one side where Jorge leaned against the wall, apparently relaxed, but Thomas knew he would be watching and learning.

The man breathed heavily, and Thomas wondered why he had been sent. He was not an impressive physical specimen, but perhaps his companions had been more skilled, though he had seen little sign of it. If this man was an example of the kind that raided the towns and villages of the region it was surprising they had managed to capture anyone at all.

Aban returned with a three-legged stool and set it beside Thomas, who unknotted the rope where it was attached to a hook in the wall. The man's arms dropped, still tied at the wrists. Thomas kicked the stool toward him.

"Fetch another seat for me," he said, without taking his eyes from the man, who reached for the stool and sat. He rubbed at the rope binding him, pulled at a tight knot.

"Leave it where it is," Thomas said.

Aban returned with a chair and Thomas sat. He stared hard for a time until the man's eyes looked away, then he leaned forward.

"Why did you come here? There are no men left of fighting age in this village."

"He is here, isn't he?" The man nodded toward Aban, who had returned to his spot in the corner of the room. "For now."

"But you didn't know that."

The man smiled. "Oh, we knew, we just didn't know how to catch him."

"Why do you do it?"

"Do what?"

"Don't make me string you up again."

"We are given orders, of course. Nobody questions them."

Thomas studied the man a moment. "When were you taken?"

"Taken?" The man looked away, not toward Jorge or Aban, but to where a blank wall waited his inspection.

"I'm not stupid," Thomas said. "I'll assume you're not, either. When?"

"Four months."

"From where?"

"Pampaneira"

"Were others taken?"

The man nodded. "There were six of us then, more later. I was unlucky—they don't take men from there anymore."

A thought occurred to Thomas. "How many have been taken altogether?"

Again the man's eyes sought an empty space and his lips thinned.

"Tell the truth and you will be free to go. Free to return to Pampaneira."

"You don't understand. None of us are free to return to our homes. None of us are free to run away or cross the sea. Our families keep us from running. That and the punishments."

Thomas glanced toward Jorge, who nodded that he understood, which was more than Thomas did.

"Explain about your families."

The man leaned closer, less afraid, as if he was starting to believe he might be able to escape from the situation he was in.

"Our wives and children, girls and the young boys until they grow older, are free to live their lives, but without us. Should one or more of us try to escape they are punished as well as us. To run and be captured seals a terrible fate."

"You know the families are punished? How?"

"I have..." The man's body tightened and he looked away.

"You have helped to do this deed yourself, haven't you," said Jorge. "Is that what you were going to say?" He remained as relaxed as he had throughout, but the man grew even more agitated. His gaze dropped to the floor, as if preferring the detritus there.

"I do what I am told. I have to do what I am told. If I don't it is my family who will be punished for my disobedience. Most of us are the same, but not all. Some men are *his* favourites."

"There are always men willing to kill," Thomas said. "Often enough for no reason at all. What is it that turned you into what you are? Four months is no great time to corrupt a man."

"You don't understand what it is like in the camp. We are not men anymore. We are animals. He has his own soldiers and they are treated well, but the rest of us have to obey. It takes a toll. Turns us into something less than men."

"This man you speak of, the leader, describe him to me."

Thomas thought he already knew but wanted confirmation.

"He is tall. Handsome. Unlike his father."

"There are many tall, handsome men—one of them is standing over there. Does this one have a name?"

The man shook his head. "No name I know of, but he calls himself The Warrior."

Thomas sat forward. "The Warrior?"

"That is what I said, isn't it?" It was the first sign of defiance from the man.

Jamila entered the room and Thomas turned at the interruption. "I told you to stay outside."

She glanced at the man slumped on the stool, her face expressionless. "There is something you need to see."

"I'm busy here."

Jamila gave a shake of the head, and Thomas knew he was being stubborn. She wouldn't have disturbed him if it wasn't important.

"Draw him up again," he told Aban as he stood. "Perhaps it will persuade him to be more talkative when I come back. Set his feet on the stool, let's see how long he can balance on that."

Jorge followed him, an expression of distaste on his face.

"What?" Thomas said.

"There's no need to torture him further, he's answering your questions."

"Did you not see when I mentioned his master? It made him bold. He needs a lesson in humility, and then I intend to feed him—perhaps even allow him to take a bath. He certainly needs one. But first I need to speak to you before Aban joins us. What is the Spanish word for warrior?"

Thomas watched a slow realisation come to Jorge, who shook his head. "It can't be, it's too obvious."

"Only if you speak Spanish. He will call himself *muharib* in Arabic."

"But he doesn't speak Arabic."

"Or claimed not to when I knew him last year, but enough time has passed since. He may have learned the language, will have had to learn some if he wants to lead a band of reluctant men who all speak a bastard version of that tongue. But I suspect he spoke it already. This is not recent—it has been planned for years."

"How long are you going to leave him strung up?"

Jamila waited to one side, arms crossed over her chest, a look of impatience on her face.

Thomas glanced at the sky. "Until after noon, until the day begins to lose its heat." Though this high on the flanks of the Sholayr the day took longer to gather heat to it, and it was quickly lost.

"And if he dies?"

"Why would he die?"

Jorge shook his head. "He's not a young man, nor a fit man."

"He won't die," Thomas said. "And when we go back, he will answer every question I ask of him."

"And afterward? What becomes of him?"

"I haven't considered that yet, but I will think on it if it worries you so much."

Jorge stared at him so hard Thomas turned away before

63

he could say anything else and walked to where Jamila waited. "Show me what is so important, then."

She led the way to where the last houses stood on the northern edge of the village. She stopped in the shade of a wall and caught Thomas's wrist to prevent him going further.

He glanced at her, then turned to scan the far hillside, for that was the obvious reason she had interrupted him. Jamila continued to grip his wrist, her hold strong, and Thomas saw what she had brought him here for. The men who had fled had not gone far. Two sat on horseback, the third not visible, and a knot of anxiety coiled in Thomas's chest.

"Did you see where the other went?" he asked.

Jamila released his wrist, as if satisfied he would not turn and leave now.

"Three of them sat there for a long time, as if trying to decide whether to attack again or not, then they argued and one rode away north. That was when I came for you."

Thomas wondered how far away reinforcements might be. They could be an hour, or they could be a day, but he suspected the shorter time rather than the longer.

"Is there some place you can go? A larger town?"

"Pampaneira is an hour south," said Jamila. "It's not a city, but it is the biggest town in the area, and safe. The Governor there has come to an arrangement with the raiders of late, or they consider it too big to attack."

"Get everyone together and start out. I'll catch up with you in a while."

"What are you going to do?"

"I need to finish questioning the man, then I'll take care of the soldiers on the hillside. I should have done it before. I was weak."

"Take care of them?"

"Just do as I say."

Thomas saw anger on Jamila's face. He waited for her to see the logic of what he proposed. He was aware he had lost something since Lubna died. She had softened him, made him consider the opinion of others. Now her influence was gone, and the anger he had suppressed for too long could be given full rein. Thomas knew he had lost any patience Lubna had ever instilled in him. He stared at Jamila, waiting without expression until she realised there was no alternative but to do as he said.

Thomas watched her go, her shoulders tense, and knew that something else had changed inside him. Before Lubna, he had taken women when he needed them, more often than not paying for their services. As a young man he had been harsher, taking what he wanted—often not even needing to take, for he was aware he possessed something that attracted women and had used the power it gifted him. As the years passed he had changed, softened, become more considerate of the needs and opinions of others. When he had been with Lubna he had never wanted anyone else. And now, he knew, he wanted Jamila. He also knew the old Thomas, the compassionate Thomas, would never have acted on such an impulse, even if, as he suspected, Jamila would not reject his advances.

Perhaps dealing with the men on the hillside would distract his thoughts.

Perhaps he should discuss how he felt with Jorge, a man who understood sensuality better than anyone else in the world. Except Jorge would tell him to lie with Jamila, that to abstain from pleasure was also a sin. But first he had a man to question, and a decision to make.

CHAPTER NINE

"You didn't have to be so hard on him," said Jorge, as he and Thomas stood on the edge of the village and watched a small caravan of people, donkeys and carts move away along a rough track that would eventually lead them to Pampaneira. Jamila had told Thomas how to find the town when he was ready, and that she would arrange accommodation for him and Jorge.

"He told us everything he knew," Thomas said. "Some of it was even useful. And I let him go, didn't I? We needed answers fast, not tomorrow, not even later today."

"Yes, you let him go, but he could barely walk."

"Then he should have answered my questions sooner."

"You hardly gave him time."

Thomas wondered whether he should have sent Jorge with the others. He could do what needed to be done just as easily on his own. It was still not too late to send him, but something told him Jorge would take a long time to forgive him if he did. Were they not partners? The only partner Thomas had in the entire world? He glanced at the sky, judging the afternoon to be half gone. Time enough for everything to happen as it must.

"Stay here, I'll be back in a moment."

Jamila had told him Ibrahim had decided to stay rather than be carried miles by women, and that he also wanted to see Thomas. He walked fast to the small house on the edge of the square where he knew the old man remained— the man he was meant to be helping, the man who was beyond all help.

Thomas found him sitting on an upright chair, his face pale

"Jamila tells me two of the men are waiting on the hill-side," said Ibrahim.

Thomas nodded and sat on the edge of the narrow cot. He wondered if he should try to persuade the old man to leave but knew there was little logic in it. He would die soon anyway. Let him die where he had lived.

"They are waiting for others to come, aren't they?" said Ibrahim.

"It makes sense. There's nothing else to keep them there. Are you sure you want to stay?" Thomas asked the question, knowing the answer he would receive.

"I stay here, where I belong. I know I am dying, and I choose to die here. There will be a great deal of pain, won't there?"

The old Thomas might have softened his answer, but the reborn Thomas had no time for such. He had been called butcher in the past, now he had moved beyond such a title.

"You will live a month at most."

"You are not going to try to persuade me to change my mind?"

"I can make it all end now, if you ask." Thomas looked into Ibrahim's eyes. "I will make it quick, and as painless as possible."

"I will not see the sun set today, but not at your hand.

67

There is something I want you to do for me, though not that."

Thomas thought he knew what Ibrahim was about to propose, and approved.

"Ask it."

"You are going to let him sacrifice himself?" Jorge's face was sweat-streaked, as was Thomas's, their hands stained by the black powder they had brought on a small cart, dragged from the hut in the quarry where Ibrahim had worked his trade his entire life.

To Thomas it seemed fitting he should end his life in the same way, in the village he called home.

He rolled the last barrel of black powder off the cart and stood it beside two others. Another four sat on the far side of the doorway to Ibrahim's house. More were set against surrounding houses where the stone walls would concentrate the force of the explosion toward the middle of the square. Trails of powder ran dark across the dry earth, each leading to where a chair was set, empty for the moment. What had taken longer than fetching the barrels had been collecting scattered rock from the quarry floor and piling it on the cart to haul to the square. It had taken even longer because of the need to bring them by a way that was not visible to the two men who remained above the village. Now the rocks had been set around the barrels of powder, partly obscuring them from a casual observer.

"What if I told you he had asked me to end his pain?" Thomas said. "A pain that will never lessen, only grow worse day by day. You would tell me to do so, wouldn't you?"

Jorge stared at him, silent.

Thomas sighed. "I thank you for your help, but if you're

going to be stubborn over this I'd prefer you follow the others. I can finish what needs to be done on my own."

"You would send me away?"

"Rather that than have you nag me the entire time." Thomas pushed at Jorge's chest, sending him staggering back two paces. "Go after them. I don't need you here and they need your protection."

"You know I can't fight," said Jorge. "Usaden tried to teach me when he trained Will, but he says I lack the instinct to kill. He's right, I'm sure, for which I'm glad. I want to kill nobody."

"But you're big, and you can look mean. I've seen you do it. Go. Now. Before we fall out over this."

Jorge shook his head. "*Before* we fall out?" He turned and stalked away, shoulders hunched, and as Thomas watched him go he wondered why he had been so harsh on him, and where his own anger had come from. No doubt Jorge could tell him, but it was too late for that.

A call came from within the small house and Thomas turned away from Jorge's retreating figure and went inside to find Ibrahim attempting to stand. Thomas went to him, took his arm and then, feeling the frailness of the man, lifted him like a child and held him against his chest.

Ibrahim smiled. "I remember when I could lift my wife this way. Where is your friend?"

"Gone to join the others." Thomas turned sideways to carry Ibrahim through the doorway then set him in the chair outside. He went back and brought pillows, tucked them around the man.

"I thank you for your kindness in allowing me this last duty."

"Do you have everything you need? It doesn't have to be this way, you know. It's not too late for Jorge to take you to the others. I can lay a trail of powder and set the fuse from a safe distance."

Ibrahim patted the small table beside him, where a flint and oil lamp rested.

"And spend a month dying in agony? I prefer to leave this life in a blaze of glory, my friend."

Thomas stared at Ibrahim, an unfamiliar sensation in his chest, and it took him a moment to realise it was admiration. He wished he could have spent more time with the old man.

"You're sure you don't want me to light the lamp before I go?" he asked.

Ibrahim gave a smile. "Best not. One stray spark and we'll both be blown to pieces before it does any good. I can manage—and if not, the men will kill me almost as fast as the powder."

Thomas stood for a moment, wanting to say or do something but failing to know what.

Perhaps Ibrahim saw the uncertainty in him because he laughed. "Go, do what you must. And once again, my thanks." He glanced at the clear sky, the sun bringing a warmth to the afternoon. "Better I die this way than being eaten alive hour by hour. Now go, Thomas Berrington. Go and do some good."

CHAPTER TEN

The two men didn't hear Thomas coming.

He had taken a wide circle around the hillside and now crouched behind them, close enough to overhear their conversation. They were watching Jorge ride away down the hillside on their companion's horse but made no effort to pursue him, which confirmed they were waiting for others to arrive.

"There'll be nobody left to kill if they don't come soon," said one.

"We know which way they're going. We can kill them later if he wants us to."

Thomas half expected the man he had questioned and released to be with these two but there was no sign of him. If he had any sense, he would make his way home to his family and take them far from these lands.

Thomas stood and shook his arms to loosen the muscles. He carried no weapons, but had no need of them. The idea of defeat barely even occurred to him as he stepped out into clear view.

"Perhaps you would like to kill me instead."

One of the men turned so fast he almost unseated

himself. The other, a better soldier, reacted more slowly, turning his horse so he was side on to Thomas. His hand went to a scabbard strapped to the saddle and drew a sword from it. Thomas knew he would have to disable him first, so stepped closer.

The man smiled. All he saw was an unarmed opponent, one too stupid to run.

"You are no hostage, are you," Thomas said, making the man frown. "I see it in your eyes. You enjoy this work. Which is all the better for my conscience."

The other soldier had finally prepared himself to fight, but Thomas ignored him. He stepped closer again, leaning to one side as the first man swung his sword. It came close, but Thomas's mind had become a thing of utter calm, the world glittering in sharp relief. He grabbed the reins of the horse and jerked them hard. The horse pulled away and he jerked again, pulling its head around and it staggered, losing balance. The soldier tried another swing but he, too, was now unbalanced, and when Thomas gripped his wrist he tumbled from the saddle. His head met a rock and bounced. He lay still. Thomas was disappointed. The fight had been far too easy.

He leaned down and took the sword from the man's fingers, which curled over and over into the dry ground, then he pivoted as the second soldier finally launched his attack. Thomas's sword slid through his tunic and emerged from his back. It wasn't a killing blow, but it hadn't been meant as such. Thomas had a use for both of them yet.

Without haste he searched the saddle bags of the first horse until he found what he knew must be there. He uncoiled a length of hemp rope and looped it around the injured man's waist, then drew his horse to where jumbled rocks allowed him to achieve what he wanted. He lifted the dead man onto his shoulder, lighter than he expected, which made what he needed to do easier.

Thomas climbed awkwardly over the rocks until he had enough height, then dropped his burden so the man sat facing the other, who clutched at his side where blood flowed from his wound. Thomas wrapped the rope around them both, drawing their bodies tight until they resembled lovers. It was a deliberate display, a shaming of them, and he saw distaste show in the injured man's face and ignored it. The man would be dead inside an hour, but not before he had delivered Thomas's message.

When he was done, Thomas mounted the dead man's horse and led the other and its occupants down to the village square. He tied the reins of the horse holding the two men to a post and left them there. Ibrahim watched proceedings from his chair, a wide-brimmed hat shading his face from the sun. He said nothing, but a smile played on his lips.

As Thomas rode away he heard the one he had struck through ask for help, for mercy. No doubt he would have seen the barrels, the dark lines of powder running from them to Ibrahim's feet, and guessed their purpose.

Thomas rode to the peak where the pair had been waiting and stared out into the far valley, looking for the men he knew would come. He didn't have to wait long, which told him two things—the other men hadn't been far away, and they had come fast in response to the resistance that had been shown.

There was a score of them, which told him a third thing. They came with intent. With more than enough men to take care of half a dozen enemies if necessary. Thomas smiled at an image of himself, Jorge, Olaf and Usaden facing these twenty. He hadn't thought of the mercenary Usaden in a long time, but missed him now. A member of the feared Gomeres, the man was a dervish in battle and would have relished this moment. A dervish also when he

73

trained Thomas's son, Will, but soft when they sat and talked about the world.

Thomas didn't need the help of others today. There would be no fighting, only death. He encouraged his horse to the peak of the ridge, better to display himself, riding backward and forward until he was sure the men had seen him, then turned and made his way to the village. He stopped beyond the outer ring of houses, laid out deliberately to offer some small show of resistance, made weak by the open roadway that led between two of them.

Thomas was hungry and thirsty. He considered looking for food and water but decided against. Depending on how fast the men came he wanted them to see him here, so he stayed in the saddle, sword in hand, as if he intended to fight them all. He wished he had thought to ask Ibrahim if he had another hat he could use, for the sun was hot against his head. Fortunately, he didn't have to wait long.

They came over the ridge in double file, their horses picking their way among rocks. Even at a distance it was clear these were hardened men, used to fighting, used to winning. Thomas scanned their number but saw no obvious leader. He was disappointed. Somehow, he had expected a leader. He had wanted a leader. Someone to make an example of. Perhaps next time, when news travelled of what had happened in this village, soon not to be a village. Thomas was sure at least some of the houses would remain standing, but people wouldn't want to return after what was about to take place here.

When the men came within three hundred paces of him Thomas jerked the horse's reins and rode unhurriedly between the houses.

He pulled up in front of Ibrahim and dismounted, knelt beside him.

"Last chance, old man."

Ibrahim grinned, showing more gum than teeth. "Last

chance to do some good." He laughed. "You know, I'm looking forward to this. One last throw of the dice. How many do you think I can kill?"

"Two, at least." Thomas nodded toward the men tied to the horse, pleased when Ibrahim laughed again. He wondered if the show of good humour was bravado, but didn't think so. Given the choice, he would have wanted to do the same as Ibrahim. He stood, then leaned down and lifted the man's hat, kissed his brow and replaced the hat carefully. "How many virgins will there be for you in heaven?" he asked.

"Oh, I pray there will be least one more than I can cope with."

Thomas mounted the captured horse and rode away without looking back. He had reached the river when he heard the roar of an explosion, a cacophony of rocks and falling masonry. He rode on, urging the horse to the side where trees would hide them both. He dismounted and left the horse tugging at a patch of sweet grass, then made his way back to where he had a view of the track leading down from the village. It took some time, but eventually a group of men rode around the outside of the houses and picked their way down the hillside. They came slowly, looking for another ambush. There was a dozen of them now. More than Thomas had expected, and he was disappointed, though several showed injuries, faces bloodied from flying masonry. There were too many to confront so he drifted back through the trees and re-mounted the stolen horse. He rode to the west until he was sure he was far enough from those attempting to track him, then turned south and picked his way down rough hillsides. Jamila had told him where the town of Pampaneira lay and he was sure he could find it.

As Thomas approached the town late afternoon was softening the air. The bulky shoulder of the Sholayr cast long shadows that highlighted the convolutions of the land. Pampaneira was the lowest of three towns which clung to the slopes of the mountain, and as he rode through the first two, children, women and old men turned to watch his passage. He noted the lack of any young men, a pattern that was becoming familiar, but when he reached Pampaneira the situation changed. He passed lean old men working narrow terraces that dropped like the steps of a staircase down the hillside, most barely wide enough for a man to stand on, each perfectly tended. As he rode into the steep cobbled streets younger men of fighting age leaned against walls to watch him pass, their faces expressionless.

He found an inn set at a corner of the town square and dismounted. A youth came running to take his horse, and Thomas placed a small coin in his hand. He watched the youth lead the horse away. He was younger than Aban, but not by much. Something was different here, and he wanted to know what.

Jamila had arranged accommodation for them in a relative's house and Jorge dispatched to the town square to wait for Thomas and lead him along near-precipitous streets to it.

"Where are the other villagers?" Thomas asked, as he sat on a bed that looked too narrow to accommodate them both.

"Some left as we came south." Jorge stood with his head angled to avoid hitting the low ceiling. "They have relatives in other towns, distant in some cases, who they hope will take them in. Others have family here, or in one of the other two towns higher on the slope. It is only the five of us in this house at the moment."

"And the men on the street? I take it you noticed them." Thomas rubbed his feet. They ached from wearing boots all day, and there was a deep throb at the base of his spine from the riding.

"I asked Jamila, but she said she would tell us when we were both here"

Thomas rose and went to where a small bowl waited, a jug of cold water beside it.

"Where is Aban going to sleep? Does he have relatives here too?"

"He wanted to sleep in the room with his mother but she told him he'd have to come in here with us."

Thomas looked around. "Where, exactly?"

"There were only the two rooms free, so yes, in here. Someone is meant to be bringing a cot, though where they will put it is a mystery."

"Perhaps they can lean it against the wall and Aban can sleep standing up."

"More than likely." Now Thomas was standing, Jorge sat on the bed and stretched his long legs out, instantly at home, instantly relaxed. "What happened back there?"

"You know what happened. Didn't you hear it?"

"We heard nothing. Ibrahim is a brave man."

"Was a brave man," Thomas said.

"How many?"

"Eight or ten. Another dozen followed me, but I lost them."

"You didn't try to fight?"

"I must be gaining sense as I grow older. That, or I'm simply too old."

"Do you think Ibrahim will have considered his sacrifice worthwhile for the death of eight men?"

Thomas suppressed a spark of irritation. "He knew he was dying and was happy at the end. Almost like he was going to a party."

"His own funeral, more like."

"I should have dragged him with me, put him through

77

unspeakable pain so he could die here, away from the place he has lived his entire life?" Thomas stared at Jorge. "Should I have done that?"

Jorge glanced away. "I'm not saying that. It's just … it seems callous to make use of him as you did."

"It was his idea."

"You could have persuaded him otherwise."

"What is it you want of me? It was you came to find me, and all you've done since is criticize. You ought to go back to Gharnatah and leave me in peace." Thomas turned and left the room, afraid he might hit Jorge if he stayed. On the stairs he met a man struggling with a cot and had to return the way he had come, but was determined to offer no assistance. Instead he stood aside as the man attempted to manoeuvre the cot, for all its narrowness, through the door.

Before he could move past the man, another door opened, this one behind him, and Jamila said, "What are you doing standing here? Are you too shy to knock?"

Thomas didn't bother turning around. He started to push past the man, who continued to find it impossible to get the cot through the door. No doubt Jorge was trying to help, which would only contribute to the problem. Thomas reached the head of the stairs before Jamila caught up with him and grasped his wrist.

"We need to talk."

"About what?" Thomas knew he could pull away if he wanted but offered only a token resistance.

"You will have seen the men, I am sure. You are not stupid."

"Ask Jorge's opinion on that."

Jamila frowned, shook her head. "Have you two had a falling out?" She smiled. "Perhaps we can re-arrange our accommodation. Dana is much taken with you."

"Dana is barely a woman, and already with child."

Jamila laughed. "I am only teasing. You are so easy to tease, Thomas Berrington, that I cannot resist. I know Dana is too young for you." She released his wrist, but her fingers lingered against the back of his hand. Dana might be too young for him, but she was making it clear she was not. Then her expression changed, became serious. "Did Ibrahim suffer?"

"He died instantly. As did eight other men."

Jamila offered a sharp nod. "Not enough, but it is good all the same. And so are you for helping him. We will remember him in our prayers tonight." Jamila's hand lifted and touched his chest, lay there. "There is something I need to show you. Only you and me. You can tell Jorge later if you want, but for now it must be only you."

Jamila removed her hand and eased past him to descend the stairs. Thomas watched her go, the stirrings of emotions he hadn't felt in months coiling sinuous threads through his body and, even worse, his mind.

CHAPTER ELEVEN

In one corner of the town square stood a substantial mosque, its doors open to admit men for evening prayer. Thomas noticed that many of those he had observed as he entered the town were not making their way to worship Allah, but remained where they were, watching everyone else. As Jamila led them past one such group the men called out to her coarsely, and one of them came close enough to grab her arm and tug her hard towards him.

Thomas moved fast and hit the man on the side of the head, and he staggered back with a cry. Thomas turned to the man's companions, expecting retaliation, but instead they only laughed at their friend's discomfort, calling him a fool and a poor fighter for not seeing the blow coming.

"Are you all right?" Thomas took Jamila's wrist, drew her sleeve up to reveal a red weal where the man had gripped her. It would bruise soon.

"I am used to such treatment when I come here. Do not concern yourself, but my thanks. It is some time since a man has come to my rescue. It felt good."

Thomas realised he had made a mistake, but it was too late to take his actions back—and besides, he would never have allowed harm to come to her, whatever price he might have to pay.

"What is it you want to show me?"

"Some of it you have just seen," said Jamila. "The men. Men of fighting age. This is the only town I know where they are allowed to remain in their homes."

"It wasn't always so, was it?" Thomas said. "The man I questioned told me he came from Pampaneira and was taken by force. What changed to make the raids stop here but nowhere else?"

"That I don't know."

As they moved into a roadway that led steeply down-hill Thomas halted for a moment and looked back into the square. Perhaps two score of men stood in small groups or sat outside eating places. Alcohol was being consumed, as well as hashish smoked, its scent sweet in the air.

"How many are here?"

Jamila halted and turned to him, stood close. "About double what you see. Less than a hundred in total. They like to gather in the evenings and threaten people. Women mostly, as you saw."

"Are they local men?"

Jamila shook her head. "The ones acting this way are soldiers. The local men are left alone. They work their fields and keep quiet. It's been known for the soldiers to attack them for no reason other than a love of mischief and inflicting pain."

Thomas turned away and they started down the slope again. It was precipitous, his feet pinching into the toes of his boots as they descended.

"Why did you being us here if Pampaneira is a base for the forces that take men from the towns and villages?"

Jamila gave a small laugh. "No, their headquarters lie elsewhere, not here. This is where they bring the women and children of the men they take. This is where they are held as hostages to their menfolk's good behaviour."

"Is that why the men are here, as gaolers? A hundred seems a lot in a town this size, but it's not enough of a force to stop an invading army. Are they here to stop people leaving?"

"The women and children are, I told you," said Jamila.

"Why here?"

"There are a few small villages like mine north of Pampaneira, a few others even smaller. Isolated farmhouses. Isolated people. It would be impossible to place soldiers in every single one of them, which is why they bring the women and children here."

"But they left you in your village."

"And came once a week, or every other week, and they knew where we were if any of our menfolk tried to rebel."

"You don't know what has become of them, do you?" Thomas asked, and Jamila shook her head, her expression serious after the earlier flirting.

Thomas continued to walk without seeing the street, thinking of what the captured man had told him. Most of it had been rambling in his desperation to answer, most of it useless, but not all, and what he had said fitted with what Jamila was telling him. They reached a corner and the roadway dropped away again. From their position Thomas could see over the town wall to the south. He watched the play of light and shade as it etched each ridge and valley in clear relief. Far in the distance the light changed to indicate where the Mediterranean lay, billowing clouds marking the coastline. Thomas found it difficult to believe he had woken in Jamila's small village. A village that no longer existed.

"How many towns lie between here and the sea?"

"None of any size. Some are bigger than here, but most are smaller. A lot of people, though. Farmers mostly. There is al-Marilla to the east and Malaka to the west. Do you know them?"

Thomas nodded. "Yes, I know them." He looked around, back to the falling land. "Why don't people just leave? Malaka is in Spanish hands now, but al-Marilla is still Moorish the last I heard." He stopped and looked at Jamila, taken by her strength, afraid of the attraction he felt for her.

"Because just as we are hostages to our menfolk's good behaviour, so is our good behaviour the same to them. Any hint of resistance or escape results in them being punished."

"How do you know this?"

Jamila looked away, a tension in her body. "Sometimes women are taken to witness the punishment. A beating is the least of it. Others are crucified until they can no long draw breath. These are not idle threats being made."

"The man I questioned said he couldn't run away because if he was caught he would be executed, his family also punished. Imagine what it would be like—to die knowing the same fate, or worse, awaited your loved ones. What if these people have recruited men in each town and village to keep watch? It might explain where Luis went to if he was one of them."

Jamila made a noise and crossed her arms beneath her breasts.

She shook her head. "No."

"The man I questioned told me his leader calls himself The Warrior. He said it like it was a title of some kind."

"I take it the man you questioned is dead, is he?"

"No. I let him go." Thomas looked at her. "What, do you think I would kill him in cold blood? He told me what I wanted to know and I let him go. He might be stupid enough to go back to his master, but with luck he'll return to his family,. If what you're telling me is true he might have a day, two at most, to find them and flee."

Jamila smiled. "You are not as harsh as you pretend to be, are you."

Thomas didn't understand what she meant and started to descend the road again. They were near the bottom now, a level area before the land descended once more. Somewhere nearby running water sounded. To the left a high, long building ran along the far side of the level roadway, steam venting from ornately fashioned holes in the walls, some in the shape of crescent moons, others as stars and circles.

"Is this why you brought me all this way?" Thomas said. "I know I must stink, but there are more important matters to deal with than my cleanliness." He glanced the way they had come. "And now I have to climb all the way back up there again."

"It will not take you long to bathe." Jamila smiled. "Even less time if I help."

Thomas laughed, the feeling of doing so strange, the emotions it raised unwelcome. "Oh, I think if you helped it might take a lot longer."

"But you would be clean everywhere." Jamila faced him, her face serious. "I make no jest, Thomas. They have private chambers, and it is a long time since I pleasured a man—and I like you."

"You like me."

"Don't be stupid. Even you must be able to tell I do."

"You should ask Jorge, not me, for he will almost certainly know. He is a far better lover than I could ever be."

"It is not the skill, but the man that is important."

"Not according to Jorge. And this man is saying no."

Jamila let out a deep sigh but didn't seem annoyed at his

refusal. "Then I might as well show you the real reason I brought you all the way down here." She turned away.

Thomas watched her go—her lithe body, the glint of evening light in her hair. He felt an unwelcome stirring and wondered how long he could resist her. Or even if he wanted to.

Lubna's memory filled his mind. His hands recalled the touch of her skin beneath them, but the memory made resistance more difficult, not less.

He wondered what Lubna would say if she was here now. Though if she was here there would be no need for words.

He waited a moment for her voice, but nothing came.

Thomas felt a wave of loss crash through him. He staggered, and a groan escaped his lips. Jamila was too far away to hear and continued walking.

"No," Thomas said to himself.

This time his cry was loud enough to halt Jamila. She turned and started back. Thomas held up a hand, dropping his head so he couldn't see her anymore.

"No," he said again, and this time the demons invading his thoughts fled. He shook his head. "I am going mad." The idea didn't surprise him. The loss of Lubna had tipped him across some divide, he knew. He had come to the mountains to end his life, but something had stopped him. And now ... now life was making itself known to him once more, and he was unsure whether he welcome it or not. He needed some distraction, one that didn't involve tearing Jamila's clothes from her body.

"What else do you want to show me?" he said.

Jamila smiled and turned away.

The house sat square at the end of the street. Wide steps led from the roadway to an arched terrace.

"It's a fine house," Thomas said. "But I have seen many fine houses. Why this one?"

"The Governor lives here."

"You may need to explain a little more."

"I believe he has made a pact with the raiders. That is the reason this town is used as it is. Why the soldiers believe they can get away with whatever they like."

"The men I saw working fields were none of them young. The same for those going to pray."

Jamila turned her head, gaze sharp on him. "Jorge told me you are looking for someone. The man who killed your wife."

"Are you saying the man I seek lives in this house?" It half made sense to Thomas. Mandana or Guerrero. Or both.

Jamila shook her head. "No, of course not. But I believe the man who does knows of who you seek. I believe he either works alongside him or is forced to work for him. More likely the latter. Don't you want to capture this man and punish him?"

"That is what I came to the mountains for, but I have lost my way since. Now ... now I don't know why I'm here anymore. Escaping, I think, but escaping what I have no idea."

"Except you cannot escape, can you? The one you lost will always be with you, as she should be."

Thomas narrowed his eyes. Jamila could have no idea of how strongly the vision of Lubna had filled him, but her words offered some small confirmation he wasn't going mad.

"It is too early to confront this Governor," Thomas said. "Night will be better. Tell me more about him while we eat. I have allowed myself to grow weak. That ends today."

Jamila fell in close to his side as they climbed the steep roadway back to the square. Thomas tried not to show how much the climb tired him. They found Jorge standing in the square, Aban to one side, Dana on the other. There was a scowl on his face.

"These men are inhuman. Why did you keep us waiting here?"

"It was your choice," Thomas said. "Besides, you are tall and look strong. I expect they avoided you."

"Not altogether. And Aban said we were to meet here then go to eat. I can't remember the last time I ate a good meal."

"There is food being prepared for us now," said Jamila. She led them back to the house they were staying in, tucked in the alleys behind the Mosque, more climbing involved. They came out into a small square. On the far side tables were set on the street, but only one of them was occupied, by a group of five men. Jamila entered the building, and after a moment Thomas followed.

He stopped just beyond the doorway, breathing in air rich with the odour of spices he had not tasted since Jorge's lover, Belia, and Lubna had worked their magic in the kitchen. Jamila embraced a woman a little older than herself. There was no resemblance other than the way they held themselves—confident, assured of their own power, and he wondered if it was this woman's house they had taken over.

After a brief conversation Jamila turned and beckoned Thomas to follow. She led the way into a small courtyard where a table had been set. Lamps swung from wooden beams stained by their smoke. A small rill flowed along one side, and the walls were tiled in Moorish style. Thomas looked around, reminded of his own house in Gharnatah.

He was the last to sit, taking the only place left at the

head of the table. Despite the Moorish surroundings two flagons of wine were set on the table, glass goblets ready to be filled. It took Jorge no time to be the first to try the wine. He smiled and nodded his approval before reaching across the table to pour for them all. Two girls appeared with trays and laid out meat, rice, sauces, flatbreads, roasted birds, even a platter of small fried fish, most likely the darting trout Thomas had seen in the tumbling streams that cut through the southern slopes of the mountains. For a moment he experienced a moment of nostalgia for the fields of England, for the clear water of the Lugge, the fish reminding him of the trout that swam there, of the bulky backs of salmon forcing their way upstream in the autumn to spawn. He had no idea where the sudden emotion came from. He missed that land not at all. His home was here now, beneath the sun of al-Andalus.

"Tell me what you know of this Governor," Thomas said, as he spooned a rich sauce onto his plate and dipped flatbread into it. The spice filled his mouth and rose to make his eyes water. He smiled and took more. "I take it you brought us here not just for the excellence of the food. We can talk in safety, can we?"

"It is why we are here and not outside on the street. We will not be disturbed unless we ask for more food." Jamila smiled. "Jorge, I think, will ask for more."

"Jorge always asks for more, of everything. So, tell me what you know. Does this Governor have a name? Is he a Moor, a Spaniard, a Jew?"

"He is Moorish," said Jamila, "though he speaks the local dialect, and has good Spanish as well. But they say the man he works for is a Spaniard."

"I suspect I know who that might be," Thomas said. "The man who killed my wife. The man I intend to kill in turn."

A silence fell around the table.

Thomas looked at Jorge. "You knew this already, didn't you?"

"Of course … but not your intention. You still plan to destroy him?"

"And his army."

"Then you'll need help, and more than just mine."

"Perhaps. Jamila, tell me more. This Governor is a link, the first I have discovered." Thomas shook his head. "I had lost my way, I see that now, but I have found it again thanks to you."

"I will help you fight them," said Aban, bringing a worried glance from his mother.

CHAPTER TWELVE

As Thomas descended the precipitous roadway toward the bathhouse he carried a coarse sack in one hand which held clean clothes. Not new, for that would have required a wait of several days, but they were barely worn. He tried to remember the last time he had changed the clothes he wore and failed. It might have been as long ago as the day he set a torch to Lubna's funeral pyre, and he wondered how Jorge and the others had managed to put up with him.

"Do I smell?" he asked Jorge, who walked beside him. His clothes were clean, though old for Jorge.

"You stink like something dead a week."

"I suspected so. I apologise."

"No need. At least you're about to do something about it."

One final turn and the bathhouse lay ahead. It was early evening and the building sat in long shadows cast by the surrounding mountains. Smoke rose from a tall chimney at the rear and steam emerged from carved vents along the top of the walls. A number of men stood outside, talking the meaningless words of all men after a day's work. Two of them looked like soldiers, standing a little apart and watching everything.

Thomas asked for a private room, ignoring the knowing look of the owner who glanced between him and Jorge. A small pool sat in the centre of the space they were shown to, a single stone spout projecting from the wall. The boy who brought them showed Thomas how to use it, splashing water across his feet, then left.

Jorge stripped, laying his clothes on a high shelf, then stood beneath the spout and let hot water cascade over his head. There were soaps and oils, and he lathered his hair before washing every inch of himself. Thomas removed his old clothes and piled them on the floor. When they were finished he would ask the boy to take them away and burn them. The sack containing his new purchases went on the shelf beside Jorge's.

He sat on a stone bench, not wanting to taint the water in the pool yet, and watched Jorge with a detached interest. He hadn't seen the man naked in a long time and noticed he had lost weight, his muscles more delineated. His body, once scrupulously denuded of all hair, now showed dustings here and there, but not as much as a full man would.

"Do you like what you see?" Jorge asked.

"You're thinner."

"Worry over you, no doubt." Jorge pulled the handle and let water flow across him before stepping away. "It's all yours. I only hope there's enough hot water. Gods, you look terrible."

Thomas stood. "My thanks." He knew he was painfully thin, his skin stained with dirt, but even worse was the weakness. He was aware age had sapped some of the strength he once possessed, but the months since Lubna died had taken a far bigger toll. Too little food, too much time sitting in a ruined hut staring at a noose hanging from a beam, whispering its insidious message of oblivion.

Jorge slipped into the warm water of the bath and stretched his arms out. His legs half-floated so he took up almost all the space.

"Jamila will no doubt want you to pleasure her once you no longer smell like the arse-end of a donkey."

"Perhaps in that case I had best not wash myself at all."

"Then do it for me," said Jorge. "Please, do it for me. I would pleasure her on your behalf, but she has no interest in me. I suppose there must be a first time for all things. These are indeed strange times we are living through."

Thomas wetted his body then used the soap, scrubbing himself hard, over and over until his skin was raw. He sluiced then lathered again, working more soap into his hair, wondering if he needed someone to check it for lice. There would be someone in the baths to do the searching, he knew, and he should get it cut, his beard too. He sluiced again until he felt almost human, then slid into the bath on the opposite side to Jorge. They had lain together in water this way more times than he could recall, and each time Jorge would tease him, except not today. Today he was serious.

"Are you convinced Mandana is involved in this?"

"And his son. Perhaps his son more so than him. You heard what that man called him. The Warrior. Guerrero in Spanish."

"Why him?"

"Why Guerrero and not Mandana? Because he is the younger, the stronger, perhaps even more vicious than his father."

"That, yes, but why are you so sure it is them? The Warrior is a good name for a leader of men to call himself. It has a strength to it. The pair of them were working for Fernando the last we knew."

"Perhaps they still are," said Thomas. His body was languid, at ease, and he had trouble concentrating. He knew, soon, he would need all his wits about him. For now he drifted, almost floating in the water. "The entire area, the whole of al-Basharāt, sits in the shadow of Gharnatah, but this is not a land controlled by Muhammed. It is not controlled by anyone. Take this region and Gharnatah becomes vulnerable. Now that Malaka has fallen there is no escape to the south. Spain controls all of the north. An army here, to the east, another to the west. That is what Fernando wants."

Jorge shook his head, stroked his hand through the warm water. "If your theory is correct then you can't fight an army alone. Not even you, Thomas."

"I wonder how many of this army consist of captured men—a quarter, a half, more than a half? Would captured men fight as hard for their captors?"

"It might be wise to know a little more before launching a foolish attack."

"Yes, it might. But I can't put from my mind that it was Guerrero killed Lubna." Thomas sat up and leaned forward. "He hunted her down and killed her because of what I did. He blamed me for the death of his wife, even though it was entirely his own fault. He killed Lubna because I uncovered his plans to steal Malaka's gold. Am I meant to turn my back on that like the Christian God says I should? Turn the other cheek? No."

"I agree, he must die. Mandana too, father and son are as bad as each other. But to kill them you have to stay alive. We need to have a better plan. Or a plan, at least."

"We?" Thomas said.

"Yes, we. Did you think I would let you do this alone? Lubna was your wife, but did I not love her too?"

Thomas sank back into the water, floating again, trying to still the harsh beating of his heart that sent tiny ripples across the surface.

"Is Usaden still in Gharnatah?"

"Of course. You asked him to look after your family, and he will. He is your man now. But you will need more than just Usaden, however good he is."

"There is none better," Thomas said.

"Agreed. But you are talking about attacking an entire army."

"I will think of something."

"Something rational, I hope."

When the boy came to ask if they were going to be long, because other patrons were waiting for the chamber, Thomas told him they were finished and pulled himself from the water. He knew he had made a decision, and the making of it brought a new confidence. He told the boy to take his old clothes and burn them, then find him someone to trim his hair and beard. Barely recognisable, he dressed his scrubbed body in fresh cotton and linen. It felt like donning a suit of armour.

The bathing and clothes were only the start of the plan, if plan it could be called. For the moment it involved little more than waiting and watching. Thomas had identified a number of locations where the governor's house could be observed from without drawing attention and led them to one such now, a small inn with rough tables set outside. A young girl came to hover in the doorway and Thomas asked if they had wine. The girl nodded and went inside without asking what kind of wine they wanted.

"Are we going to be here all night?" Jorge looked at their surroundings, making clear his opinion of them.

"There are other places, but this is convenient, and no doubt as good as any."

"What are you expecting to see? Or perhaps I should be asking who."

"Mandana or his son. Perhaps both. Killing his men will have angered him. I expect the man to come here to see if this is where we have fled to."

"It would help to know who this governor is," said Jorge, "and whether he can be trusted or not."

"Why? According to Jamila he's involved. You've seen this town. It's a gaol. So we sit here and wait until the gaoler arrives."

"How long?" Jorge leaned to one side as the girl brought a jug of wine and two cups.

"As long as it takes."

"What if he doesn't come for two weeks, or a month? We can't stay here forever."

Thomas looked around. "Why not?" His attention returned to the house at the end of the street. People moved along the cobbles, most of them coming from the higher part of town to bathe. Nobody else came to the inn, and Thomas realised that should have been a sign. Instead of rising he stayed where he was, continuing to watch the house. Nothing was happening, but he was patient.

"I'm not staying here watching an empty house," said Jorge. "You do what you like, I'm going back to the others."

Thomas nodded, his eyes not moving from the building.

After a while Jorge rose and walked away.

The girl came out and picked up the almost full flagon of wine.

"Do you want food?" she asked.

Thomas shook his head.

"If you're not drinking and not eating there are other customers waiting."

Thomas looked around at the empty tables and said nothing. After a while the girl went away again. He wondered what he would do if Jorge was right, but knew he would never find Guerrero and Mandana by searching the countryside. The area was just too big, too difficult to navigate. He would wait for them to come to him. They may not come tonight or the next night, but they would come eventually.

The sky grew dark and stars appeared, glittering like pinpricks cut through black velvet cloth. In the house a light moved beyond the wide front door as someone approached. The door opened and a tall man walked onto the terrace. Thomas sat up. He recognised him.

He rose to his feet, staring at the house, trying to decide whether to approach or not. He had not seen Don Domingo Alkhabaz in several years. The last time had been in the palace sitting atop *al-Hamra*, and then he had been in the company of Faris al-Rashid and others who were plotting the downfall of a Sultan. Not the Sultan who now ruled there but his father. Now his son sat on the throne after taking it, losing it again, and then regaining his position. It was a sign of the chaos al-Andalus had sunk into that such a thing could even be comprehended.

At one time Thomas had considered Don Domingo a friend. Not a close friend, but neither an enemy like his master, Faris al-Rashid. But that had been almost six years ago, and much had happened in the world since.

Thomas realised he could sit where he was all night, but to do so would bring no enlightenment. He watched Don Domingo stand at the top of the steps. He was waiting for somebody, and that thought sparked an excitement in Thomas. He wished Jorge was still with him to provide courage, then shook his head at the notion he could even consider such a thing. Where had his own courage gone?

He dropped coins on the table and stepped around it, just as another figure appeared at the end of the roadway. Don Domingo Alkhabaz moved forward and descended the wide steps to the street. It was clear this was who he had been waiting for, and Thomas stepped backwards until he was obscured in the shadows of a narrow alley.

The other figure walked slowly toward the Governor's house. This man Thomas had seen more recently, the last time only an hour before Lubna's life was taken. Abbot Mandana held a staff in his right hand. His left was missing. Thomas glanced along the road but saw no companions. It was all he could do to restrain himself from leaping out as the man passed close by. He knew the old Thomas, the fearless Thomas, would have done so whatever the consequences, and he wondered if he had truly changed so much. He missed that man, the one who knew his own mind, who never doubted.

He watched as Mandana reached Don Domingo. There was no embrace, no touching of arms. Mandana spoke for a moment, then Don Domingo turned and led the way into the house. The door closed, a matter of minutes since it had opened and changed everything. Thomas remained in the alleyway, attempting to work through the implications of what he had just witnessed.

Thomas recalled Usaden's words when he had returned to the courtyard of yews where Lubna lost her life. He said he had pursued Mandana's son before losing him, and that Mandana himself had not been involved in the attack on Lubna and the others. Will confirmed the story even through his own shock. Yet here the man was again, in a town where the families of captured men were being held. It was no coincidence, and Thomas wondered if his son was close—for more than Mandana it was the son, Pedro Guerrero, he sought. The man who had killed his wife. The man whose name, in Spanish, meant Warrior.

CHAPTER THIRTEEN

When Thomas returned to their shared accommodation he found Jorge flirting outrageously with both Jamila and Dana, neither of whom offered the usual response to such efforts. Thomas drew him aside without explanation and led the way to the room they shared with Aban, who remained downstairs with the two women.

"I was enjoying myself," said Jorge, attempting to look petulant and failing.

"Clearly. I've just seen Mandana enter the Governor's house."

"Already? You have the luck of the devil, Thomas. But it's not so surprising, for it confirms your theory."

"Do you remember Don Domingo Alkhabaz?"

"Of course. One of the more civilised companions of Muhammed and his so-called friends." Jorge sat on the edge of the bed and stared at Thomas. "Does the fact that it's Don Domingo have some significance? Is there more going on here than you thought?"

Thomas pulled up a rickety stool and sat, for the roof was too low to allow him to stand without bending and his neck was starting to ache. "Mandana is here for a reason, either something to do with the captives or something else —he may even suspect this is where we fled to. Whatever it is involves Don Domingo."

"And if that man you tortured told the truth, Guerrero can't be far away." Jorge stared at Thomas. "Unless father and son fell out over what happened in Malaka. I genuinely believed Mandana liked Lubna—that he had changed. But if what we were told is true and Guerrero is Mandana's son—though how such a thing could be possible I have no idea—they may well be working together now.

"Mandana could never be trusted. He's reverted to what he has always been—a wolf, a killer. His change was no more than a mask he hid behind. I just wish I knew the reason for what he is doing here. It doesn't make sense. He should be with Fernando, doing his bidding."

"Perhaps he is." Jorge smiled. "Can we go and kill him?"

"Not yet. I'm going back to watch the house when the town grows quiet, then follow when he leaves to find out where he's holed up. This town is different to the others so I don't think he'll be far away."

"And then we kill him?"

Thomas stared at Jorge, trying to decide if he meant his threat or not. Then he realised Lubna's death would have hit him hard too. They had been friends. Good friends. Lubna would go to Jorge to unburden herself of the fears she couldn't admit to Thomas. They would have shared secrets he wasn't privy to.

"Mandana can live or die, it's his son I seek. The man who took Lubna's life."

"Father and son," said Jorge. "If they're working together you will have to kill both." He tilted his head to one side. "Would you still consider Don Domingo a friend?"

It was a good question—a relevant question—but one Thomas had no answer for.

"I haven't spoken to him in years. It puzzles me why he's here, in the position he is. When I knew him he was a rich man."

"We live in hard times. Even rich men are not immune to trouble." Jorge smiled. "We are rich men, are we not? Though it would be hard to tell looking at us now."

Thomas thought of the wealth they had liberated over the years. None of it stolen, not in truth—liberated was the word he preferred.

"Are we still rich men?" he asked.

"We were when I left Gharnatah, I made sure to check. Whether Muhammed has discovered our chests and stolen them by now I doubt, but you can never tell with that man. He stole Helena from you and keeps her captive. You should have returned to Gharnatah with me and freed her like we were going to do. It would have been a better tribute to Lubna than hiding in these mountains."

"She wasn't stolen from me," Thomas said. "She was never mine. But you're right, I should have freed her before coming here. How well do you know Don Domingo?"

"I doubt he even remembers who I am. Why?"

"I was hoping you could talk to him, find out how he ended up here, and what his relationship is with Mandana."

"And what will you be doing?"

"Following Mandana, of course, to find out where he goes."

"He'll have a horse and you won't. Besides, Don Domingo won't tell me anything."

"I can find a horse, but there's little point if Don Domingo won't talk to you."

"He knows me as a palace eunuch, nothing more—a

creature he would never even acknowledge. I should follow Mandana instead."

Thomas only stared at Jorge.

In the end Jorge had wanted to come even though Thomas had no use for him. If Jorge couldn't interrogate Don Domingo he would have to do so himself and let Mandana ride away. He had told Jorge the women needed his protection, but here he was beside him in the dark roadway, watching the Governor's house. The inn they had frequented was shut, all the houses dark except for the one where lamps flickered behind expensive glass windows. Even the town's dogs had stopped their endless barking and fallen silent. Thomas wondered what had become of Kin and determined to ask Jamila in the morning.

"What if he stays the night?" asked Jorge.

"He won't. He'll have men waiting for him beyond the town walls, but I admit he has been in there longer than I expected."

"What if he left when you returned to our lodgings?"

"Then Don Domingo would be in bed and the house dark. Mandana is still there."

"So we wait?" said Jorge.

"In silence," Thomas said.

Half an hour passed before there came movement at the end of the street, but instead of Mandana's men appearing a boar came along the roadway, as if this was its natural habitat. It rummaged in piles of rubbish that had been thrown out. When it came to where Thomas and Jorge stood it stopped and sniffed the air. Thomas laid a hand on the hilt of the knife at his waist. He had seen boars attack before—both in France and England, and later here in Spain, so he knew the danger they offered—but this one seemed to find them unthreatening and continued on its way. Thomas smiled as it passed within a dozen paces, totally unconcerned. The boar continued on, then stopped and looked around before breaking into a run along the street.

The door of the Governor's house opened and Mandana stepped out. He was alone. From within the door a lamp moved, but whoever held it didn't reveal themselves. Mandana looked left and right, up at the dark sky, then came slowly down the steps and started along the roadway toward them. Thomas caught Jorge's sleeve and pulled him deeper into the alley they were sheltering in. Jorge's foot caught on a discarded sack of offal and he tipped sideways into a pile of wood, sending it clattering.

Mandana stopped, only forty paces separating them. He glanced back at the Governor's house, then directly at the opening of the alley. Thomas was sure he couldn't see them, but the noise was enough to tell him someone must be lurking within the shadows. Thomas didn't want to confront the man, not yet, nor did he want him to know he was on his trail. He grabbed Jorge's arm and pulled him deeper, praying the alley would let them out at the far end. He saw Mandana take a few steps toward them then suddenly jerk away. A sound came, a clattering of horned feet, and the boar came running along the road, right past Mandana without even seeing him and on down the roadway. The town's dogs broke into a high-pitched clamour. Mandana watched the boar disappear then shook his head and continued on his way.

"Close," said Jorge.

Thomas held a finger to his lips. He waited until the sound of Mandana's progress had faded. "Follow him. Tell me how many there are with him and in which direction he goes, but do *not* go after them."

Jorge stared at him, the whites of his eyes almost all

that showed. "I'm not sure I'm the right person after all. Perhaps I should try to talk with Don Domingo."

"Follow Mandana—not close, but find out where he's going and how many men he has with him. You can do that, can't you?"

"I'm a better talker."

"You said he thinks of you as a palace servant. It won't be dangerous, so long as you don't fall over any more rubbish." Thomas pushed at Jorge, who hesitated a moment then turned away. At the end of the alley he stopped and looked back, even though Thomas would be hidden by the shadows, then went on.

Thomas waited for the town to fall still again before making his way toward Don Domingo's house. He tried the wide door from the terrace but found it barred from within. He hadn't expected getting inside to be easy, so took one of the smaller roads that led along the side of the building. He chose the one the boar had appeared from for no other reason than it pleased him to do so. It pleased him even more when he came to a wall twice his height that must enclose a space behind the house. He reached up, fingertips searching for a hold. The mortar between the joints was soft, crumbling away in places. He pulled himself up until he could straddle the top of the wall and take stock of what lay beyond.

There were gardens that might once have been impressive but had been left to run wild. The expected rill along the centre had dried up and grown choked with weeds. At the rear of the house sat a terrace with a terracotta tiled roof. The flagstone floor had been recently swept, though why anyone would want to sit out there was a mystery. Thomas turned and let himself hang then dropped to the ground, the sound of snapping stalks loud in the night. He waited, but nothing showed to indicate he had been heard, and he made his way to the terrace. Here he was rewarded with a door that opened to his touch, giving access to a narrow hallway. At the end a lamp burned. Thomas waited, listening, hearing nothing. He closed the door and walked along the corridor, trying to work out where Don Domingo's rooms would be. On the upper floor, almost certainly, and when Thomas found a staircase he climbed it, grateful for the occasional lamp that offered enough light for him to make his way without knocking into furniture. The servants would no doubt have rooms downstairs in the cellars, but there might well be someone else on the upper floor—a female companion perhaps, because Thomas recalled Don Domingo was much taken with beautiful women.

At the top of the stairs Thomas stopped to work out a strategy. Don Domingo had recently been talking with Mandana. The night was more than half gone, so it was likely he had gone to his bed, but unlikely he had fallen asleep yet.

Thomas slipped his shoes off and left them at the head of the stairs, then walked barefoot along the upper hallway. Where doors had been left ajar he peered inside, saw offices, a dining room, another where the sweet scent of hashish hung in the air. He ignored the doors that were closed for the moment, knowing he would have to try them at some point if he failed to find Don Domingo.

Ahead, on the right, he heard a soft female voice offering words of encouragement. Then a male voice, an edge to it urging the woman to try harder.

Thomas turned back and entered one of the rooms he had passed, a place for reading, with documents on shelves and deep cushions. He sat cross-legged and waited, fighting off the urge to sleep. He listened to Don Domingo and the woman struggling to achieve some manner of conclusion. Grunts of passion and squeals of delight. He tried to work out if the sounds held genuine passion or only a pretence at such. He jerked awake from a dream where Lubna lay atop him, her skin silken, warm beneath his touch, and he almost cried out at the surge of loss that rose through him.

Bare feet slapped on the floor, light feet, and he glimpsed a shape as a woman passed the doorway. He waited, listening as she descended the stairs. After a time a door below closed and Thomas rose to his feet.

Don Domingo's door stood a little open, but Thomas ignored it and walked to the end of the hallway where he found a window looking across the neglected garden. He sat on the sill, waiting. It didn't take long before he heard snores, but still he waited. Only when he knew Don Domingo was deep asleep did he enter the room and approach the wide bed. He looked down at the man he had once known well enough to call friend, despite the company he kept, and wondered what had brought him to this far-flung remnant of the Moorish kingdom of al-Andalus. He smiled to himself. Time to find out.

He drew his knife, not because he expected to need it, but because the encouragement it might offer would be useful. Then he knelt on the bed and put his hand across Don Domingo Alkhabaz's bearded mouth.

The man's eyes snapped open and he began to struggle. Thomas showed him the knife, letting the lamplight glint off the blade until Don Domingo stilled.

"I mean you no harm. Do you remember me?"

He watched Don Domingo's eyes track his face, saw a failure of recognition. It was not a surprise. Thomas knew he had changed these last months, enough that even close friends might fail to recognise him.

"Thomas Berrington," he said, and saw Don Domingo frown, felt him try to give a shake of his head. "When I remove my hand you will remain silent. I trusted you at one time, but now I am a desperate man and won't hesitate to hurt you. Do you understand me?"

Don Domingo tried to nod. Thomas withdrew his hand, the knife coming down to rest against the man's neck.

"I heard you were dead. You disappeared into the wilderness and were never heard of again."

"True, some of it at least. But as you can see, I am still alive. What brings you to a place such as this?" Thomas withdrew the knife but didn't sheath it yet.

Don Domingo sat up, arranging a surfeit of pillows behind him.

"Better I ask the same of you, Thomas Berrington. What are you doing in my house, and how did you find me?"

"Not find," said Thomas. "It wasn't you I was looking for, but the man who was here earlier."

"Ah ... I see." Don Domingo swung his legs from the bed, unconcerned at his nakedness. "We will be more comfortable having this conversation somewhere else."

Thomas watched Don Domingo walk to a wardrobe and pull out a robe. He slid it around his shoulders and tied it at the front. Silk pooled at his feet, dragging as he walked toward the door. He stopped and looked back.

"You can stay here of course, if you wish. I will even send someone to entertain you, but I suspect you have come in search of knowledge, unless you have changed a great deal since last we met."

Thomas rose and followed Don Domingo, who led the way to a large room at the end of the corridor. A single lamp burned when they entered, but Don Domingo went around lighting others before indicating a chair fashioned in the Spanish style. Wide windows looked out into darkness, reflecting the two of them as they sat.

"It appears we have both fallen on hard times, Thomas.

Tell me what brings you here, and then I may be able to offer a little information in return."

"I seek the man who was with you tonight. Abbot Mandana."

"Why?"

"I intend to kill him. His son, too."

"Ah ... so you know about the son, do you? Then we will need coffee." Don Domingo rose and left the room.

Thomas remained where he was, wondering if he was a fool to trust the man. He might have gone to rouse his servants. No doubt there would be guards. He wiped a hand across his face, slapped his cheeks, and wondered when he had started to want to live again.

CHAPTER FOURTEEN

Thomas stood at the window, looking out into the night. All he saw was his own distorted reflection staring back, and he wondered when he had started to look so old. His face was gaunt, that of a man nearing the end of his life. *Is that what this is*, he wondered? *Have I come to these high places to die?* When Don Domingo returned he welcomed the distraction from his own thoughts, which had grown as dark as the night.

"The girl will bring us coffee. She was asleep, so it may take a while." He indicated the chair where Thomas had recently sat then took his own. "There are few people that know Mandana has a son. I'm surprised you do."

"It was Pedro Guerrero who killed Lubna," Thomas said.

Don Domingo stared at him, his face showing nothing. "I heard she had died. I was sorry to hear it, and sorry for your loss. I know how much you loved each other."

"How?"

Don Domingo frowned. "How did I know? People talk of you, Thomas, for you always seem to be involved in the heart of events that are none of your business. So I hear things. As does my master." He held a hand up when he saw Thomas's expression. "No, not Mandana. I talk of Muhammed, for it was he who sent me here after I fell on hard times. I was grateful, until that man turned up and made my life difficult."

"How long have you had dealings with Mandana?"

Don Domingo raised a shoulder. "Half a year, perhaps a little less."

"How long have you been here in Pampaneira?"

"Two years. It was a good life, an easy life until Mandana turned up. He brought Guerrero to see me. He is handsome but his eyes are dead. I suspect he came to frighten me into doing as they asked, and it worked."

"You are rich, you could have left this place."

"I was rich, but no longer. Muhammed has placed other men he trusts, or who he has a hold over, in towns to the east and north of Gharnatah. You know how he is. Those men took land that belonged to others, and some of that land was rightfully mine. Muhammed does not punish them, so they grow ever bolder. He worries over everything. He worries the Spanish will come from the west and the east both. Then he worries they will come from the south, then the north. I heard a rumour Yusuf was planning to oust him before he died."

"He was a brave man, a good man," Thomas said.

Don Domingo gave a soft smile. "He used to worship you when he was younger. Everyone saw it, how he followed you around whenever you came to the palace. It was as if you were tied together with a length of string. How did he die? Were you there?"

"Not when he was struck down, but he died protecting others, as you would expect."

"He would have made a good Sultan."

"It would have meant more fighting."

"Muhammed is a coward. The fighting would not have

lasted long." Don Domingo sighed. "And I would still be a rich man."

The woman Thomas had last seen leaving Don Domingo's bedroom padded into the room on bare feet. She placed a tray holding fine porcelain cups and a steaming jug of coffee on the low table between them, then turned and left. Thomas watched her go.

"She is yours for the rest of tonight if you wish it," said Don Domingo.

Thomas smiled. "My thanks, but I want of no-one since my wife died."

"It was the news of the hour in Gharnatah when Olaf Torvaldsson returned."

"He serves Muhammed now?" Thomas asked.

Don Domingo offered a nod, leaned forward and poured thick, dark coffee into their cups.

"Why do you want to kill Mandana so much? Is he worth it?"

"I will kill them both," Thomas said. "Guerrero murdered Lubna."

"How can you be so sure? I heard she died in the chaos of battle."

"Is that what Olaf says?"

"No, he tells it the same way as you—but others carry a different tale." Don Domingo reached for his cup and sipped at it.

"Those others were not there. I was. What are they doing here, Don Domingo?"

"You should ask your other friend, not me."

"Jorge knows nothing of it."

Don Domingo smiled. "The eunuch? No, I mean the Spanish King. Mandana is here on his business—though I doubt his master knows exactly what it is the man is doing."

"Are you in Fernando's pay as well?"

"I am in nobody's pay. I scratch out a living where I can. Small taxes here and there, some income from iron mines on the other side of the mountain."

"And empty property? Abandoned goods when men are taken?"

Don Domingo said nothing.

Thomas reached for his coffee and drained the small cup.

"No more lies. Tell me everything you know."

"Can you trust him?" asked Jorge.

Thomas had returned to their lodgings in the first grey light of dawn. Already the peaks of the Sholayr were splashed with pink, but the deep valleys held night close like a cold lover it was reluctant to release. Aban was curled in sleep on the narrow cot pushed against the wall. Jorge had been sprawled across the other bed when Thomas woke him. They had come downstairs to sit at the table.

"He has no reason to lie, and I believe I scared him enough to shake the truth from him in the end."

"You're beginning to specialise in scaring people," said Jorge. "Though it's always been a trick you've had."

Thomas ignored the comment. "He says Mandana came to him with an offer that allowed for only one answer. This is the largest town in forty miles and has empty houses after its scouring."

"Why bother? It might be the largest town, but that doesn't make it a city. Mandana can simply take whatever men he wants by force, like he has elsewhere. I doubt those he's taken even know their families are held here. What kind of a threat is that?"

"Don Domingo claims the captives know well enough.

Mandana and Guerrero are Spaniards, and the Spanish are nothing if not efficient—it's why they are going to win this war. Women and children are taken now and again and displayed to their menfolk. Mandana has told Don Domingo to make a record of where every man comes from, another record of who their family is. It's a simple matter to match one up with the other. He told me more, even though he didn't want to."

"Which is?"

"It is how hundreds of captured men are controlled. It takes only one or two examples to be made, and I wager one is usually enough. If a man tries to rebel or escape he is held and his family, if he has one, brought to him. The wives see their husbands in chains, the husbands see their wives and children, vulnerable." Thomas breathed hard, the telling of it difficult, but the act not surprising when Mandana and Guerrero were involved. "The man knows his own life is forfeit, but not that one of his family will also be executed. One is chosen—son, daughter, wife, father, mother. It doesn't matter which. They are killed in front of the rebel, then the remaining family members are made to witness his fate in turn. It's demonic."

Jorge was silent for some time, his gaze turned inward, and Thomas allowed him to come to terms with the news. If he could. Thomas knew he hadn't fully done so yet himself.

Jorge looked up, his face set hard. "Did Don Domingo tell you how many men Mandana has?"

"Close to a thousand, perhaps more."

"Gods, as many as that? Does he know why they have brought an army here?"

"Mandana hasn't told him—or he claims he hasn't, and I see no reason why Don Domingo would lie to me about it, he told me everything else. He believes Mandana continues to work under Fernando's orders, except I'm not so sure he does anymore. He has broken loose. I'm sure Fernando would not countenance what I heard."

"And this town—is it little more than a prison?"

"Wives, children, entire families are brought here so they can be held in one place. So they can be controlled. The man we questioned said he obeyed to keep his family safe. I have no doubt they will be somewhere within the town walls of Pampaneira." Thomas shook his head, barely believing the tale he was telling. "Don Domingo showed me records, detailed records of every woman and child that has been brought here. Their names, their captured menfolk, where they live in the town. If I didn't know it already, that alone would be enough to implicate Mandana and Guerrero. Mandana was involved in the Inquisition in Ixbilya, and they did so love to record every minute item of information—exactly as is being done here."

Jamila came to wipe the table with a damp cloth. Thomas had not been aware she had come into the room, so involved was he in the telling of what he knew, but she had obviously overheard much of what he had told Jorge.

"Men came to our village," she said. "They made us tell them our names and wrote them in a book. They came back every month or so and compared the names to make sure none of us had left." She set her knuckles on the table-top and looked at Thomas, Jorge all but ignored. "We were as good as prisoners. Hostages to our menfolk, but prisoners to them as well. You are right, Thomas, it is a work of genius. Evil, but clever."

"Mandana isn't that clever," said Jorge, as Jamila moved off.

"No, I'd say that, too. But I know barely anything about Guerrero. This isn't the work of Fernando, it will be one of those two who has come up with the idea."

"Which of them is in charge?" said Jorge. "An army can

have only one leader, one man to look up to. Is it Guerrero or Mandana?"

The thought hadn't occurred to Thomas, and he knew Jorge was thinking better than he was these days. He grasped Jorge's arm and pulled him close. "You're right. Of course you're right."

"Well, that's another first from you."

"It has to be Guerrero. Mandana's too old, too sick, but his son is in his prime and kills without a second thought —I know that to my cost. The man we captured spoke of him with both reverence and fear."

"So why is it Mandana and not Guerrero who deals with Don Domingo?"

"Because, strange as it seems, I believe Mandana is the more rational, the more open to reason." Thomas thought of his first meeting with Guerrero a year before, when he had carried his dying wife into the infirmary in Malaka. How the man had been unreasonable, irrational. How he had blamed Thomas and Lubna for his wife's death.

"We came through other places on our way here—all of them the same, stripped of men. There were abandoned villages, too, their inhabitants no doubt brought to live here. Whatever is going on must be happening close to here. If Mandana has a thousand men they will have a camp, and I mean to seek it out."

Jorge laughed. "You will fight a thousand on your own?"

"Do you think me stupid?" Thomas held out his arms to display how gaunt he had become. "Look at me. I don't scare people anymore. I can barely fight one man." Thomas was aware that something had broken inside him and feared it might never heal. It was nothing physical, despite how thin he had become. The strength that had leached from him could be recovered with time and effort, but there was a void within, shaped in the form of Lubna, that could never be made whole again. He didn't want it made whole, because that would mean forgetting her. Even killing Pedro Guerrero, the man who had stolen her life, would not heal the void. Not that it would stop him. The man was living on borrowed time, Mandana with him. Thomas would wipe the entire family from the face of the earth. He knew he should have done it sooner. If he had Lubna would still be alive. Mandana's show of atonement had seduced him, made his resolve weaken.

Jorge offered a smile, unaware of the dark thoughts in Thomas's head. "It's true you aren't the man you once were, but a week or two of good food, some exercise, and you'll be back to your old self." Jorge glanced to where Jamila was busy preparing food and lowered his voice. "Tumble her into bed. Sex is good for both the body and the mind. But even after that you'll need help."

"I've been a fool," Thomas said, knowing Jorge would agree, which he did. "When Mandana and Guerrero first came here they couldn't have had more than the hundred men we saw in Malaka. My grief blinded me. If I had pursued them immediately, with Olaf and Usaden and a dozen others, I could have destroyed them both. Now, it's too late."

"You need more men, that's all," said Jorge.

"Enough to fight a thousand? It would need an army."

"Olaf has an army."

Thomas shook his head. "Olaf leads the Sultan's army. Can you see Muhammed allowing him to take his troops into these mountains in pursuit of a ghost? Mandana and Guerrero are no threat to Muhammed."

"But they are a threat to us," said Jorge.

"Which is why I have to hunt them down and kill them."

"You don't see it yet, do you? You are right, this place is a prison. There is nothing to stop people leaving except fear, and the knowledge of what their punishment would be. And now we are also here. No doubt our names will be added to Don Domingo's list, and Mandana will hear about our presence. Perhaps he was given a list of new arrivals in the town when he came last night. What if he has read it already?"

Thomas stared into space, teasing the logic of Jorge's argument, annoyed it hadn't occurred to him before.

"Then it's even more important we hunt them down before they come for us."

"I've told you, we can't do anything. The two of us?" Jorge shook his head. "We should flee, I agree, but flee to safety."

"Where is safe anymore?"

"Gharnatah, almost anywhere in Spain. You can throw yourself on the mercy of your queen. Isabel will offer you protection."

"I have unfinished business here," Thomas said. "And now I also have a plan."

"Which is?"

"If I tell it you'll want to come, and I need to do this alone."

Jorge sat up. He stared hard at Thomas for a long while before speaking.

"That is exactly the attitude that got you into this trouble in the first place. Instead of trusting your friends, you set off on your own. You're lucky to have survived this long."

"Or unlucky," Thomas said.

"Don't be stupid. Did you think I wouldn't be with you wherever you led? Or did you truly come here to die?" Jorge shook his head. "No, of course not, otherwise you would have used that noose instead of letting it hang there like some pointless promise. And now I'm here I won't let you leave without me again."

"Nor will I."

Thomas and Jorge looked across to where Aban stood in the doorway.

"Did you think I wouldn't hear you arguing? Those men have taken my father and my friends. If you go to fight then I come too."

"There will be no fighting," Thomas said. "Even with three of us we are still a little outnumbered." Even as he spoke, he knew there had been times in the past when such thoughts would never have occurred to him. That was something else Lubna's death had stripped from him, the certainty he could not be killed.

"So what were you going to do alone that the three of us cannot do just as well?" asked Jorge.

"Track them. Find their hideout."

"And then?"

"I haven't thought that far ahead, but something will occur to me."

"I've already told you, you need Olaf's army."

"Not yet. Not until I'm sure."

CHAPTER FIFTEEN

Jamila refused to allow Aban to go with them. The boy pleaded, argued, lost his temper, but in the end he couldn't go against his mother's wishes. So it was only Jorge who accompanied Thomas from Pampaneira a little before noon. They left on foot, because horses would make them too conspicuous, and in this land of precipice and gorge two feet were as good as four. They had been walking an hour when a dark shape came bounding down the hillside toward them. Kin fell into step at Thomas's side, face turned up, tongue lolling.

"I'd forgotten you had acquired a dog," said Jorge.

"I didn't think I had. Where has he been all this time?" In truth, in the melee of leaving Jamila's village, the laying of black powder and the death of Ibrahim, Thomas had forgotten all about the dog. "Besides, he's not mine. If I'd thought on it, I would have assumed he had gone off with someone else. Someone he already knew."

"He must like you. God knows why. Perhaps he'll save your life and someone can write a tale of your brave, dead dog."

"I'd rather he didn't make the effort and lived."

"That too, then."

Kin grew tired of waiting for either of them to feed him a scrap and bounded ahead.

"He's going to be a problem when we want to pass without being seen," Thomas said.

"Nobody notices a dog," said Jorge. "Besides, we're probably going in the wrong direction anyway."

"If we see no sign by the end of the day I'll think on where else they might be. But you said this is the direction Mandana left in, and I see no reason for him to try to hide where he was going."

"Other than being Mandana."

"Yes, other than that. He had no idea anyone was watching him, and he probably believes me dead, like everyone else seems to."

Jorge made a show of looking around at the desolate landscape. They had climbed slowly, following narrow trails created by animals. "I'm glad you're so sure we're going the right way."

"Not me, Kin. Look." Thomas pointed to where the dog was snapping at the remains of a fire. Thomas started to run, almost immediately breathless. "Kin, no!"

But his cry was ignored as the dog retrieved what it was trying to pull from the still warm embers—a good-sized cut of meat, burned almost to a crisp. Kin tore at it with sharp teeth, swallowed the charred meat in two sharp gulps before looking up and wagging his tail. Thomas knelt and felt the embers. Still warm. He looked around as Jorge made his way more slowly toward them. The ground was disturbed, but he could make out where men had slept. He rose and walked the ground, studying it. Four men, but when he went further out he found where five horses had been tied to a wizened almond bush.

"Do you plan to live off the land again?" asked Jorge as he joined him.

"Mandana was here, together with four of his men. The fire is still warm, so they can't be far ahead." Thomas looked to where Kin was crisscrossing the ground, nose to the dry earth. "He's got their scent." He glanced at Jorge. "Are you ready to run?"

Jorge opened his mouth to object just as Kin began a steady lope to the north. Thomas started after the disappearing dog, knowing Jorge would follow. Where else would he go?

Kin was waiting for them beyond a low ridge when Thomas crossed it, the air burning his lungs with each breath. Jorge had caught up with him but stayed at his side, moving the more easier of them, and Thomas knew he had to take more care of himself. He was no use to anyone in the condition he was.

"Has he lost the scent?" asked Jorge.

"No, just lazy." Thomas almost smiled before he caught himself. "He's waiting for us."

"Are dogs clever?"

"Some appear to be so, others are as dumb as rocks."

"Which kind is Kin?"

"One of the clever kind, I think. Did you ever have a dog as a boy?"

Jorge laughed. "If I had my father would have cooked it. No, I never had a dog, nor since. I never felt I was missing out by not having one."

"We always had dogs," Thomas said.

"In England?"

"Yes, and since. I had a dog in France, and for a time I looked after another in a range of high hills, but none since. I had my own dog from the age of four when my father considered me old enough to care for and train one.

An untrained dog is dangerous and no good to any man, so I know this one has been trained both to hunt and track." A thought occurred to Thomas. "If Kin was raised by Luis, he might be able to track him. I've seen it before. Their senses are far more acutely attuned than ours, particularly to the scent of their master."

"And that helps us how?"

Thomas turned to Jorge. "Pretend for a moment you have a brain inside that handsome skull."

"Do you really think I am handsome?"

"Of course you are, but you know I admire knowledge more than beauty."

"It is your loss. But yes, I see what you mean. If the dog smells Luis he might lead us to their camp." Jorge shook his head. "Though I don't see it. If Mandana has a thousand men, how can a dog smell a single man among them?"

"Likely not, but I think he's going to track Mandana and his men, and that will lead us to where we want to go."

Kin set off again, going more slowly now so Thomas had no need to run, for which he was grateful.

"And when we get there," said Jorge, "we do nothing but watch, agreed?"

"Agreed."

"Good. I am too pretty to die a horrible death. Or any kind of death. What if the dog tries to go to Luis? They'll kill it, won't they?"

Thomas slowed. The thought hadn't occurred to him, and he knew it should have. It made sense. Kin wasn't his dog. According to Aban he belonged to Luis, the son of the dead farmer and his wife. The possible father of the child Dana carried inside her. Family, relationships, love and loyalty. Thomas thought he had left such things behind on the hilltop when they raised Lubna's ashes to the sky, but perhaps such things could never be escaped. He thought of all the people he had loved over the years, all those he had hated, those who had loved him, and those who had hated him. Many, many people, and he felt a stirring at the memories coiling through him. There had been a girl in Lemster, two years older than he was, who had set her sights on Thomas because he was the son of an important man. And Eleanor, a girl the same age as him, in the south of France. Many women between and since, and he wondered when he had lost the need to only bed them and found a need for love. Except love had betrayed his trust. Both Eleanor and Lubna had been torn from him, and he vowed not to let love seduce him a third time. It seemed great joy and great pain were the bookends of love.

"Kin isn't my dog," Thomas said. "I have no hold over him."

"And if his master is dead? You know it more likely than not, don't you?"

"I'll worry about that if it happens." He looked to where the dog was two hundred paces ahead, skipping its way up a long hillside, front and back legs sometimes working together, other times almost completely unconnected. Now and then Kin would dip his nose to the ground, but the scent of what he followed was strong in the air and he tracked it without effort. This is what he had been born for, this was the dog's world of scent and sound and instinct, and Thomas knew they would have wandered aimlessly had Kin not been with them. Inside he felt a spark of something that seemed suspiciously like hope, but so unfamiliar was the sensation he chose to ignore it as a false promise.

They followed Kin over scarred and shattered hillsides until gradually the land began to fall away ahead. A deep valley lay below, while beyond it the snow-capped peaks of the Sholayr loomed, majestic in their cold isolation. The day was slowly leaking away, light gathering in pools between the peaks.

"What do we do tonight?" asked Jorge.

"Sleep on the ground, unless we happen on a ruin or another village. We have passed no habitation since we set out."

"Is that significant, or just an observation?"

"It tells me two things," Thomas said. He waited for Jorge to show impatience before telling him what he thought, half ashamed at the spark of pleasure it raised. "Mandana and Guerrero don't want to be observed, and this country isn't one their men raid."

"Are those the two things?" Jorge seemed unimpressed.

"No, just one. The other is that he is heading back to his lair."

Jorge stopped walking, and it took Thomas a moment to realise. When he did, he turned.

"I'm not sure I want to get close to his lair," said Jorge. "I didn't like the way you said it."

"Don't worry, we'll keep well back and stay hidden. We do nothing other than watch and plan."

"We have a plan now?"

"Not yet, but we will do."

Thomas started off again, knowing Jorge would follow.

They passed no ruined houses, not even a tumble-down hut like the one Thomas had made his home in for a month, his only companion a rope that swung in the almost constant wind. But he did find a sheltered hollow that offered some scant refuge. Kin disappeared, gone so long Thomas feared he had continued on ahead, the scent of his master too strong to ignore. Instead he returned an hour later with a plump hare in his mouth, by which time Thomas and Jorge had gathered what little wood there was and made a small fire. Thomas climbed from the bowl of their shelter and walked a little way down the slope until he was satisfied no light showed. Daylight had faded around them so the smoke was invisible. He skinned the hare, tossing the offal to Kin, who made short work of it, then skewered the hare over the fire and let what little fat it contained drip and sizzle. After a while he cut the carcass into four, passed the largest piece to Jorge, the smallest to Kin, then bit into his own portion, saving the remainder to break their fast in the morning. His stomach cramped with need, and he had to force himself to swallow past the spasm. Later, when his belly was at least partially full, he and Jorge lay together, their robes wrapping them close as their bodies warmed each other. Kin lay on Thomas's other side, his long head resting across his lap. Thomas laid his hand on the dog's deep chest and stared at the array of stars that cut through the deep black of the sky, counting them, making patterns until sleep found him.

Thomas woke to the sound of Kin growling, a deep sound, and when he reached out he felt a vibration in the dog's chest. He stroked him until he stilled, then lay listening for what had disturbed him. At first he thought there had been nothing but the dreams dogs have that seem to always involve running, but then he heard what had disturbed Kin. A man's voice, a response, and the soft rattle of harnesses and horses' hoofs on hard rock. Whoever was passing would not see them, for the fire had died completely and their shelter was well hidden. Thomas listened as the men passed, waited until there was no trace of them. Kin had fallen asleep again, comforted by Thomas's touch, and soon Thomas followed him, a small hope flaring into dreams of retribution. More men making their way back to camp, which meant they were close to finding out where Mandana and Guerrero had their headquarters. What happened when they did was less clear, but Thomas knew there was only one end point for the knowledge he would gain in the morning. Either he would die, or they would. He also knew that Jorge was right and he couldn't do it alone, and a seed of an idea traced its way through his dreams.

CHAPTER SIXTEEN

Thomas woke alone on cold, hard ground. He couldn't recall the last time he and Jorge had slept side by side and it was he who had risen first. Kin was also missing, and for a brief moment Thomas feared they had been stolen away in the night, until he realised such a thing was impossible, for why not him as well? He rose and walked up the small rise, washing his hands across his face to dispel the last traces of sleep.

He saw Jorge and the dog sitting side by side on a ridge a quarter mile away. When he reached them he discovered they were watching Mandana's camp spread across the valley below as it came alive. Thomas settled beside them, took a sliver of last night's meat from Jorge when he passed it across, tore a little off and fed it to Kin, then took in what lay below.

"That dog has had more meat than you or I."

Thomas smiled. "Well, he did do most of the work yesterday, and it was him caught the hare. What's been going on so far?"

"I don't like it," said Jorge. "And watch, you'll see why."

Thomas rested his hand on Kin's flank, taking comfort

from the touch without even being aware of it. Below, smoke from fires rose to be trapped in the windless valley. A large tent stood at the upper end of the slope, a few others scattered about it, but most men appeared to have spent the night like Thomas and Jorge, sleeping on hard ground huddled around makeshift fires.

"Any sign of Mandana or Guerrero?"

"Wait," said Jorge.

Thomas narrowed his eyes as something caught his attention. Close to the base of a low cliff rough wooden crosses had been erected—four of them. Men hung from two, arms tied to the cross pieces, legs hanging free. One had been dead some time—birds had taken his eyes and pecked openings in his ribcage to get at the delicacies within. The other had died more recently, in the last day or two.

"He's teaching them a lesson," Thomas said, his voice so soft he wasn't sure whether Jorge heard him or not, but he had.

"And about to teach someone else another." Jorge inclined his head toward the large tent. Men had gathered around it, a lot of men, perhaps a quarter of the camp. The crowd appeared well attired, standing tall, joking amongst themselves as they waited for what they clearly knew was about to happen.

Five men emerged from one of the smaller tents, but none were who Thomas sought. Four of them dragged the fifth between them through the gathered soldiers, who parted to allow them passage. The prisoner's wrists and ankles were tied, and whenever he hesitated the rope was tugged hard, almost causing him to fall. The small group reached the largest tent and stopped. The prisoner stood with head bowed, no doubt aware of his fate but unable to do anything about it.

A flap was drawn aside and Abbot Mandana stepped

out. His pale robes, his height and bearing, made him unmistakable. He moved slowly, using his remaining hand to lean on a staff. A second figure, dressed in the same way, emerged, equally as tall but far younger. Pedro Guerrero, Mandana's son. Thomas had seen him only twice before, but there was no mistaking the man who had killed Lubna. Beside Thomas Kin whined, perhaps sensing his anger, or grief.

Thomas watched a pair of men approach the prisoner, who began to struggle. Gripped between them was a woman. Thomas scanned the crowd until he found what he was looking for. Set to one side stood a group of children, none over the age of fourteen or so. A man stood behind each, holding their heads so they were unable to look away from what was about to happen.

Guerrero stepped forward and began to speak. His words were lost in the distance, but it was clear what his instructions were.

The woman was to die first, her husband forced to watch. It was a lesson to every other man who had been captured and brought here. This is the punishment for rebellion or escape.

Guerrero went to the woman and gripped her around the waist, her body tight against his own. He turned so she faced her husband before unsheathing a knife and drawing it across her throat. This time the man's screams reached as far as Thomas and Jorge.

Guerrero held the woman until her body was still, then let it drop. He walked to the man, still held between two others, and Thomas expected him to use the knife a second time, but he did not. Instead he spoke again, almost certainly promising what would happen to anyone else who tried to flee.

"I wonder what he did to deserve this?" said Jorge.

"It could be nothing at all. He's being punished to dissuade others. You've seen the children?"

Jorge nodded.

"They are here to witness what happens here for when they return to Pampaneira."

Far below Guerrero loomed over the man, who had been pushed to his knees, his captors trying ropes tight so his arms were pulled out to either side.

"A whipping, or something worse?" said Jorge.

Below, a conclusion was approaching. The two hundred or so men watching began to disperse, but instead of returning to wherever their places were they began to move among the captured men, cajoling them to their feet. After a quarter of an hour the majority of men were lined up in two ranks facing each other, a wide space between. They were here to witness the event. The volunteer soldiers stood behind the ranks, no weapons in their hands but their threat obvious.

"No, not a whipping," Thomas said.

He didn't want to watch but made himself, knowing what he was about to see would harden his resolve. He had allowed himself to be drawn in by Mandana. That had ended with the death of Lubna.

The punishment was worse than he had feared. The man was dragged shouting to stand behind a tall stallion. The ropes holding wrists and ankles were tied to the pommel of its saddle, and then the horse was whipped hard. This time the sound of yelling men reached up to them, a dissonant roar of hatred, but whether toward the man or those punishing him Thomas couldn't tell, and doubted it mattered. The man's body was dragged flailing along the ground, bouncing from rock to rock, falling limp mercifully quickly.

Thomas heard Jorge turn aside and vomit up the scrap of meat he had eaten. Thomas felt nothing, not even anger.

Now he knew for certain that Mandana had reverted to the devil he had always been, and Guerrero was worse.

Below, the stallion came to a halt and men untied the broken remains of the deserter. They were all forced men who were made to perform the task, then told to carry the remains and dispose of both bodies. There would be no burial here, only the throwing of the remains over some cliff to be picked clean by vultures and vermin. No need to display what was left of the man's body on a cross, because everyone below had watched the manner of his dying. A lesson to them all.

"We need an army," said Jorge, and Thomas nodded.

"When we know more we'll get help." He glanced along the valley to where it descended toward the east. "Gharnatah is less than half a day's march. If Muhammed has any sense he will have set guards in all directions, including this one."

"That's Olaf's job, isn't it?"

"He might suggest it, I'm sure, but the ultimate decision is the Sultan's. It makes me think–" Thomas broke off what he was about to say as he felt Kin stiffen beside him and emit a small yelp. "No," Thomas said. He twisted his fingers through the long hair behind the dog's neck as he felt it try to rise.

"What's he doing?"

"He recognises one of those men," Thomas said.

Four of them carried the remains of the dead man and his wife, climbing the slope, and Thomas knew they meant to carry the corpses to a higher place where the birds would more easily find them. He rose, tugging Kin after him, pushing at Jorge's shoulder, but the dog jerked around, snarling as it snapped at Thomas's hand. Then it was free and bounding down the hillside.

Thomas saw one of the men look up as if in recognition of the animal, and Thomas in turn recognised Luis, who released the arm he was holding and, unbalanced, the body fell to the stony ground. Kin ran at a sprint to him and leaped around his legs, barking wildly.

"No," Thomas said, his voice soft, knowing he could do nothing. He pushed at Jorge again. "Go, we have to hide. The dog is lost." He glanced behind. Luis was trying to stop one of the others, who had drawn a knife and was attempting to catch hold of the dog. But Kin was too fast and continued to bark, over and over, thinking it was all a fine game to play.

Thomas led the way over shattered rocks, climbing ever higher until they came to a steep rock-face where Jorge took the lead. He had always been the better climber, and Thomas recalled how they had ascended the three hundred foot cliff at Ronda with nothing but the light of the moon to show them the way, and felt a foolish hope rise in him that they would succeed again, the two of them. Except when they had completed that feat, Lubna had been at the foot of the cliff to encourage them, something she would never be able to do again.

Jorge came to a deep ledge and turned to offer a hand to Thomas, who reached up and took it, feeling the man's greater strength as he pulled him over the lip. He fell panting to the rock, trying to suppress the urge to laugh because there was nothing to laugh at, but still he felt his chest shake. He knelt and looked over the edge. Far below, the four men had reached their destination and laid the bodies of husband and wife on the ground. There was no sign of Kin, and now with distance Thomas was unable to tell which of the men was his master. He wondered if one of the others had used a knife on Kin and felt a sense of loss, even though the animal had never been his.

"Do you think Luis knows we're here?" asked Jorge, who came to kneel beside Thomas, his shoulder pressing against his as it always did.

"More than likely. He must know Kin didn't find him by accident."

"I can't see the dog. Did they kill it?"

"I expect so." Thomas shifted position, an impatience growing in him—a need for action he tried to ignore it but knew he was going to fail.

"Four men," he said.

"You count well. What about them?"

"Luis was taken only recently. They won't have corrupted him yet."

"And?"

Thomas glanced at Jorge then rose. "You can stay here if you want, I can probably manage the other three on my own." As he began to descend the cliff he heard Jorge make a sound and start to follow.

The men had turned back but were not yet visible from the camp when Thomas stepped from behind a rock and confronted them. He held a knife in one hand because he had no sword with him. He noticed none of the four carried one either.

The men stopped and stared at him.

"Hello, Luis," Thomas said, staring at the young man. "Which of these men killed your dog? He will be the first to die."

Thomas saw one of the men look away and wondered if it had been him.

"We should get back," said one of the others. "He'll punish us if he thinks we're trying to run off." The man washed his hands together, as if wanting to cleanse them of the task he had been forced to carry out.

Thomas wondered who the man referred to, Mandana or Guerrero, though he believed he knew the answer. Mandana's men always called him the Wolf. The leader here they called Warrior, so it was Guerrero who led them. An old evil making way for a new one.

"Is that what he did? Tried to escape?"

Luis offered a nod. "What are you doing here?" He turned to his companions. "Go back, all of you. Tell him I'm gutting the bodies to make sure the animals get to them sooner. I'll catch you up."

The other three looked at Luis, then at each other. One of them shrugged and set off. A moment later the other two followed.

"Don't say anything about these men," Luis called after them. One of them raised a hand, but Thomas wasn't sure how long they might have before someone came in search of them.

"They won't say anything," said Luis, no doubt reading his expression. "We look out for each other as best we can."

"Are you sure? One of them killed your dog."

"No, Kin ran off."

"Were you taken before or after they killed your parents?"

"After. I fought them but was too valuable to kill. They tied me hand and foot and strung me across the back of a mule to bring me here. They've beaten me every day since. I want to fight back but dare not."

"You have no-one left to lose anymore, not like some of the other men," Thomas said.

"There is Dana and Aban," said Luis. "Jamila and a few others. They are as much family to me as my own parents. It was made clear to me from the first day that they are hostages to my obedience."

"How did they know about them? You are no relative."

"They know everything." Luis looked down at the ground and his shoulders stiffened. "I tried to fight them but they killed…" He turned his face away, as if afraid of showing emotion. "They killed them both, and then they took me. I could do nothing. I had to leave them bleeding on the ground…"

"We buried them," Thomas said.

Luis's lips thinned. "I thank you for that." He glanced around, put two fingers to his mouth and whistled loudly. A moment later Kin appeared, approaching slowly. "I scared him off. It was either that or kill the others and make a run for it, and I couldn't do that. I've seen what they do when they catch you. What they do to your family." He looked up at Thomas from where he had knelt to stroke Kin. "Do you want a dog? I can't keep him, not here. Somebody in camp will only eat him. We don't get as much food as the regular soldiers."

"Why take you at all? If they're trying to build an army they need the best soldiers. Untrained men can't fight."

"But they can die. That is our role and we know it."

"Come with us," said Jorge, speaking for the first time.

"They'll chase us all down and kill you as well, they always do. Nobody escapes." He nodded his head in the direction of the bodies they had taken to the hilltop. "They know the village my friends live in. They will take one of them before they kill me. You too. Do you want to die like these two?"

"Many have tried to kill me in the past," Thomas said. "Both of the men who lead you have tried and failed. I am a difficult man to kill."

"He is," said Jorge.

"You don't understand."

"Yes, I do. You have been taken against your will, no doubt beaten, starved, threatened and worse. Those men have leached the will from you, but you don't have to let them. Come with us and fight back. Your friends are safe, Jamila has taken them to Pampaneira."

"Which is where they take everyone. They are less safe there than they were before." Luis looked between them, his eyes returning to Thomas as the more reliable of the two. "If I come with you and they catch us, will you promise me one thing?"

"Agreed."

"You don't know what it is yet."

"Still agreed," Thomas said. "And yes, I will kill you before they can take you. It is my promise."

Luis stared at him, then clicked his fingers and Kin came close. He stroked the tall dog's ears, his own face softening. "They're planning something new, the one they call the Warrior and his father—and it's big."

CHAPTER SEVENTEEN

As they made their way south Thomas tried to tease more details from Luis, but the boy knew little other than something was being planned, but not what. Thomas wondered if it was the reason Mandana had been in Pampaneira. Wondered if it was a mistake to return to the town, but he knew Jamila, Dana and Aban had to be taken somewhere else. Somewhere safe.

They kept away from any tracks, such as they were, in case someone came in search of Luis, which they would eventually. Deserters were not allowed to escape. As far as Luis knew nobody ever had, and Thomas saw that knowledge worried him.

"If you don't know what's planned, how can you be sure there is something?" They had reached a narrow defile between two steeply rising slopes. The vista provided a clear view of the ground falling away to the south, and if anyone was following them they would be seen.

"Because they're making preparations."

Thomas thought for a moment. "Explain to me what life is like in the camp."

"Gruesome."

"Other than that. Day-to-day, tell me what happens."

So Luis explained how the camp worked. One day in two raiding parties would be sent out. Luis had gone with them twice because he said they were starting to trust him. Each time men were brought back, to be beaten into submission until they did their master's bidding without question or died.

"Are you like them?" Jorge interrupted at that point, and Thomas knew why. Luis showed a spark of rebellion, of self-belief at odds with how he told them the captives behaved.

"I pretend to be like them, and there are others who do the same. We want to meet to discuss escape but can't for fear of being discovered or betrayed. There are many spies. It is not safe to trust anyone."

"How often are men punished as harshly as we witnessed today?" Thomas asked.

"What you saw is rare. That kind of torture is reserved for those who try to escape and get caught. But punishment is meted out for any infraction, however small."

"Tell me, what's changed that makes you so sure something is being planned?"

"There's been more food lately, and the random beatings have stopped. Guerrero and Mandana spend long periods shut away. Everyone knows they're planning something." Luis had theories, but they didn't seem reason enough for what he proposed. Bigger raids would be pointless in this country of small towns and villages. The existing raiding parties would capture just as many men.

"Who is in command," Thomas asked. "The father or the son?" He assumed he knew the answer, so was surprised when Luis told him.

"Guerrero, of course. He listens to the old man, but it is Guerrero who makes all the decisions, Guerrero who leads."

"Someone's coming," said Jorge who, though listening, had sat at the top of the slope watching the land below.

"Coming here?"

"No, down there. A dozen men on horseback. I expect they're looking for Luis."

The youth crawled to the edge and peered over. He watched for some time, then wriggled back.

"There's no decent tracker with them," he said, as he settled beside Thomas again. Kin had stayed at his side the entire time. "They don't expect anyone to get far, let alone have the wits to go to high ground. They'll have a note of where they took me from and assume that's where I'll go back to." He raised his eyes to meet Thomas's. "Where are we going?"

"I had planned to take you to Pampaneira, where Dana is, and others from her village, but I've changed my mind."

Luis continued to stare at Thomas. "Then I'll go alone." He reached out and stroked Kin.

"If you do they'll catch you and take you back. Drag you behind a horse, or worse."

"I can look after myself."

"I don't doubt it, but you'll be going in the direction they're expecting, so they will catch you. I can't make you stay with us, and I refuse to make threats. Dana will be safe for now. They've only been in Pampaneira a short time, so their names will not yet be recorded. If you stay with me I'll make sure you get back to your girl."

"When?"

"That I don't know."

"What are you going to do?"

"Watch."

"Only watch?"

Thomas raised a shoulder. In truth, he had no clear idea what he intended to do, only that if Guerrero was planning something he needed to know what it was, and the only way of finding out was to watch, and wait.

"They've gone," said Jorge, from the edge of the narrow cutting.

"Which way?"

"South. At least, I think that's south." Jorge pointed, and Thomas nodded.

"They'll be back. We'll be long gone from here by then."

"Where are we going?" asked Luis.

Thomas smiled. "Into the wolf's lair."

———

He had been exaggerating, but not by much. They had crept far closer to the edge of Mandana's camp than Luis was comfortable with, but he seemed to trust Thomas, and like Jorge. Even so, his unease was clear. He kept Kin at his side, one hand almost constantly stroking the dog's fur. Darkness had come and the spot they observed from was little more than two hundred paces from the outer line of fires. Close enough to overhear conversation. Thomas crept a little closer to hear them better still, but nothing he overhead hinted at what Guerrero's plans might be. He doubted anyone but the man himself and his father knew what those were.

Thomas tried not to think too deeply about what he was doing here, why he was putting all three of them in such danger. He had come to these high mountains in a rage of revenge, but that had eventually faded, as all rages do, to be replaced by a deep emptiness, and an urge to end his pain. He knew why he had not succumbed. The fight for life, even his own life, was too deeply ingrained in him.

But he wondered why, if he had chosen life, what he was doing so close to a thousand men, any one of whom would take his life without a moment's regret. He was putting Luis in even more danger.

Thomas knew his rage had cooled, hardened into something more dangerous to those who had stolen Lubna's life. He had re-discovered a reason to live, and it sparked a cold thrill through his core. Exactly how he might revenge Lubna he didn't yet know, only that he couldn't turn aside until he had.

When the camp began to settle for the night, Thomas left Luis to keep watch while he and Jorge slipped back to a place of safety to sleep. He wondered about trusting the youth, but knew he couldn't remain awake all night, and asking him to take the first watch would show his trust. Even so, sleep took a long time to come as he lay awake waiting for soldiers to come.

When he woke the air had chilled and darkness still cloaked the land. He left Jorge curled on the ground while he descended to where Luis was when they had left him, except now he was curled around Kin, both of them fast asleep. Thomas didn't even think of berating him, just left him to continue enjoying his dreams as he sat and watched the glow of fires which had settled into little more than embers. The camp wasn't silent, no camp ever is, but it had slipped into those deep night hours when a stillness descends. Thomas's few hours of sleep had left him refreshed, and the internal decisions of the previous day brought a sense of renewal, of purpose. He sat and watched the sky lighten to the east, the darkness between fires gathering substance as it turned deep grey, then a lighter shade. A few men stirred, walked to the edge of the camp to relieve themselves. Others woke. Fires were encouraged into fresh life. And then Guerrero emerged from the tent and Thomas stiffened. He turned and shook Luis, putting fingers across his mouth in case he cried out. He sent him to fetch Jorge, then watched as horses were

saddled and a band of fifty men gathered, most on foot—
the horses were for their leaders and captains. Only when
the group was ready did Mandana emerge to be helped
into a saddle. Luis returned with Jorge, and Thomas led
them in a wide circle to get ahead of the men, always
seeking cover, until they were crouched in a cleft of rock
waiting for them to appear.

Foot soldiers came first, with Guerrero and Mandana
protected in the middle of the troop. There were no carts,
which told Thomas their journey would be completed
before day's end. He considered where they were and what
lay nearby, and an obvious conclusion came to him, though
quite what it meant he couldn't decide.

Gharnatah lay half a day west. Thomas had grown
increasingly convinced that since being captured by the
Spanish several years before Muhammed had been
working on behalf of them. And as long as he remained
Sultan, Gharnatah was doomed.

"We should go or we'll lose them," said Luis. He had
become a convert to their cause since his desertion, and
there was no more talk of giving himself up or leaving to
return home. He had become a part of their small band.
For how long was open to question, but Thomas knew
Luis would not have to remain with them much longer.

"If I was leading them I'd have a smaller group set half a
mile behind looking for anyone taking an interest in our
passing."

Luis smiled. "You over-estimate them."

"Mandana might be insane, but he's wily. Better over-
cautious than dead. We wait a while longer. Besides, I
know where they're going." Thomas turned to look at Luis,
and for a moment the sight raised a memory of himself at
the same age, his whole adult life lying ahead, and he
realised how long ago that had been. "Did you make
friends in the camp?"

Luis shook his head. "Friendship isn't encouraged, and there are turncoats who draw you into conversation, pretending a friendship that doesn't exist. Then if someone lets slip any sign of discontent they are exposed. A beating is the least punishment. You saw what lay at the other extreme. Are we going to do nothing but watch?"

"For now. Do you think we should fight them? Fifty men?"

"Jorge told me you and he have faced huge odds before."

"He did, did he?" Thomas glanced at Jorge, who seemed to have discovered something interesting in the valley below. "The secret to fighting against large odds is knowing when they are too big." Even as he spoke the rational words, Thomas knew he had rarely heeded his own advice, surprised he had survived as long as he had, knowing he had come close to death on many occasions. His survival was more a matter of luck than skill, and judgement barely came into it.

Finally, Thomas stood and began to clamber down the slope to the valley floor where walking would be easier. Kin ran ahead, but a single whistle from Luis brought him loping back to join them.

The valley widened, the walls dropping until they formed a low bluff. Ahead and below, Mandana's men had spread out, but still with the main cohort ahead, another smaller one behind. Beyond them the city of Gharnatah was visible spread across its two opposing hills. On one sat the glittering wonder of the al-Hamra palace, on the other the twisting jumble of alleys and houses of the Albayzin. Beyond the city walls, rich farmland spread as far as the eye could see.

Somewhere down there, Thomas knew, his son and daughter lived. He wondered what they were doing at that moment. Was Will still as curious as ever? Still too brave for his own good? Had Usaden continued to train him?

And what of Amal, the daughter Lubna had carried inside her for almost nine months but never lived to see? Thomas knew if it hadn't been for Jorge's lover, Belia, Amal would have also died. He had been unable to do what he had done for others and act with the cold rationality he was known for. It had been impossible to find that lack of emotion which earned him the name of *qassab*: butcher. It had been Belia who cut Amal from the belly of her dead mother to free a new life.

"We wait here until we know exactly where they're headed." Thomas tried to close down his thoughts, even as he felt guilty for doing so. He recalled the many times he had told people it was better to know the worst than live in hope. He had been a fool.

He expected Guerrero's men to head toward the city gate, though exactly what kind of reception they might expect was a mystery. Instead, they stayed high on the hillside, moving north of the main roadway, making their way into the vast hunting grounds beyond al-Hamra before descending toward the palace itself.

"Where are they going?" asked Jorge.

"To meet with Muhammed."

"But they're enemies."

Thomas smiled. "Are they?"

It took a moment before Will realised who had walked into the shaded courtyard, but when he did he sprinted toward Thomas, leaping the final three feet. Thomas plucked him from the air and held him close, breathing in the scent of him.

"Pa!" Will kissed his face. "Why are you crying, Pa? Did I jump too hard?"

"No, not too hard." Thomas kissed the top of his son's

head and looked beyond him to where Usaden Hamid, the Gomeres mercenary he had hired away to train his son and protect this household, stood with feet planted apart, a sword in his hand. It had no doubt appeared there the moment he heard the courtyard door open. He almost looked as if he wanted to smile but managed to control himself.

"Aiii!" The cry erupted from Belia as she came from the house to see what all the noise was about and saw Jorge. She ran to embrace him, holding his face in her hands while she studied it. "Why did you not send a message? I would have prepared a feast. I still can, I will go into town and buy meat and fresh spices. You will come with me to help carry it." She glanced aside. "Who is the good-looking one?"

"Luis. Is he good-looking? As handsome as me?"

Belia kissed his mouth. "There is no-one as handsome as you, and you know it full well, so do not go seeking compliments. How long are you staying?"

"Ask Thomas."

Belia glanced in his direction—a beautiful woman, with lustrous dark hair and even darker eyes. Not as beautiful as Jorge, but with a mystery about her Thomas had never fully understood. Which, he supposed, is what made her a mystery. She came to embrace him, her familiar scent bringing a fresh wave of emotion. Thomas wondered when he had become so weak to be crippled by grief so easily, and he turned away, lifting Will onto his hip even though the boy was heavier than he remembered. Then he realised he had not seen him in half a year. It was a long time. Far too long.

Will wriggled in his arms and noticed Kin for the first time.

"Pa, a dog!" A frown crossed his young brow. "Does it bite?"

"Only bad men." Thomas set Will on the ground. "Why don't you go and say hello?"

Will glanced up, then glanced at Kin, torn between the father he loved and a dog. A big dog. It was no contest, not to a boy of five.

Thomas sat on a stone bench near to where Usaden continued to stand, as if he could stay there until the end of time and not show fatigue.

"Have you been hard on him?" he asked.

"As hard as you asked me to be."

"Good. Does he learn well?"

Usaden offered a nod. "He does, and fast. He will be a great warrior one day."

"I hope he never has to use what you teach him." Thomas patted the stone beside him, making it clear he wanted Usaden to join him, and after a moment the man came across and sat. Thomas wanted to embrace him but knew it would not be welcome. Instead he offered his hand. Usaden sheathed his sword and offered his in return —the best he would ever give, and more than he offered most men.

"Better to have the skill and not need it, than need it and not have it," said Usaden, more words than he had likely spoken in a week, other than to bark commands at Will.

CHAPTER EIGHTEEN

Thomas knew getting into the palace would prove difficult because most of the guards would recognise him, but there was someone he knew who could help. Several years before a builder by the name of Britto had extended Thomas's house when Lubna first came there, and had completed more work since. Now the man was a friend, and if he was still working at the palace Thomas was sure he would be willing to help. After sunset he walked through the steep alleyways of the Albayzin to Britto's house and invited him to an inn. Brito accepted, despite commenting that he preferred not to drink with dead men. Thomas wondered how many others in the city believed he had perished, and knew he had been away too long.

When Thomas told him what he wanted Britto laughed and reached for his hand, examining the palm. "Just as long as the guards don't see this soft skin it should be easy enough." He turned the hand over, turned it back. "You have grown too thin, Thomas Berrington."

The following morning, Thomas carried two wooden pails which clanked with builders' tools. He had dressed in stained clothing and covered his face with the tail of a tagelmust. As they approached the first guard Britto made a coarse joke and Thomas laughed, the sound false in his own ears, but the guard appeared convinced enough. Britto nodded to the guard, the guard nodded back, and they were inside the outer wall.

"I take it you have no intention of assisting me in laying tiles, do you?"

Thomas shook his head. "Did you expect me to?"

"No, but a good apprentice is hard to find these days. All the good ones want to go to war and make their fortune."

"Then it's lucky I wouldn't make a good apprentice, isn't it? I'll come as far as your work, so you don't have to carry everything, but then I go to find Olaf. You did say he's here, didn't you?"

"He was the day before yesterday, and as far as I know there are no new battles, so I expect he'll still be around somewhere."

"What does he think about serving Muhammed?" Thomas asked.

"Strangely, he and I spend little time discussing his feelings about the Sultan ... or anything else. He's the Sultan's general and I'm a simple builder—what else do you expect?"

They were almost at the second gate where four guards stood, stopping all those who sought entrance, checking their clothing and whatever they carried.

Thomas turned to Britto. "What if they recognise me?"

Britto shook his head. "I barely recognise you, and these men have no idea who you are. Don't start believing you are so important you cannot pass unnoticed, particularly dressed as you are. It's only a shame we couldn't have made you shorter." They reached the guards, who had started to harass a young woman who wanted to take a basket of bread inside. "Hey, Fariq, give her a couple of years and she'll be old enough to be your daughter. In fact, she probably is your daughter from what I hear tell."

The guard swiped a hand at Britto's head, but missed. He was laughing, which was a good sign.

"Take her if you want. I like a bit more meat on their bones."

"I heard that, too," said Britto, and this time he deliberately allowed Fariq to slap the side of his head as he took the girl's arm and led her through the gate and on toward a set of rough steps that rose to the final entrance. The guard hadn't even looked at Thomas.

The last barrier, which offered access to the inner palace, was the most secure, with two barred metal gates set eight feet apart so those entering were trapped between them until the far one was opened. Two guards stood at the first gate. They nodded at Britto, allowed their eyes to strip the clothes from the girl, then moved to Thomas. He didn't recognise either, but ducked his head as if struggling with one of the buckets as the outer gate swung open to allow them to enter, their bodies pressed together in the confined space. The outer gate closed with a clang, but the inner remained locked.

Thomas leaned close to Britto, who was talking softly to the girl.

"Does it always take so long? What if one of them recognises me?"

"I told you, the guards have no interest in you. As long as you're with me you're just another badly paid workman."

"They're talking to someone, I can hear it," Thomas said. "What if it's someone who knows me?"

Britto shook his head and went to the inner gate, which remained barred. He rapped on the iron bars with a hammer until one of the guards turned.

"Wait your turn."

"It is my turn," said Britto. "I'll let you explain to the Sultan why his tiles are taking so long to finish. I should have him offer me rooms here so—" Britto cut himself off abruptly as a figure appeared beside the guard.

Thomas turned away, making himself busy with the buckets, as Abu Abdullah, Muhammed XIII, Sultan of Gharnatah peered into the dimness between the gates.

"Your Sultan is grateful for your work, Britto, but we are busy at the moment." Muhammed's gaze took in the girl, lingered for a moment, then shifted to Thomas, who busied himself once more with the buckets, trying to make himself look shorter.

"As I should be, Your Grace. Tiles do not attach themselves. Ask these men to let us in and I promise the new walkway will be finished by the end of the day."

"Open the gate," said Muhammed. "And send word to the Spaniard I am ready to see him in the courtyard of lions." Muhammed peered into the dimness of the chamber again. "Who is the girl?"

"Daughter of a friend," said Britto. "The guards scare her, so she prefers to come in with me."

"And your workman?"

Thomas wondered why Muhammed was so interested in workmen all of a sudden.

"Him? He's new." Britto grinned. "You keep sending my good apprentices off to war, Your Grace."

"To keep Gharnatah safe." Muhammed waved a hand, and a guard unbarred the inner gate and swung it wide.

Britto let some curse go under his breath and pushed past him. The girl followed, Thomas bringing up the rear. He kept his gaze down, despite wanting to drink in the beauty of the palace. Even here, outside the inner chambers, fabulous gardens sported plants from all the known world, while water played soft music everywhere. Beyond the gardens pink walls rose into the sky, picked through with crenellated windows. Once, this place had almost been home to Thomas, but those times seemed distant now and his life had since been shattered into a thousand shards, each of which dug into his flesh and soul.

"You, stop!" Muhammed's voice cut through Thomas's thoughts and he slowed, knowing he had run out of luck. He should have done as Britto said and cut a foot from his height, if such was possible. He started to turn as Muhammed came past him and went to the girl. He took out one of the flat loaves she had no doubt baked herself that morning. He lifted it to his nose, sniffed, all the time staring at the girl, who was too afraid to look away. Muhammed dropped the loaf on the ground and turned away.

"Bastard," said Britto, but not loud enough for Muhammed to hear.

Thomas knelt and picked up the bread, but when he offered it to the girl she shook her head. It was tainted now, so he kept hold of it, not knowing what else to do.

"Off to the kitchen with you," said Britto, slapping the girl on the backside, and she nodded and trotted off, casting a glance back just before she disappeared.

"She's too young for you." Thomas fell into step as Britto began to walk toward the inner palace.

"Do you think so? You saw how she looked at me."

"Perhaps I need to check your eyes."

"She looked at you, too. You should—" And then Britto stopped as he realised what he had been about to say. "Sorry, Thomas. I liked Lubna."

"Everybody liked Lubna."

Thomas didn't want to talk of her, but knew that without Britto he would never have made it inside the palace. They entered a courtyard, passed through it to a wide corridor that arched high overhead. Almost every surface they passed was etched with the same words, over and over, in ornate Arabic script: *There is no victor but Allah*. Thomas wondered if the sheer repetition might stop the Spanish, but suspected it was a vain hope.

Britto stopped and put down his tools. Thomas set the buckets on the flagstone floor as Britto turned to him. For a moment he hesitated, then drew Thomas close and kissed his cheeks, Britto's dense beard coarse against his skin. "I will come to visit tonight and find out how you got on. I take it Jorge is with you?"

Thomas nodded, strangely touched at the show of affection. Britto had once been nothing more than a workman to him—now the man had become a friend, someone Thomas would trust with his life. Someone Thomas *had* just trusted with his life. It would have been more sensible for Britto to have unmasked him in front of Muhammed, but he would never do such a thing.

"You will be more than welcome, you know that. And bring your wife."

Britto pulled a face, then grinned. "Perhaps I'll bring the bread girl instead."

Thomas cuffed him across the shoulder, handed him the bread still in his hands, and turned away. He was inside the palace. Now there was only one person he wanted to see.

Thomas thought be might have a broken rib, possibly two, before Olaf's wife Fatima released her hold on him. She stepped back, but not far, and held his face in her hands, turning it from side to side as if she couldn't quite believe what she saw.

"You are too thin," she said.

Thomas nodded in acknowledgement.

Tears filled Fatima's eyes, but she made no move to wipe

them away. Instead her fingers tightened painfully on Thomas's face. He made no attempt to loosen her grip, sharing the grief that must be filling her. Lubna had been Fatima's daughter, the single issue she had borne for Olaf Torvaldsson. His other daughters had been carried by his first wife, a woman of the north who must have possessed extraordinary beauty if those daughters were any indication.

"I am sorry," Thomas said. "I would not have had it happen." But even as he spoke the words he once more felt a certainty that Lubna's death was his responsibility.

Fatima embraced him again, held his face. "I know you would not. You loved her more than anyone. Perhaps even more than me." She touched his chest, her hand flat over his heart. "It must hurt so much." Tears continued to streak her face to drip from her chin.

Thomas put his arms around Fatima and drew her against him, comforted by her grief because he knew it matched his own. She buried her head against his chest, and he felt her sob. He waited until she stilled, then held her a moment longer before unwrapping his arms.

"Right," said Fatima, only now wiping an arm across her face—a face Thomas studied, finding elements in it that reminded him of Lubna. "You need fattening up."

"Belia started that process last night."

"And I am continuing it today. Besides, Olaf is out doing soldiering, so we have plenty of time." She patted his arm. "Sit and tell me about Malaka, about how clever my daughter was there, and how much you loved her." She glanced at his face. "If you can, of course. I know men find it hard to express what lies locked in their hearts."

"I will tell you everything," Thomas said, a sudden ease flooding him, and he knew it was because he had not spoken of Lubna since she died—not the real Lubna, the woman who made him laugh and made him cry out in ecstasy. Fatima would understand that Lubna. But perhaps he might skip over the ecstasy part.

"Olaf is still in Gharnatah, then?"

Fatima looked back at him from where she was sorting through what she would feed him. "For now. These are not easy times for him. He hurts too, but refuses to show it even to me." She offered a brief smile. "I am pleased you can." Another smile. "And Amal looks just like her mother, doesn't she?"

Thomas nodded, though he was not convinced she did. He had sat and stared at her the night before while she slept, trying to find some similarity and failing. Belia told him it was understandable. Amal had only six months and would not come into her true looks for many years yet. But still he tried, desperate for some familiarity, impatient to find out how his and Lubna's daughter would develop. Would she be as beautiful, as wicked, as clever, as stubborn as her mother? He knew it didn't matter. Amal would be both herself and part of her mother and father. Just as Will was part of Thomas, despite Helena refusing to offer him any certainty he was his true father. How could two sisters be so different?

Fatima brought food and he ate until he could eat no more, and they talked of Lubna and their love of her, laughing as much as they cried. And then, as noon came and went, and the shadows on the floor had moved half way across the tiles, the door opened and Olaf Torvaldsson came in, making the room all at once too small. He stopped at the sight of Thomas, and for a moment it was unclear how he would react. Then he came forward and plucked Thomas from his chair, and this time Thomas was sure his ribs were broken.

"We need to talk," Thomas said, rubbing his side.

"Not here." Olaf turned away, stopped when his wife

called out that food was ready. "We will eat later. Thomas and I have matters to discuss."

Thomas glanced at Fatima, shrugged, and followed Olaf out into the afternoon sunlight, having to run to catch up.

"Are you aware–" He was interrupted when Olaf raised a hand.

"Not here. Do you have wine at your house? I assume that is where you are staying. Is Jorge with you? And how are my grandchildren?"

"Yes, I have wine. As for your grandchildren you will see how they are, but I spent an age getting into the palace, so I hope you know an easier way of getting me out."

"I am Olaf Torvaldsson. If you are with me no-one will dare question who you are, or where we are going."

CHAPTER NINETEEN

When Thomas and Olaf entered the courtyard Usaden was training Will. Olaf stopped to watch, his keen eyes measuring every move, every thrust and parry, until he was sure Usaden was doing a good enough job. He turned and walked into the house without a word, leaving Thomas to catch up.

"Does he train him in the axe as well?" Olaf asked, as Thomas sat across the table from him.

"Usaden doesn't know the axe, but Will practices everything you taught him in Malaka."

"The axe is good for a boy to learn. It is easier than the sword at his age."

Thomas didn't point out that Will had used a sword effectively enough in a doomed attempt to protect his mother, when Pedro Guerrero and his men stormed the courtyard they had been sheltering in at the climax of the battle for Malaka.

"I will make sure he continues to practice. Perhaps you should give him lessons in the axe."

"I do. I come as often as I can, to see them both." Olaf

looked across the room to where Belia was preparing the evening meal. "Is she awake?"

Belia gave a nod and left the room, returning a moment later with Amal. She placed her in Olaf's arms, a tiny bundle clutched against his broad chest. Thomas watched a softness settle across Olaf's face, and felt something stir inside himself without knowing what it was until he recognised it as jealousy. Olaf knew Thomas's daughter better than he did himself. He had been wrong to flee to the mountains. His responsibilities lay here, in this house.

"We need to talk," Thomas said.

"Are you back for good?"

"I don't know. For now, at least, but I have unfinished business in the hills. When that is done I will come home."

"Has this business anything to do with Mandana and his son? I saw them ride in yesterday to be greeted like some kind of royalty."

"Is Muhammed dealing with them both?" Thomas sat up as Belia laid plates on the table, dropping them down with a clatter to indicate she didn't approve of what they were about to discuss. "Do you know why they're here?"

"Muhammed hasn't told me. He hasn't even mentioned they were coming. Which makes me think he'd rather I not know about it."

"Then he's a fool."

Olaf smiled as if his face was unused to such an expression. "You get no argument from me on that."

"So why do you still serve him?"

Olaf reached out and picked up a chicken wing. "Because his brother Yusuf, who you and I hoped to place on the throne, is dead. Someone has to keep Muhammed in check. There are people buzzing around him like flies on dung, all trying to get him to make them even richer than they already are."

"Nothing changes. His father was the same."

"But not al-Zagal. He was a steadying influence. It is a pity he was forced out. Tell me why you are here, Thomas. Have you come to rescue my daughter? I can help with that if you will let me."

Thomas was aware he had given Helena barely a thought since abandoning his family and friends in Malaka.

"Is she still his captive?"

Olaf nodded and sucked the meat from a chicken bone before reaching for another. Amal snuggled against him, a smile on her sweet face. Perhaps she sensed the man who held her would lay his life down for her.

As I should have done for Lubna, Thomas thought, then dismissed the notion. He couldn't carry the guilt forever, because to do so would stop him punishing those who killed her. It was revenge that filled him now. The trembling chaos of it hovered in the air around him, the tension of it coiled within his body waiting to be released. He knew Olaf must feel the same, perhaps even more so than he did, and the suddenness of the idea surprised him, together with the thought that Helena was another of his daughters—and one Thomas might be able to free.

"Does he still beat her?" Thomas recalled the news that had been brought to him in Malaka, when he had been unable, or unwilling, to do anything about it. Perhaps now he could.

"Not where it shows. Outwardly she is as beautiful as ever, but when I see her, as I do occasionally, there is something broken. Nothing physical, but up here..." Olaf tapped his brow. "Sometimes Muhammed deliberately displays her to me. He taunts us both, because she knows I am close and can do nothing." His gaze met Thomas's. "But you can."

"Why would I? I'm not here for her."

"Because she is Will's mother, and my daughter. If you won't do it for her, do it for your son—and for me."

"What does Muhammed want with Guerrero and Mandana?'

"How am I supposed to know that? Nothing good, I'm sure, but what they are plotting together I have no knowledge of. So, you will do it, Thomas?"

"How?" He knew the decision had been made, not unhappy with it—only unsure whether any plan could work.

Olaf tipped his head in Jorge's direction. "He can help. Jorge knows the palace better than anyone. There are others, too. I have prepared a way, if you are willing to follow it." Olaf reached for more food, before realising Amal was still in his arms. He lifted her and held her out to Thomas, who took his daughter and buried his face against her tiny body to breathe in the scent of her. He felt something twist inside him—an uncoiling of love that had been frozen far too long.

"When?" he asked.

"Tonight. There is some kind of celebration being planned for Muhammed's new friends. The palace will be chaos, so tonight is your best chance."

"Do you miss this place?" Thomas asked. They were close to where the harem lay, Jorge's natural home.

"A year ago I would have said yes. Now? No, I don't think so. Like you, I'm a changed man."

Thomas knew a year ago he would have objected to the description, but not now. He longed for old certainties, longed for Lubna to still be at his side. At least what he and Jorge were doing might make up a little for the neglect of his wife, and his part in her death.

Olaf had spirited them inside the palace walls. Thomas had stayed with Fatima at their house, but Jorge had slipped away. Thomas wondered if he had gone to visit Bazzu, the palace cook, and if they had spent the intervening hours in her bed. He knew Jorge loved Belia, but knew equally well that fidelity was not a philosophy he embraced, or even understood. Jorge had loved Bazzu long before he met Belia, and there was some deep connection shared between them. Thomas had long since stopped trying to understand the ways of the man he called his friend.

It was dark before Jorge returned, but they remained in Olaf's house eating food prepared by Fatima while she amused them with palace gossip. She knew what they intended to do, but there was no mention of Helena—perhaps because to do so might bring bad luck.

Outside, the noise of the celebrations reached them, and when they left after midnight wavering lights still showed in the courtyards they passed and men called to each other in loud voices. There were women, but no wives, only harem girls and others brought from the city and the Albayzin. Thomas glanced into the places they passed, but saw no sign of Mandana or Guerrero, no sign of Muhammed. They would be within the inner chambers, the most beautiful women placed at their disposal—and there was none more beautiful than Helena.

"Muhammed will almost certainly have Helena close," said Jorge, as they passed along a corridor scented with oils from a nearby bathing chamber.

"Where will she have a room?"

"In the harem—no, near the harem. She won't be allowed to enter that place again, but close by."

"Then that's where we go. I'll recognise her room when we find it."

Jorge smiled. "Indeed, her scent is not easily forgotten,

is it."

"As hard as I have tried."

There had been no guards on the way into the palace and now Thomas saw why. Men were stationed at all of the entrances to the inner rooms. He came to a halt, looking around. To the right, a party was winding down, people slumped across cushions. Thomas took Jorge's sleeve and drew him toward a side chamber that was empty. He didn't know if where he was headed would still give them access or not, but he had sought out Britto earlier and quizzed him about which of the passages he had once used still remained open. Only a few, Britto had told him, but he knew which because he had been involved in the filling in of them. At one time, Thomas had known his way around them as well as he knew the inside of his own house on the Albayzin. He only hoped Britto was right, and a passage remained which would allow them to pass through the ring of guards.

Thomas began to examine the places where an entrance might lie, running his hands over the stones and tiles before moving on. At one point a sudden noise made them both press back into the shadows of a narrow corridor as a woman's laugh sounded close by. When she appeared— running, but not fast—Thomas almost believed it was Helena. The woman had bright blonde hair, but as she passed, unaware of their presence, he saw it was not her. A moment later two men followed, laughing coarsely.

"I hope she is willing," said Jorge, his voice less than a whisper, the judgement in it clear.

Thomas was about to move away when he felt something beneath his fingers where they pressed against the wall. He turned and went to one knee, examining a small opening set between the tiled lower wall and the stone upper. He hooked his finger in, found a catch and pulled at it. Something within the wall made a noise, and a small section swung out. Thomas pushed his hand inside to find a second catch. When he released this a wider entrance opened. He grinned and slid sideways into a tight space.

"All I can say," said Jorge, "is it's lucky I didn't eat all Fatima put on the table." He followed Thomas, the entrance barely allowing him access.

When Thomas pulled the door closed the interior was pitch black.

"How do we find our way?" Jorge's hand came out, searching, touched Thomas and clung on.

"There is only one way to go. We don't need eyes to guide us. Just be sure to keep hold of me."

Thomas turned away, his own hands going out in front, feet sliding along the gritty floor. He tried not to think of what he might be disturbing, what spiders and insects had made this dark place their home.

The corridor turned slowly to the right and began to descend. A moment later Thomas almost pitched forward as his foot found empty space. He leaned back against Jorge and waited while he caught his breath, then explored with the tip of his foot to discover steps leading down. He found the first, the second, then descended a score until once more the floor levelled out. Ahead a light showed and he moved more confidently, sound reaching them as they came closer.

Light spilled through an opening above his head, too high to see through, but Thomas had been shown how to climb these walls a long time ago. He used that knowledge now until he peered into a large room. Fine wall hangings displayed hunting scenes, and silk cushions were scattered across the floor. Low tables held tiny cakes, flagons of wine and water pipes. The sweet scent of hashish and opium hung thick in the air. It should have been a scene of debauchery but was not. Muhammed sat to one side of the table, Pedro Guerrero and Abbot Mandana on the other.

There were women, but they sat apart from the men, talking amongst themselves. Thomas craned his neck to take in as much as he could, until he found who he expected to be there.

Helena sat alone, head down, her white hair hanging to touch the tiled floor. She appeared to be thinner than Thomas remembered, but it had been several years since he had last see her, even longer since she shared his bed. She had been made a gift to him, as much a joke as a gift, from the old Sultan, Muhammed's father. Helena had been scarred in an attack and considered no longer perfect enough for the harem. Thomas had managed to restore most of her beauty—but not enough for a return to the harem. Except here she was, though he knew beauty had little to do with her presence. Muhammed kept her close as punishment for Thomas. Why he carried such hatred was a mystery, but the man himself was a mystery. A Moorish Sultan who was also a vassal of Spain. Was that why Guerrero and Mandana were here—was it a sign of an escalation of the battle between Spain and al-Andalus? Or even the start of an end to the war?

Thomas turned his head so his ear was pressed against the opening, but there was too much background noise to make out what the three men were saying. He slid down and faced Jorge.

"She's inside with Muhammed and the others, but they're talking business."

"They won't let her go until they're done. They might have need of her when they're finished."

Thomas nodded, knowing Jorge was right. Helena was nothing to him anymore, though still the mother of Will, and for that he would do all he could to set her free.

"How did she look?" asked Jorge.

"Broken."

"That's not like Helena."

Thomas turned away, searching for a way out of the tunnel. They were within the gilded enclave of the palace now. There would be guards, though not many, and there would be eunuchs, but few of those, and they would be known to Jorge.

When he found an exit, it brought them out on the edge of the harem, which was no surprise. The purpose of these secret chambers was to provide access to and from such places.

The scent in the air was heady. Thomas pushed Jorge forward. At least if he was recognised he might be able to talk himself out of trouble, but he returned a moment later to say the harem was empty. No doubt the Sultan's concubines had been moved elsewhere, away from any possibility of corruption. Jorge led the way through, both of them walking fast to a corridor beyond. Rooms without doors opened on one side where concubines were housed and where, Jorge assured him, Helena would have a place assigned.

They went slowly, both of them glancing into each chamber to check the clothing, any books or journals that might be on display, breathing deep of the scent of whoever lived there until they came to a room where Thomas stopped and sat on the narrow bed.

"Here," he said, and Jorge nodded.

"She is unmistakeable, isn't she?" He sat beside Thomas and patted his leg. "You were a lucky man."

Thomas laughed, but there was no humour in the sound.

They waited, for there was nothing else they could do. Jorge stretched out on the bed and slept. Some time later came the sound bare feet on stone and then Helena entered the room.

She stopped in the entrance, and for a moment Thomas saw her almost perfect mouth open to scream, then she recognised who sat on her bed, and who lay across it. She cocked her head to one side and took a pace inside, glanced back and took another.

"They may yet come for me," she said. "I think the young one has not finished with me."

"I expect there is business still to discuss." Thomas stood, awkward. Should he embrace her? He thought not.

But Helena did. She came to him and put her arms around his neck and pressed herself against him, her unmistakable scent enveloping him with an insidious familiarity. He tried not to respond, but his body betrayed him.

"Oh, I think their business is concluded," Helena whispered into his ear. "Muhammed has taken them to see the lions in his menagerie. He does so love to show them off. He told me to wait here and he would send a message when they are ready for me. I am to be made a gift to both of them, though I expect only one will be able to perform."

Thomas put his hands on Helena's waist and peeled her away from him. "Then we have to go now."

"Have you come to rescue me? Oh, Thomas, you are such a hero. How can I ever repay you?" Even here, even now, she had to tease.

Thomas turned to wake Jorge, but he was already sitting up. No doubt he had taken everything in, as he always did.

"Can we get out through the harem?" Thomas asked.

"It's the wrong direction," said Jorge.

Thomas thought hard, trying to work out the layout of the inner rooms, but he was not as familiar with them as other parts of the palace. He had visited the outer levels of the harem when treating women in his role as palace physician, but these deeper spaces were forbidden even to him. Only those such as Jorge, who were considered incapable of violating the inhabitants, were allowed access.

"How far is the bathing chamber used by the Sultana?"

Jorge frowned. "Close, but it's in the direction of Muhammed's rooms."

"If he's showing off his animals for the moment, we have time." Thomas grasped Helena's wrist and drew her into the corridor. For a moment she resisted, then the resistance faded, and she padded along beside him as Jorge pushed past to lead the way.

The deep bath was empty, a small pool of water all that remained in one corner.

"Why are we here?" asked Helena. "I have bathed already, unless you want to wash me as you once did?"

Thomas released his hold and went into a corner. In this chamber a Sultana had died, her attacker disappearing like smoke in the wind. How such a thing was possible was a mystery, until Thomas and his young companion had solved it. There had been a secret opening deep in the corner, and Thomas went there now. He was certain it must have been closed off, but was surprised to discover the release mechanism still in place. When he thrust his arm in to pull on it he was even more surprised when it moved and a section of wall swung open. When he turned back Helena was staring at him, her mouth open. He was glad he could still surprise her in at least one way.

Inside, the tunnel led away, light entering through high openings. Jorge entered last and they had to shuffle around each other so Thomas could close the entrance, wondering as he started off how many of the passages remained in place. He considered staying in these hidden places to try and find a way to access Muhammed's rooms, to listen in on whatever was being discussed, but when he made the suggestion Helena said, "There is no need, I heard every word they spoke. I can tell you exactly what they are planning."

CHAPTER TWENTY

"What I want to know is where she is going to sleep." Belia sounded close to losing her temper, and Thomas wondered if she had grown too fond of his house and was starting to consider it her own. Not that he was ever likely to find much use for it again, so she was welcome to have it.

Olaf had brought them down from the hill on the same secret tracks he had taken them up on, and now sat in the main room while three of them stood on the edge of the courtyard trying to settle Helena's sleeping arrangements. *As if we have nothing better to do*, Thomas thought.

"She should sleep with Thomas, of course," said Jorge.

"No, she can't." Even the prospect sent a chill down Thomas's spine.

"Why not? She's shared your bed often enough before," said Jorge. Belia had crossed her arms across her chest and stared at them both, waiting for a decision.

"Perhaps Luis would like her beside him." Thomas said.

"She'd kill the boy. There is only your bed available."

"Then she's welcome to it, but without me beside her. There's a cot in the workshop. It won't be the first time I've

slept there. In fact, it will prove quieter than in here."
Thomas stared at them both.

Belia eventually unfolded her arms and slipped a hand around Jorge's waist. "Just so long as she doesn't try to join us."

Thomas wondered what kind of tales Jorge had been entertaining Belia with—or possibly not tales, for he had lived in the harem with Helena far longer than she had lived under Thomas's roof, and no doubt knew more of her wiles.

"Will they miss her?" asked Belia, as Thomas started to turn away.

"Not for a while. Dawn is close and those on the hill will be sleeping most of the day away."

"Will they know who took her?"

Thomas looked at Belia until she lowered her gaze, making him feel a moment of guilt. "They don't even know I'm in Gharnatah."

"But Olaf is," said Jorge. "They'll go to him first, and when they discover he's not there..."

Thomas left Belia and Jorge in the courtyard and went into the house. He wondered if Muhammed would care enough to send men in an attempt to find Helena.

The woman herself sat at the table next to her father, as if his presence alone could protect her. Opposite, Luis stared at her with his mouth open, and Thomas wondered if perhaps they had been too dismissive of Jorge's suggestion. It would be an experience for the boy, if nothing else. Not that it was ever going to happen. Helena ignored him as if he wasn't there, but her eyes found Thomas as soon as he entered the room and she straightened her back. She was still dressed in the clothes of the harem, fine silk that clung to her body to accentuate the shape beneath. A shape Thomas had once known intimately.

He went to the head of the table and sat. Exhaustion

clung to him, but he needed to know what Helena had overheard of Muhammed's discussion with Guerrero and Mandana before he could even think of sleep.

"Tell me what they said." He leaned forward, his eyes on Helena despite what he felt about her. He knew she was grateful, knew she would want to express that gratitude in the only way she could, but he would deal with that situation if it happened.

"I'm tired," she said. "They kept me awake all night and I haven't slept. We should go upstairs, Thomas."

"None of us has slept. You can go to bed when you tell me what you heard."

"Can it not wait? My head spins and my body hurts."

"Did they abuse you?" It was Olaf who spoke, still the concerned father despite knowing the nature of his daughter, of what spite she was capable of—a father's love able to accommodate all things. Thomas assumed he would be the same himself with Will and Amal, that it was the role of a father to forgive, even though his own had never forgiven him for anything, except at the very end.

"Muhammed abused me every single day. Sometimes it was physical, sometimes only threats, but those can be worse. Tonight, he hit me. He displayed me to those men and beat me with a cane. I saw the young one enjoyed my plight."

"And Mandana?"

"He is the old one?"

Thomas nodded. "And his son is Pedro Guerrero."

"I was not told their names. The old man is father to the young?" Helena frowned. "Now you say it I can see the sense—they have the same look, the same height. But the young one … Pedro, you said? He is cruel, like Muhammed. Worse than Muhammed. I was offered to him."

"What did he do to you?" It was Olaf again, still the

protector, though he must know it was too late for protection.

"Nothing. He said he would enjoy me later, when he was less tired and less drunk. The way he looked at me when he said it made me afraid."

"You're safe now," Thomas said, and Helena smiled at him. She reached out a hand, but Thomas withdrew his. She left hers on the table as if that had not been what she intended. "Tell me what you heard."

"Muhammed grew tired of humiliating me. By this time, they were discussing business and forgot I was even there. Muhammed was drunk and had been using the pipe. They talked of Spain, but of other things too. Muhammed hates his uncle. He is plotting with the men to attack al-Zagal and kill him if he can."

"Muhammed has soldiers of his own to do that," Thomas said.

"You know Muhammed," said Olaf. "He worries about everything and nothing. He won't attack al-Zagal until he is sure of victory. I can see how he might prefer someone else to do it for him."

"How many men does al-Zagal have?" Thomas asked.

"Not as many as he once did. He is a broken man since the fall of Malaka. He was defeated even before the main battle, ousted from his position in Gharnatah. He's made a place for himself in al-Marilla but has less than a thousand around him. He rules the town but not much else. I heard he was considering crossing the inner sea to Africa."

"Muhammed wants his uncle dead," said Helena. "He offered those men a thousand trained soldiers if they attack al-Zagal." She glanced toward Olaf. "He said you would lead them." She stared at her father for a long time before continuing, as if she wasn't sure whether to tell him everything that had been said, then made her decision. "He wants you gone from the city, father. He doesn't trust you."

"I serve the Sultan," said Olaf. "I have always served the Sultan. Muhammed knows that."

"He also knows you are privy to every secret he has. He was never rational even before he became Sultan, now he is worse. He sees threats everywhere. He believes in portents and signs. If a bird flies through a courtyard without resting in a tree it is bad luck. If the wind blows south one day and north the next, it brings danger. He is no longer rational." Tears glistened unshed in Helena's eyes, a sight Thomas had never seen before—one he believed he would never see. It told him how badly Muhammed had treated her, how deeply her spirit had been broken.

"Who will lead this attack if Muhammed sends you and a thousand men?" Thomas asked Olaf. "Guerrero, Mandana, or you?"

"I will not go," said Olaf.

"Refuse and he will arrest you."

"Muhammed told them they would be in charge," said Helena. "They told him they already have two thousand men of their own, and with Muhammed's soldiers they will take al-Marilla in a matter of days."

"They have a thousand at most," Thomas said. "Is that not right, Luis?" He wanted to include the youth, who had spent the entire time staring at Helena as if he had never seen her like before, which might well be true. "And not all of those are fighting men, are they?"

Luis nodded, but made no comment. He reached down and stroked Kin's head, the dog sitting beside his master the whole time.

"That will still give them two thousand," said Olaf. "More than enough to defeat al-Zagal. It would extend Muhammed's territory and take in all of al-Basharāt, with strongholds at either end."

"What good will it do him?" Thomas said. "He'd be

better served building his strength here in Gharnatah rather than spread it too thin. It is this city the Spanish want, not some scatter of towns to the east, not even al-Marilla. They have taken Malaka, and Gharnatah will be their next prize."

"Muhammed doesn't see that," said Olaf. "As Helena said, he is no longer rational."

"Mandana and Guerrero agreed to this plan?" Thomas asked.

"More than agreed," said Helena. "It is they who came to Muhammed with it, not him to them. They are here for another reason than simple conquest, but what it is I did not hear. Other than ... but no, that has nothing to do with anything."

"Other than what?" Thomas said.

Helena's eyes tracked the table, paused on her father, then came to meet Thomas's. "They mentioned your name. Both of them."

"Me?" Thomas almost laughed, until he recalled the hate that had driven Guerrero to kill Lubna.

"They wanted to know if you had returned to Gharnatah."

"Did they say why?"

Helena shook her head. "Muhammed said you had not, but that you still had a house here on the Albayzin."

"Did he ... and what did they say to that?"

"They asked where. And when Muhammed wanted to know why they were so curious about you, the young one–"

"Guerrero," Thomas said. "Mandana's son."

Helena waved a hand, names unimportant to her. "The young one, *Guerrero*," she emphasised the word deliberately, then paused. "Yes, he might be Mandana's son, but power has shifted. The father has made way for him, that was clear—or been pushed aside. It was Guerrero who did

171

the talking, Guerrero who said it didn't matter if you were here or not. If the house is yours it has to be destroyed and everyone in it killed. He said if you fled, or were not here, he can always find you and kill you later."

"Muhammed agreed to this?" Thomas thought about what Helena had told him, and other things, before nodding. "Yes, he would. Of course he would. This isn't Gharnatah, this is the Albayzin, and the two are as good as at war. It would concern him not at all if the pair of them laid waste to it. Except Guerrero only has fifty men with him, and it would take four times that to stand any chance at all."

"Muhammed said he would provide troops to help."

Thomas stared at Helena. "Why did you keep this news to yourself until now?" He stood, hesitant—unsure of what to do, missing the old Thomas who was always certain. "Once Muhammed discovers you are missing, he will know who has freed you. Did they say when they were coming?"

"No, but it won't be today. They will all be asleep after last night." A frown settled on Helena's face, an alien expression for her. It seemed to have occurred to her she had escaped one danger only to place herself in an even greater one. "What will you do, Thomas?"

Thomas glanced at Olaf. "Are you going back to the palace?"

Olaf gave a shake of the head. "Not today. Maybe never."

"You always told me you were the Sultan's man."

"Muhammed is no Sultan." Olaf's voice held an unfamiliar note of distaste. "He never was, but I was too obsessed with my own sense of loyalty to take the action I knew I should. Now ... he is sending men to kill you, Thomas, and everyone here. He has stepped beyond the realm of any civilised behaviour."

"What about Fatima?"

"I will send a message. She is safer where she is for now, she's no danger to him."

"And if Muhammed takes her captive, as he did Helena?"

"He won't. He knows if he does I will kill him. Without my presence on the hill there is a possibility my men will follow his orders. They might not, but at least he has a chance. He dare not jeopardise that chance." Olaf stood. "They won't come in daylight, so we have some time, and everyone is exhausted. We should get some sleep, and then, after noon, we must leave Gharnatah." He looked around at those gathered at the table. "All of us. Agreed?" Olaf waited until everyone nodded.

Thomas was the last of all. He had only just returned to this house he loved, and would have welcomed more time to let its familiarity ease his soul. But he knew Olaf was right. It was go or die, and dead he could never avenge Lubna.

CHAPTER TWENTY-ONE

Thomas could barely believe what Guerrero was planning, but knew he shouldn't be surprised. It had been Guerrero who was involved in the plan to steal the wealth of the Malaka Guild a year before, a plan that had resulted in Lubna's death. Thomas thought he had prevented the theft, but when he returned to the place where he had killed one of the plotters, the wooden crates that had lain there were gone. No wonder Guerrero had the funds to finance an army—enough even to bribe a Sultan.

"You're right," Thomas said to Olaf. "We should all try to get some sleep." He stood and made for the door to the courtyard. He wanted to think about what Helena had told him, wanted to think about the real reason Guerrero and Mandana were here. Not to kill him, despite what Helena had overheard. The pair might hate him, but nobody could hate that much. The son and father were both irrational, but they weren't stupid. Far from it.

He saw Helena began to rise, ready to follow him. Saw Olaf put a hand on her arm and shake his head.

Thomas walked outside, breathing deep of the cool air. The house held a multitude of memories that tumbled together in his head, one merging with another so he could barely tell them apart. He wondered if he would ever accumulate more, or whether this was the last time he would see this house. He would miss the place, but his whole life had been one relocation after another for as far back as he could remember. He stared across at al-Hamra, then on to where the snow-capped peaks of the Sholayr loomed to overlook the foolish ambitions of men.

When he entered the workshop he found Usaden lying on the cot. He had forgotten it was where the Gomeres slept, and started to back out.

"Who are you trying to escape, Thomas?" Usaden had not been there for Helena's telling, and Thomas realised he had probably slept most of the night through, sure of their success.

Thomas laughed despite the tension inside him. "A demon nestled within the body of a beautiful woman."

"You make her sound appealing." Usaden rose. "I was about to get up, so you can have the cot. It is surprisingly comfortable."

"For someone more used to sleeping on desert sand, it probably is." Thomas clapped Usaden on the shoulder as he passed, then lay on the cot, his head and shoulders propped against the side of a bench. If anything, this room held more memories than the rest of the house and he was glad he had come here.

Usaden pulled out a three-legged stool and sat as if it was a padded chair.

"Tell me true," Thomas said, "how does Will fare in what you're trying to teach him?"

Usaden's dark eyes studied Thomas before he answered. "Truth? He will be a great fighter—if he can control his temper. I think there is a little of his grandfather in him, but he also fights like you. He is instinctive, and possesses the same cold logic I have seen when you fight. It is a combination that will make him invulnerable … or kill him."

Thomas wondered when Usaden had found the time to watch him in battle, for they had always fought side by side, with little spare capacity to look around. "I am still alive, though."

Usaden almost smiled. "Indeed you are."

"We have to leave this house," Thomas said. "Guerrero and Mandana are coming to kill everyone here, most likely tonight when they believe us asleep, but we will be long gone before then. It's your decision what you do, but if you wish it I would like you with us."

"Why would I not be with you? I have not finished training your son yet."

Thomas stared at the man. A Gomeres mercenary who had fought like a dervish during the fall of Malaka, who had almost caught up with Guerrero but was rebuffed by the chaos of soldiers fighting at the entrance to the Gibalfaro fort. A man who fought for money but no longer did so. Thomas knew Will worshipped the man, and perhaps a little of that worship, or friendship at least, was mutual.

"Have you come here to escape the ice woman?" asked Usaden.

"I thought you were asleep when we came back."

"I was, but you made so much noise I thought it better to find out what was going on. I remained outside, in case you did not consider it any of my business. Now I know better. I assume she is the devil you spoke of?" Usaden glanced at the light filling the courtyard beyond the workshop door. "All of you should sleep now, recover. I will stand guard. I will wake you if anything happens."

Once Usaden had gone Thomas stretched out on the cot, aware it felt wider than the last time he had lain there, aware he had lost too much weight, too much strength. He would need all his strength before Guerrero and his father were dealt with. He didn't believe either were here to help Muhammed—more likely some kind of betrayal was involved. He thought about the pair and came to believe they might well have come to Gharnatah in search of him. Not because Thomas was important enough, but because both men knew he wouldn't rest until he had hunted them down and killed them. He smiled as sleep called, and the thought of revenge filled him.

"Men are coming."

Thomas woke fast, on his feet before he knew where he was. Usaden stood nearby, waiting, patient—used to watching men come awake from deep sleep and having to prepare to fight.

"How many?"

"I do not know. Many, I think."

"How far?"

"We have a little time. I can hear fighting, so they have met resistance."

Thomas smiled. "This is the Albayzin. Soldiers aren't welcome, particularly Muhammed's soldiers. Where are the others?"

"You can help me wake them."

Olaf was ready in an instant, as was Luis, who had spent weeks in Guerrero's camp, no doubt always ready for some kind of threat. Jorge took longer, and Thomas left Belia to hurry him along. Will was awake, having slept at least some of the day, and Amal lay in her cot with a smile on her face. Thomas stared down at her. So much like her mother—dark-haired, olive-skinned, good-natured. He lifted her and grabbed Will's hand. He stopped on the landing to look through the window, high enough here to see over tumbling rooftops to al-Hatabin square and the

177

river Darro. Three arched stone bridges linked the red hill of al-Hamra with the opposite slope of the Albayzin, and soldiers blocked them all, with others standing in the square. Thomas went down the stairs and handed Amal to Belia, Will to Helena, and went outside with Jorge and Luis following.

"They're coming, but slowly," said Usaden. "It seems half the population are trying to stop them."

"It's Muhammed's doing," said Olaf, standing tall, his long blond hair tied in a plait at his neck that hung halfway down his back. "The Albayzin is a thorn in his side he can't stop picking at." He glanced at Thomas. "How do we leave?"

"You aren't staying?"

Olaf waved a hand at the noise. "How can I?"

"He doesn't know you're here," Thomas said.

"He doesn't need to. This is not about me, it's about him. He's attacked his own people and is now throwing his lot in with the men who killed my daughter. I have had enough. He can fight the rest of this war without me. It is time for you and me to revenge Lubna. I am with you, wherever it leads."

Thomas wanted to embrace Olaf but knew it would be the wrong thing to do. A nod of acknowledgement was enough before he took on the responsibility he had spent too long trying to run away from.

"We'll need food and clothes, and weapons of course." He turned to Jorge. "Take Luis to the cellar and bring some of the coin there, we may need it."

"And the rest?"

"We can't take it all with us. Hide it as best you can, but don't take long about it."

"That is my entire wealth," said Jorge.

"Is it worth more than your life?" Thomas stared at him, waiting until Jorge looked away, shaking his head. "Bring no more than can be carried. With luck, they won't search for it if they don't know it's there. Besides, it's only money."

"It's easy for you to say that. I've never had any." But Jorge turned, Luis following, and they descended into the cellar.

Thomas watched the pair disappear, then turned back to Olaf. Usaden had climbed the low wall and now clung to a corner of the house so he could look across the jumble of houses that descended the steep hillside.

"They're closer. I can see men now. There are some in grey uniforms, not Moorish soldiers."

"Guerrero and Mandana's men," Thomas said. "It's time to go."

Belia had spent part of the morning packing what she could, and handed sacks to them as they entered the house. There was still no sign of Jorge and Luis, so Thomas went down to the cellar to find them emerging from a dark corner.

"We're leaving. Now."

"I wanted to make sure the boxes were hidden well," said Jorge. "There's that escape passage Britto built for you, we've put them in there and locked the door."

"It's us they're looking for, not gold." Thomas turned away, hoping Jorge would finally stop worrying about the wealth they had managed to accumulate over the years. It didn't matter anymore, if it ever had.

They left the house to find the alleyway deserted and began to climb its turns toward the crest of the hill. Most people had locked their doors, so their progress was unimpeded. The sound of fighting came clearly from below. Guerrero's men were meeting fierce resistance.

Olaf took the lead, but Thomas knew he was holding himself back so the rest of them could keep pace. Even so, Thomas's breath burned in his lungs, and once more he cursed his weakness even as he knew cursing was useless. He would have to do something to regain the strength he had allowed to drain from him. How could he expect to take revenge on those who took Lubna's life if he wasn't strong? He knew he had lost sight of his goal, had allowed himself to be seduced by the temptation cast from the darkness beyond life. So immersed in his own thoughts was he that he ran straight into the back of Helena, almost knocking her to her knees. He grabbed her, then went past to where Olaf had stopped on a corner.

"Men," said Olaf, never one to waste words.

Thomas leaned around him and looked into a small square. They were almost at the top of the hill, close to where Muhammed's mother maintained her own miniature version of the al-Hamra palace. Beyond lay the town walls and their promise of escape.

"I count fourteen," Thomas said. "And five of us."

Olaf nodded. "One of whom is Olaf Torvaldsson, and another Usaden Hamid. The rest of you can wait here if you wish."

Thomas shook his head and offered a tight smile at Olaf's words. He was probably right, but he couldn't let the two of them fight while he stood aside.

"It will be quicker if we all do it," he said.

"Can the boy fight?"

"We'll find out."

Olaf thought a moment. "Tell Jorge to stay at the rear. I have grown strangely fond of him and would not have him killed."

Thomas left Olaf on the corner and went back to tell the others of the plan.

Usaden already had a sword in each hand, bouncing on his toes. No doubt he was impatient to use his skill, and Thomas was pleased the man had decided to stay with Will to continue his training, knowing it must have been hard to turn his back on the fighting that continued in other parts of al-Andalus. Now the fighting had come to him.

Thomas drew his own sword, a dagger in his left hand. He turned to Luis. "This is not your fight. You can stay and protect the women if you wish."

"Those men held me prisoner," said Luis. "They killed my parents in front of me." His eyes were cold, his shoulders tense, and Thomas hoped he possessed enough skill to keep him alive.

Olaf left the corner and came back to them.

"They're just standing there waiting. They have been sent in case we come this way, but they don't really expect us. If we go in hard and fast it will be over before it starts. Is everyone ready?"

Thomas nodded, letting an anger settle through him, once more aware of its difference, a hot rage that was alien to him. He wondered if this is how it would always be from now on, if he had changed so much. He shrugged. If he had, so be it. He pushed past Olaf and began to run. Like Usaden, he was impatient for mayhem.

CHAPTER TWENTY-TWO

Thomas lay on his belly as he watched six of Guerrero's men steer their horses up a steep track. He narrowed his eyes, trying to see if any conscripted men formed part of the party, but he thought not. It made him feel better about what they were about to do.

A day had passed since three of them had separated from the rest of the group who had escaped Gharnatah and sent them on to Pampaneira. Luis hadn't wanted to go, but Thomas insisted because the youth knew the trails better than anyone else. For a moment, as their party moved away, Kin had tracked backward and forward, clearly unsure who to stay with—then fealty won out and he had gone with Luis. Now only Thomas, Usaden and Olaf remained, and they had a plan, of sorts.

"Where are they going?" Olaf lay close beside Thomas, his voice a whisper.

"Looking for more recruits, I expect. Muhammed hasn't sent any of his soldiers yet, so Mandana won't attack al-Zagal until he's assured of victory. For that he needs more men." The day before they had lain on another hillside and watched as Guerrero and Mandana led their small band away from Gharnatah. If they had been expecting Muhammed's soldiers to accompany them, they were disappointed. Once again, Muhammed had shown himself too timid to commit to a course of action for fear of failure.

"Drafted men don't fight well," said Olaf.

"They don't need to fight, only to die. They will be placed in the front ranks to protect the others. Some will fight in an attempt to save themselves, and that is all he needs. They know if they refuse their families will be punished."

"It is a waste of lives."

Thomas glanced at him. "Do you think he cares? Do you think either of them care?"

"Can I go down there now?" asked Usaden. He appeared completely relaxed, but Thomas knew Usaden was always ready for mayhem. He nodded, and watched as the Gomeres darted away, as sure on his feet as the ibex that roamed these slopes. A few minutes later he appeared on the trail, sauntering down the slope. His hands were empty of weapons, but that could change in an instant.

"Should we go to help him?" Thomas asked Olaf.

"Why would he need help? There are only six men."

Thomas watched as the riders caught sight of Usaden. They slowed a little, but only to give themselves time to judge the situation. Thomas imagined their thoughts: one man, alone, and they were in search of men to add to their number. A single man was still an extra man, and they had built their forces in just such a way.

The leader drew a sword and encouraged his horse forward. His mistake was in leaving the others behind, but Thomas doubted it would have made much difference. Usaden waited, an unthreatening figure, except something in his manner made the lead rider slow. Perhaps he saw that Usaden was not afraid. He slowed further, but by then it was too late.

Usaden moved fast. A run to one side, a leap from a rock, a second jump to land behind the rider, and a knife appeared in his hand. Usaden pushed the dead rider from the saddle and took his place. He bullied the horse around and rode hard toward the remaining five. It was an uneven contest.

Thomas and Olaf picked their way down the slope to help lift the fallen men back into their saddles and tie them in place with rope from their saddlebags. They slapped the horses' rumps and let them canter downslope, knowing they would find their way back to Guerrero's camp.

As they watched the horses disappear Olaf said, "How many do you think they will send next time?"

"No more than a score, I'd say—for now, anyway. They may think this is nothing more than a random attack. So yes, they will send more to find out what happened, but not many more."

"We can take twenty," said Olaf.

Thomas glanced at him. "Can we?"

"Of course. There are three of us, remember."

Thomas saw the logic of it, and for a man who had so recently sought his own death he was surprised at the thrill that sparked through him. The three of them together, each of whom had loved Lubna in their own way. This was the start of the punishment for those who had stolen Lubna's life, and he knew it would only get bloodier. He smiled, pleased at the thought.

Thomas discovered he had been wrong, and he wondered if Guerrero might not have some inkling of who had killed his scouting party, because he sent not a score of men but more than twice that. They came by a wider trail, riding at their own pace, a small knot at the front testing the way.

"I count forty-seven," said Usaden.

Olaf nodded. "The same as do I. Too many?"

"For a direct assault, yes."

"Agreed." Olaf turned to look at Thomas, who sat against a rock eating an orange as he watched the soldiers pick their way south and east. "They are looking for us, aren't they?"

"What would you do if six of your scouts were sent back to you dead?"

"I would send more men next time."

"How many would you expect to be looking for?" Thomas asked.

Olaf smiled. "More than three. More than six if it had been my men. A dozen at least, most likely more."

"So you would send a large enough party to attack between ten and twenty, or more. Would you judge fifty enough?"

"Certainly."

"So would I."

"Is there a point you are trying to make?" asked Olaf.

"What is the last thing you would expect?"

Olaf's gaze flickered across the hillside as he thought, then he grinned. "I would expect my quarry to run away from me."

Usaden laughed. "So, we ignore forty-seven men and attack a thousand instead?"

"You were with al-Zagal before the siege of Malaka," Thomas said to Olaf. "When he was routed by the Spanish."

Olaf offered a nod.

"The best leader in al-Andalus was with you, yet still you were almost killed. How did the Spanish do that to you? Did they confront you directly? Come into your midst?"

"They had a larger force than we did," said Olaf.

"But they didn't attack directly, did they?"

"They were cowards. I am no coward."

"Is victory a cowardly thing?"

"If it means fighting from the shadows, yes."

Thomas raised a shoulder and glanced at Usaden. "What is your opinion?"

"Victory is victory. I am with you. Burning arrows?"

"And rocks," Thomas said.

Usaden smiled. "It is a shame we have no powder. I have seen mules with kegs of black powder strapped to them sent into a horde and flaming arrows sent after them."

Thomas thought of Ibrahim, of his black powder and his bravery, and nodded. "Yes, it is a shame."

"No," said Olaf. "It is a coward's way to fight. A warrior confronts his enemy face to face. I want nothing to do with it."

"Then stay here. Usaden and I are more than capable of scaring them. That's all I want to do for now—keep them on edge, not allow them to see who's attacking. Fear is our best friend in this endeavour." Thomas watched Olaf, seeing his stubbornness, his sense of chivalry. There was another weapon he could use to persuade the man, but would prefer not to unveil it—though of course Olaf knew of it as well as Thomas himself.

"I know Mandana," said Olaf, "but not his son. What is he like?"

"I know more about him than I used to, but still not enough."

"But you know the father. Are they alike? Mandana is a snake who cannot be trusted. Is his son the same?"

"Worse, I suspect." Thomas believed they had come close enough to risk the final toss of the dice. "You know as well as I do what he is capable of. The slaughter of innocent women and children." He felt the prick of unshed tears behind his eyes, determined Olaf wouldn't see them. "You can't negotiate with a man like that. You can't fight him like you would other men. All you can do is destroy him like the rabid animal he is."

Olaf stared at Thomas, but it was clear he wasn't going to change his mind.

Usaden was going through their small cache of weapons, picking out what they would need. Long swords were not required for what was planned. Instead he set aside two bows, together with a dozen arrows each, and a long knife for each of them. But if it came to hand-to-hand fighting Thomas knew they would be as good as dead.

"Will you stay here?" he asked Olaf, as he sheathed the knife and hung a bow across his back.

"I might take a look around, judge the lie of the land for when it comes to a real fight."

"There's no point fighting them."

"There was a goatherd's hut we passed a half hour since," said Olaf. "I will wait for you there until sunrise tomorrow. If you don't appear by then, I will find the others. Pampaneira you said the town was, didn't you?"

Thomas nodded, then turned and followed Usaden, who was already a hundred paces ahead.

Usaden climbed steadily, his feet as sure as if he walked a city street. Thomas tried to emulate him but knew he had lost the skill, together with his certainty. He needed to find both again if he wanted to destroy Guerrero and Mandana. He knew both would have to be destroyed, or he would die in the attempt.

After a while Usaden slowed and let Thomas take the lead, because he knew better where they were going. They came to a cliff edge that looked down into the valley where Mandana's forces had been arrayed only days before. Now it lay empty, only the rubbish scattered across the ground testament to the horde who had resided there. Thomas picked his way down, examined a fire which was cold to the touch.

"I wonder which way they went, and when?" said Usaden.

"They must have broken camp as soon as Guerrero and Mandana left for Gharnatah." Thomas looked east along the valley, then west in the direction Guerrero had gone to meet Muhammed. He rose and started east, the ground rising. Grey snow-melt foamed around rocks in the small river, ice cold as they crossed it. They had gone no more than half a mile before he stopped, frowning. He saw no sign of a large force travelling this way, and yet this was where he would have expected them to go—away from Gharnatah and toward al-Marrilla.

He turned and started back the way they had come, moving faster, wanting to make up for his mistake. Usaden kept pace, saying nothing because he never wasted words in idle conversation. They passed the place where the men had camped and went on. Now there were indications a large force had passed this way, and Thomas cursed himself for a fool not to have seen his mistake sooner.

The river turned sharply, as did the valley, and before long they came out on a broad shoulder of the Sholayr with the land falling away in waves of peaked hillsides to a distant glimpse of a haze-covered sea.

"I know where they're going," Thomas said when they came to a distinct roadway, made more distinct by men's feet and horses' hoofs. "This road will also take them to al-Marilla, but turn off it and you will be in Pampaneira in a day's ride."

"I thought they were attacking al-Zagal. Why would they go to Pampaneira? They have no idea you sent the others there."

Thomas started to say something, then stopped as the pieces fell into place in his mind.

"They are a thousand men, but more than half have been stolen from their homes. How do you make reluctant men fight?"

"All men will fight when they stare their own death in the face."

"Or when those they love are threatened. Pampaneira is where the families of the captured men are held. Guerrero is leading them there so they will see their loved ones, and then he'll leave enough men to kill them if they refuse to fight." Thomas turned and looked at the flank of the Sholayr. Cloud clung to the peaks. "We need to find Olaf and reach Pampaneira before they do."

"We have already had this conversation," said Usaden. "We can sting their hides, but not hurt enough of them. They are too many."

"But we can take the people away from there, if we can persuade them to come."

"And if they refuse?"

"Then we take our own people and leave the rest." Thomas cursed. "I thought I was sending them to safety—instead I have placed them in the wolf's lair."

Usaden studied the roadway, his eyes following it until it disappeared in the distance.

"You go ahead, I will fetch Olaf. It will take too long if we both go. Try to get ahead of them and warn your friends, take them somewhere safe if you can."

Thomas looked around as if some insight would come to him, but nothing did. "There is nowhere safe."

"Does the town have walls?"

"Some."

"What is the point in only having some walls?"

"The ground is precipitous, so it doesn't need a full set."

"Can it be closed up, made safe?"

"I have only been there the once, but I believe so."

"Then go a second time now. I will bring Olaf as fast as we can travel. Watch for us, but do not wait."

Usaden turned and began to lope across the ground. Thomas watched him, aware how much the man had been holding back so as not to tire him. Then he began to jog along the roadway, pushing his body hard. There was no evidence Guerrero's men were heading for Pampaneira, but Thomas had a bad feeling about the situation. It was as if everything was slipping away from him, his uncertain grasp on a new life already fading. Will and Amal would be in Pampaneira by now. Helena, Belia and Jorge, too. Thomas pushed himself harder, ignoring the pain that racked his body, knowing pain would make him stronger.

CHAPTER TWENTY-THREE

Thomas could have travelled faster on the roadway, which had widened as he came ever closer to Pampaneira, but had been forced to leave it when he almost caught up to the tail of Guerrero's column of men. Their detritus had become ever more evident until, on a low rise, he saw in the distance the rear rank and stopped. He crouched in the shade of a boulder in case someone thought to check behind. The head of the column was hidden from sight where the land dropped into a valley. Thomas wasn't exactly sure where he was, but thought Pampaneira lay no more than two hours ahead. He checked the position of the sun. Three hours of daylight remained. With the town gates open and the walls unmanned, Guerrero would be able to ride in without opposition. Thomas turned aside and climbed a low ridge to the north until he was on the far side, then began to move as fast as he could, running when he was able, cursing his own lack of fitness and promising never to allow himself to grow so weak again. If he lived long enough to fulfil the promise.

As the sun crept toward the rock shattered western horizon he climbed a narrow goat trail until he caught sight of Guerrero's soldiers again, pleased to find he had managed to get ahead of them. He lay on his belly for a moment while his breath grew easier, and judged their numbers. Not the thousand that was claimed—less than half that—but still more than enough to take Pampaneira if such was the intention. He watched a little longer, noting that the trained soldiers stayed on the flanks of the column, herding the captured men between them.

As shadows filled the valley a commotion broke out to one side, and a dozen men made a break through their guards. Why there, in that place, wasn't clear. Perhaps some had been taken from this area and familiarity sparked a flare of courage. Perhaps it was no more than the constant strike of sticks, the snap of words Thomas couldn't hear. He saw it in the way the guards moved, how the men flinched in their presence. Whatever had triggered the move, a dozen men broke free and began to run. Had they stayed together they might have stood a chance, but each took their own path, spreading out like ripples across a pond.

Men on horseback came after them. One was Pedro Guerrero, his height and manner distinctive even across the distance. He struck out at a running figure, his sword cutting into a shoulder, and the man fell to the ground and lay still. Guerrero used the weight of his horse to gather the others, until seven of them were surrounded by mounted soldiers. The other escapees bled the last of their lives into the poor soil.

Only once the captured men were made safe did Mandana ride out to join his son. They exchanged words, heads almost touching, then Guerrero issued an order. Helena had convinced Thomas that Guerrero was now the leader of this army, but what he witnessed told him that Mandana might still hold some power over his son—at least for now.

Thomas held his position, knowing what was about to happen but unable to turn away. The conversation between Mandana and Guerrero came to an end and the two made their way back to the head of the column. The small group of captives remained surrounded by the mounted men. Thomas expected the column to start moving again, knowing he had wasted time in observing them, but was surprised when they began to spread out. Men were sent out in search of something. Four came close to Thomas but made no attempt to climb to the crest where he lay. He saw them gather meagre scraps of wood from the hillside, cuttings from almond and olive trees that had been discarded during winter pruning. They and the others carried the wood back to the camp and began to build fires, unlit for the moment. Only when Thomas saw what was going to happen did he slide back and move away. He had no wish to witness more of Guerrero's cruelty. Shadows gathered around him, both without and within, as he hurried toward the hidden town. Darkness fell, broken only by starlight. As Thomas emerged from a side valley and saw the rising jumble of white houses of Pampaneira he heard a sound from behind. He spun around, drawing his knife. He feared some of Guerrero's men had been sent to scout ahead for any resistance, but instead he saw a dark shape within the greater darkness and went to one knee as Kin approached, his tail circling madly. Thomas stroked the soft fur, smelled the rough scent of the dog, and smiled. Here was one creature who never judged, never doubted, never turned aside. He wondered how long he had been out here, and why. He had already witnessed how Kin could follow a trail, however faint, and believed he might have caught his scent and come in search of him. He looked beyond the dog, wondering if Luis was somewhere nearby, but there was no sign. Nothing moved, the night as still as if it held its breath. There was no sign of Guerrero's men, and Thomas thought it possible they had stopped for the night and would enter Pampaneira in the morning. Would more lessons be inflicted then?

"Where are the others?" Thomas whispered to Kin, as if the dog could understand. He hoped Olaf and Usaden were close, because it would be better if they entered the town together. He moved away from the track, wider here where it was used by men going to tend their precipitous terraces. Thomas found a comfortable rock, or as comfortable as a rock could ever be, and sat to wait.

Other men would have announced themselves with their conversation, but if Olaf had not been so tall, his hair not so blond, Thomas would have missed them. Even as he followed Olaf's silent progress he was unable to make out Usaden and wondered if the Gomeres hadn't come. Then he felt a tap on his shoulder and laughed as Usaden sat beside him, pushing him across with his hip to make space.

Usaden reached out and scratched Kin's ears, surprising Thomas. "He's a good dog. Never barked once— he must have known it was me. I can see the point of a dog if it is like this one, but they are still filthy creatures."

When Thomas looked up Olaf stood in front of him. Thomas rose to his feet and snapped his fingers, not expecting Kin to follow, but pleased when the animal trotted to fall in step beside him.

At the town gate Thomas looked around for a guard but found none. He made a mental note to send someone to stand on the wall and watch for Guerrero's men. Meanwhile the three of them swung the heavy gate shut and dropped a wooden bar inside. Olaf held the bar and shook the structure.

"This will not hold determined men for long."

"We'll have to hope there are some here willing to fight," Thomas said.

"Will they?" asked Olaf. "Do they have something to fight for?"

"Their families, their homes, their town. Is that enough? We need to find out tonight before Guerrero arrives. If they won't fight we'll need to leave here."

"Do you have somewhere to go?"

Thomas thought about it as they began to climb the steep hillside between white walls. They couldn't flee to Jamila's village—it was too open, and the explosion would have destroyed at least some of the houses. They might be able to go south in hope of reaching al-Marilla and the forces of al-Zagal, but he doubted they would receive any warmer a welcome there than they would from Guerrero. And besides, a battle would be fought there before long. A germ of an idea came to him, but Thomas kept it to himself for the moment. It was irrational, dangerous, and he wasn't sure if Olaf would agree to it.

Thomas knew Guerrero's men must have made camp by now or they would be at the walls. It occurred to him that just as the women and children in the town were held hostage against their menfolk's good behaviour, so it worked the other way. The people of Pampaneira would put up no resistance because to do so would endanger those outside the walls as well as within. The realisation made it even more important a decision was made quickly. Stay or go? Fight or flee?

They saw few people as they climbed to the central square. Thomas considered sending the others ahead while he went to talk with Don Domingo, but he was tired, his body ached, and an hour or two wasn't going to make much difference.

There were more people in the square, some returning from worship in the mosque, others sitting at tables, eating and drinking, wrapped against the cold. Nobody paid any notice of the three men as they crossed the square and started up another steep climb to the house. Thomas hoped Jamila and the others still remained there, though he knew with the arrival of Belia, Jorge, Helena and Luis space would be in short supply. He supposed Helena and Belia could share with Jamila and Dana, and Luis with Aban. Olaf and Usaden would just have to squeeze in with Thomas and Jorge somehow. Not that he intended them to remain in the town long.

As the alley finally began to level out Kin let out a single bark and ran ahead.

"He must be keen to return to his master," said Usaden.

They were almost at the house when Thomas caught sight of Kin again. He was standing stiff-legged, the fur on his neck raised and a deep rumble sounding in his chest. Two figures faced each other close to the opening of an alley: Luis and Aban. Their posture made it obvious they were arguing, and that the argument was about to escalate into violence.

Thomas started forward, leaving Olaf and Usaden behind. Something glinted, catching what little light was cast by the occasional burning torch, then the two figures lunged at each other. Kin sped across the ground, leaping at them. Thomas expected to see the dog attack Aban, but instead his strong jaws closed around Luis's wrist and a knife clattered to the cobbles. Aban struck out at the pinned Luis, but Thomas was close enough now to wrap his arms around the youth and drag him away.

"What's going on here!" he demanded.

"I told him Dana wants to be with me," said Aban.

Thomas turned to Luis, who was massaging his wrist. The dog sat looking up at Luis, loyalty to its master returned now the danger had passed.

"Give me your side of the story," Thomas said.

"He wants to break the three of us apart. The child is as likely mine as his. He doesn't own her, no more than I do."

Thomas looked between them, finally working out the relationship between the three, and wondering which of the two had instigated such a thing. Or could it have been Dana herself? He knew he would have to ask Jorge.

"You can't just turn up and think everything will go back to the way it was." Aban took a pace forward, but Luis stood his ground. Thomas knew if it came to a fight which of them would win. What he didn't understand was if the relationship involved them all, why the sudden falling out? Unless Dana believed Luis was never going to return and had made a promise to Aban.

"Let's go inside to talk about this. I'm tired and I'm hungry, and my friends are the same. Is Jorge in there?"

"And the ice woman," said Luis, a strange expression on his face that Thomas put down to either lust or fear. Helena was different enough to confuse men who had never seen her like before. He had witnessed it many times over the years, and knew Helena took pleasure in encouraging both the lust and uncertainty she could spark in men.

Thomas turned away, thinking of distant times when, like these two, he had been caught up in the heat of youth —though he had never been involved in the manner of relationship they appeared to share.

He nodded to Olaf, who had watched the brief encounter with a faint smile. As Thomas reached Usaden he heard a cry from behind and spun around, ready to strike out. Luis had one hand around Aban's throat. The other at his waist was dangerously close to the hilt of a second knife. Thomas moved fast. He reached Luis and punched his wrist so his hand fell away from Aban's neck.

Luis turned fast, a rictus of anger on his face. He pushed at Thomas, who pushed back even harder. He laid his forearm across Luis's chest and slammed him against the wall, even as he did so recognising the youth was stronger than him.

"Go now, while you can," he said to Aban, then turned back to Luis. "What is wrong with you? Have you been with Guerrero too long? Aban is your friend. More than a friend."

Thomas expected Luis to wilt, to back down, but all he saw in the youth's eyes was an anger that threatened to swamp all rationality. Thomas stopped pushing but kept a hand on Luis's chest. He opened his mouth to speak again when he was suddenly thrust away. For a moment he thought Aban had returned, but then as he staggered, he saw Usaden had taken his place and grasped Luis's wrist where a knife was held in his hand.

"He was about to stick you," said Usaden, without looking away. "What do you want me to do with him?" He twisted Luis's wrist until he had no choice but to release the knife.

"Let him go."

"He was going to kill you."

"Better men have tried and failed." Even as Thomas spoke the words he was aware of how much his life had changed. Half a year ago he would never have allowed someone to draw a knife on him. He would have handled the entire situation himself. Now he didn't know if he was doing the right thing by asking Usaden to release Luis, but the Gomeres obeyed his order and stepped back out of immediate range of another attack.

Thomas saw Olaf hadn't moved an inch, trusting Usaden to take care of the situation. Luis looked between the three of them. His expression changed, losing the anger that had been present for the last minutes. Thomas saw him make an effort to appear less hostile, but a fire remained in his eyes that was at odds with his forced demeanour. He picked up the knife and pushed past

Thomas with it still in his hand, but both he and Usaden watched him carefully.

"Guerrero has changed him," said Olaf. "Where is this food you promised? And a bed. I would like to sleep in a bed tonight."

"That may not be possible. I have to go talk to someone before deciding how long we stay here."

"If we do leave, perhaps we should not take that boy with us," said Olaf.

"He claims to be father to the child Dana carries."

Olaf waved a hand in dismissal. "You worry too much about people who are not your family." Olaf shook his head and stalked away. Thomas watched him go, not knowing what was wrong with everyone. He glanced at Usaden, who stood patient, emotionless, but whether such was better or not Thomas didn't know.

CHAPTER TWENTY-FOUR

Thomas was relieved to discover everyone had made it safely to Pampaneira. He embraced Belia and Jorge, ignored Helena even though he was aware of her eyes on him. He knew she had an expectation of something he refused to offer. Despite her beauty she held no attraction to him, if she ever had. Sometimes he wondered how he had allowed her to seduce him, astonished at how much he had changed since those days—those nights. So close in years, so distant in the way he felt about her.

Jamila busied herself preparing food for them all. Thomas watched Aban, who sat beside Dana. A foot of space lay between them, but both were clearly tense with the need to close it. Another thing that had changed since Thomas had seen them last, and he wondered if the change was in Dana or Aban. Had the boy finally discovered his courage?

Thomas wondered how Aban felt at the prospect of raising someone else's child—if indeed the child Dana carried was Luis's—and if not, how they could tell. The two young men looked similar enough to make any distinction difficult. Thomas was aware Helena had never offered him the comfort he was Will's father. Not that it concerned him anymore, if it ever had. As far as he was concerned Will was his, and he knew that for Will Thomas was his father and always would be. He saw his son now, sitting on Olaf's lap while the big general cradled Amal to his chest. Olaf's face had lost all trace of sternness. Usaden remained outside and Thomas knew he would be watching, protecting them all, and there was nobody better to perform the task.

Thomas approached Jamila, uneasy at the knowledge she would submit to him if he made the slightest gesture toward her. He laid his hand on her shoulder, knowing he did it to spite Helena despite her not even being in the room, but was surprised at the warmth the touch brought.

"How long before the food is ready?"

"We are working as fast as we can. Go and talk to the others." She didn't push him away but he felt her tense beneath his hand.

"I didn't mean to press you. There is something I need to do and thought I could do it now if there is time."

"It will be an hour yet," she said, her voice cool. "Helena is asleep in your room if you want to go to her. I will call you down when the food is ready."

Thomas gave up the effort as futile, wondering who Jamila had been talking to but aware it might have been any of them—or more likely Helena herself, talking of how they had once been. He turned away and went to Olaf.

"I need to visit someone in the town. Can you protect them while I'm gone?"

Olaf looked up but said nothing, no doubt sure Thomas knew the answer.

Outside Thomas had reached the top of the steps leading to the square when Usaden appeared at his side and fell into step.

"I will be perfectly safe on my own," Thomas said. "I go

to visit an old friend, someone who might be willing to help."

Usaden nodded and turned back. Thomas wondered how long the three of them would have to be in each other's company before either Olaf or Usaden uttered another word. He suspected he might grow old waiting.

The town governor's house appeared the same as the first time Thomas had seen it, a torch burning either side of the wide door, a dimmer light showing within. He knocked and waited, turning to study the street, seeing nothing. There was no boar to disturb the stillness tonight. The inn where he and Jorge had drunk foul wine was dark, its shutters closed. When Thomas heard the door open, he turned. Don Domingo's servant stood watching him, a faint smile on her lips.

"He is not expecting you," she said.

"I'm not sure I'm expecting myself. He is at home though, isn't he? And he will see me?"

She moved aside to let him pass. As she did so, Thomas wondered why he had never seen any other servants. The house was large enough, and Don Domingo's position important enough to warrant a staff of more than one, however beautiful that one was.

Don Domingo was in the wide room that looked across the dark terrace where they had last spoken. He appeared unsurprised at Thomas's entrance, rose and offered his hand.

"I wondered if you would return. I hear you have sent some of your own people here. Are you sure it is wise?"

"It seemed so at the time, but no longer. I need to both ask you and tell you something, and for you to make a decision."

Don Domingo indicated a chair. "Sit. Ask what you will, though I may be unable to provide answers."

"That in itself may be enough for me to make a decision." Thomas took the chair. It was well-upholstered, and the comfort of it made his body relax for what felt like the first time in days. "Has Mandana or his son been to see you since I was here last?"

Don Domingo shook his head. "Did you achieve what you went to do?"

"I'm not sure. I freed Helena, but may have stirred up a hornet's nest in turn." Thomas stared at Don Domingo. "Did you know Muhammed, Guerrero and Mandana are planning to work together?"

Any answer Don Domingo might have had was interrupted by the servant, who entered with a tray holding coffee and a plate of small delicacies. She set the tray on the low table between them, made a small bow and left, leaving her perfume behind.

"Help yourself, I have already eaten."

Thomas reached out, trying not to stuff two of the tiny bites into his mouth at once.

Don Domingo smiled, then his expression lost all trace of humour. "Of course I know they are working together. It is one of the reasons I am here in this sad excuse for a town, but beggars have little choice, and it is a beggar I am."

"You don't like your situation, do you?" Thomas spoke around a mouthful of soft meat encased in pastry, reached for another before he had swallowed it.

"Of course not, but it is better than the alternative. If I do as I am asked, then a better position might be found for me."

"Muhammed has little time left to rule, you must know that."

Don Domingo acknowledged the words with a soft nod.

"Then I may be of use to the Spanish. Ask what you came here for. Do you want me to send for more food?"

Thomas glanced down to where a small delicacy lay in each hand, then shook his head. "I have not eaten in some time."

"As I can see. So, what is it you want?"

"Guerrero and Mandana will be at the town walls by mid-morning. Or did you know that, too?"

Don Domingo sat straighter. "No, I did not. Mandana calls on me every four or five weeks, but is not due yet—as you should know well because you saw him here recently."

"This time he has over five hundred men with him. There is going to be trouble. I believe they come to make an example, to encourage those they have stolen from their families. He will want to consult your records, no doubt. Has he done so before?"

Don Domingo sank back into his chair. "Once only."

Thomas stared at him, knowing there was no need to ask what had happened. He could see it clearly in the expression on Don Domingo's face.

"Was it someone who ran?" he asked.

Don Domingo nodded. "That is what I was told. They took a woman and two children away. I was not brave enough to ask the reason, and they would not have told me in any case. I was told to cross their names from the record." He raised his eyes to meet Thomas's. "Unless you have brought an army with you there is nothing can be done. When they come I will give up the names they ask for."

"This time they might be taking everyone," Thomas said, and Don Domingo made a noise. "And no, I have no army, but Pampaneira is protected by strong walls and steep hillsides. A small force could hold the town for a long time. Longer than Guerrero would want to besiege it."

"They have men inside the walls," said Don Domingo.

"How many? I have seen no more than two dozen. Women and children do not need many to keep them controlled. My friends and I can take care of two dozen. Are there any others? Would the old men fight?"

"We have been spared the fate inflicted on other towns. Nobody would believe you if you said they are under threat now."

"I want you to ask them in any case," Thomas said. "They won't listen to me."

"Nor me. I am sure they consider me a joke. The governor before me was a farmer who worked his own land here. He was one of them. Spoke their bastard language, born within a mile of where we sit. I am an outsider and will not be missed when I leave. So no, they will not fight if I ask, nor will they obey. How many men do you have, Thomas? Can you offer any resistance at all?"

"We are six, but only four of those I can trust to fight."

"Six? Gods, then you have already lost, but there is still time for you to leave. I like you, Thomas Berrington, I always have, but your habit of helping people has finally gotten you into more trouble than you can handle."

"What will you do when they come?"

"Whatever they ask."

"Will you tell them I was here?"

Don Domingo offered a smile. "Were you? I do not recall such."

As Thomas passed through the central square, he noticed the men set to guard the inhabitants. They stood in doorways, or sat outside small establishments serving the means to obtain oblivion or dreams. He saw only two women, both of whom kept scarves over their heads and walked quickly, ignoring the shouted insults.

In the house the scent of cooking brought a pain to Thomas's stomach. The sweetmeats offered by Don

Domingo had done little more than sharpen his hunger, and he sat at the table across from Olaf waiting for the food to be served. Will tried to climb across the table to him, but Olaf made him go around. Thomas lifted his son onto his lap, surprised at how heavy he had become. Taller than when he had left him in Jorge and Belia's care after the death of Lubna, stronger from Usaden's training. Thomas knew he had failed as a father, abandoning both Will and Amal to the care of others.

"Where have you been, Pa?" Will asked.

"Out."

"Take me next time. This house is full of women."

Thomas tried not to laugh. "I expect they spoil you, don't they?"

"I'm too old to be spoiled."

Thomas looked around, but couldn't see who he wanted. "Do you know where Jorge is?"

"Sleeping. He sleeps all the time. Sleeps and tumbles with Belia."

"You are too young to know such things," Thomas said.

"Why?"

"You just are." He lifted Will down. "Go find him and tell him we need to talk."

"What if they are tumbling?"

Thomas tried to hide a smile. "Knock on the door first."

"Can I talk too? And can I play with Kin?"

"Of course, to both. But go get Jorge first."

Thomas watched Will run off then turned back to Olaf. "Once we have eaten we need to make a decision."

"Your friend turned you down, did he?"

"He can't help us, and I understand his reasons why." Thomas glanced up as Belia and Jamila brought clay platters heavy with spiced stew. Dana followed with flatbread. Thomas studied her for a moment. Her waist was still slim, with little sign of the child she carried. He wondered how far along she was, his old training sparking a clutch of questions he pushed to one side. Her birthing was months away yet, and no doubt none of his business. He reached for the bread and piled stew into a pocket he made with his thumbnail. The food was good, and for a time he lost himself in the simple pleasure of filling his belly. Jorge came down, seeming to be wide awake. Will went across the room to Kin, who allowed himself to be hand-fed small nuggets of meat and pigeon.

Jamila took a place at the head of the table near to Thomas and nodded toward Helena, who had come down and now sat at the far end, eating without raising her eyes. "Is it true what Jorge told me, that she was once your woman? I would understand if she becomes so again. She is very beautiful."

"A beauty that is only surface deep," Thomas said. "And no, not my woman, not anymore. Not in a long time, and I wish she never had been." He wondered why he had to qualify his answer when a simple no would have been sufficient.

When the table was cleared, the men gathered at one end while the women took Amal away. But when they tried to lead Will to bed he resisted, and Thomas said it was all right if he stayed.

"We have a choice," Thomas said. "The town walls are strong, but they need men to protect them. I'm also worried about the men that control the streets here. Even if we can find enough others willing to help, those Guerrero left behind will try to stop us."

"How many are there?" asked Usaden. "I have seen them, but their number is small. A score, possibly one or two more." He looked around at them, at Thomas, Olaf, Jorge, Luis and Aban. "We are enough to kill that number, particularly if they don't expect an attack."

"We could disable some of them, but not all. And we

would have to find them first. I think we should leave before Guerrero and Mandana arrive."

"Olaf Torvaldsson does not run away from a fight," said Olaf.

"We will not be running away. We will be making a sensible retreat. I still mean to kill them both, but how can the five of us fight a hundred times that many?"

"One at a time, of course," said Olaf.

"I agree with Thomas," said Jorge. "Now isn't the time to throw our lives away. Leave, plan, return."

"It will still be only the five of us," said Olaf. "I say confront them now. Send the women and children away. The rest of us stay. This is a good place to defend once we have killed the traitors."

"What if there are others we haven't seen?" Thomas said. "Half the menfolk in the town might be under the control of Guerrero. All it takes is a few of them to open the town gates and his army will stream in to kill everyone they find."

Olaf shook his head, but said nothing.

"We need a show of hands," Thomas said. "Who thinks we should leave?"

"No show of hands," said Olaf. He lifted his gaze and stared at Thomas. "You are our leader. The decision is yours. Tell us what you want and we will obey." He looked around at the others, waiting for any objections, but none came. The women had come to sit with them, and each of them nodded, even Helena, who usually objected to everything.

Thomas didn't feel like a leader, and he certainly didn't want the responsibility. He wondered why Olaf had not taken that role for himself. He was the Sultan's general—a true leader of men, and far more suited to it. Even when Thomas had been strong he would have let Olaf lead him. And then he knew why the statement had been made. If this was Olaf's decision he would order them to fight, order them to sacrifice themselves in a final blaze of pointless bravery. It was his nature. Olaf was born a Northman, and saw dying with honour as part of his destiny, so his children and grandchildren could tell his saga around firesides long into the future. Except none of his children, all girls, would do such. Lubna would have, but Lubna was no more. Thomas realised the task would now fall to him, to Will, and to Amal.

Thomas raised his gaze and studied each of them in turn until he was looking once more at Olaf. "We leave as soon as we can. Jamila, you and the other women prepare food to take, something that will last a few days at least. The rest of us will go out and warn who we can that Mandana is coming. What they do with the information is up to them."

Luis stood, pushing his chair back. "I want to fight. If you won't, then I will stay and fight alone." He turned and left the room.

When he was gone, making a lot of noise on the stairs, Jamila touched Thomas's arm. "He grieves for his parents. You must make allowances for him."

"We all grieve for someone." Thomas brushed past Jamila and followed Luis upstairs. He had a proposal to make. It would be dangerous, but it might appeal to the youth's frustrations.

CHAPTER TWENTY-FIVE

Thomas climbed through darkness to the highest point of the town, then onward to the highest point of the wall. He stared south until he found what he knew lay there. It was not exactly where he expected, because this land was so twisted it was hard to work out what lay in which direction, but at last he glimpsed the glow of fires in the distance where Guerrero's camp lay. The sight reinforced his decision to leave. They were too many of them, and he had witnessed their brutality in action, both during the fall of Malaka and since. Well-trained, lacking all mercy, caring little for their own lives if it meant they could take the lives of others. It was time to leave even if he had no destination in mind, only an unformed idea, and an even less well-formed plan.

When he returned to the house the others were ready, makeshift packs waiting to set on their shoulders. Luis stood apart, perhaps still thinking about the conversation Thomas had had with him. All faces turned toward Thomas except for his daughter's, who was cradled against Belia's breast in a linen sling. For a brief moment Thomas wondered if he was doing the right thing taking all of them with him. There would be hardship and danger, but he knew it was impossible to leave anyone behind, not with Guerrero and Mandana coming. He had done that once before, and the pain of the consequence would remain with him forever.

The town was quiet as they made their way to the northern gate. Dawn was a few hours off yet, but a quarter moon provided enough light to travel by. There was a good roadway that led across the flank of the Sholayr through two higher towns, beyond which lay only small villages such as Jamila's, and bare mountainside.

Thomas stayed at the rear of the group, Will's hand in his, taking comfort from the touch. Now and again as they climbed he slowed to look back, the spread of Mandana's troops growing clearer each time. They passed through the silent, single street of Bubion and then, shortly after, Campaneira. When the road twisted back on itself Jamila showed them a track that would lead them west. Thomas wondered where they might find themselves before the end of the day that was barely started. They needed a place of refuge, somewhere safe, dry and warm. As they walked he tried to think of where, but his mind was fogged with exhaustion, and he kept finding himself drifting into a state devoid of all thought, one foot moving in front of the other—Will's hand clasped in his, the backs of his friends ahead. The first grey light of coming dawn cast shadows, caught silver against the snow-capped peaks of the Sholayr, and still Thomas's mind remained vacant. And then a voice came to him, as clear as if Lubna lay with her mouth against his ear.

Go home, my love. Go to where you belong.

There was no need for the impossible voice to state where. There was only one place it could mean. Will's fingers tightened against his and he said, "Who said that,

Pa?" And Thomas stopped walking and looked down at his son.

"There's only me and you here."

Will shook his head. "I heard someone. Not Belia, she's too far ahead. It sounded like…" Will's eyes glistened with unshed tears and he shook his head.

"We're both tired," Thomas said. "Our minds are playing tricks on us, that's all."

"So you heard Ma, too?"

Thomas started walking again, already thinking of the words spoken to him—and whether they had been her words or nothing but imagination. He had thought on the matter since the first time it happened on the side of the mountain. He knew if he believed Lubna still spoke to him it would bring some small comfort, but his rationality rejected the notion. Thomas almost preferred to believe the words had been conjured directly in his own mind—memories of the woman he had loved, the woman he still loved. The words were his own, couched in the form of her familiar tones. Except … if that was true, how had Will heard them too?

He walked faster, passing Helena who travelled alongside Luis, strode on until he reached Olaf.

"We need to go back," Thomas said.

Olaf glanced at him, his expression unchanged, but a question clear in the tilt of his head. "Back? We have only just left."

"Not back there. We need somewhere we can protect, somewhere we know. Gharnatah is close."

"We should go to al-Zagal," said Olaf. "Throw ourselves in with him and fight, maybe even put him back on the throne. Make him Sultan again. Give this land hope again."

Jorge heard them and dropped back from where he had been walking with Belia on one side and Jamila on the other.

"He's a spent force," Thomas said. "He was strong once, but when he was defeated it broke something in him. It's changed him, and not for the better."

"Who is a spent force?" Jorge fell into step with them. When he held out his hand Will took it, a hand in each of theirs, a smile on his face that made Thomas wonder if his son didn't love Jorge more than he did his own father. And if he did, so be it—he had hated his own father and was the stronger for it.

"Al-Zagal. He cowers in al-Marrilla and does nothing."

"But we would be protected," said Olaf. "Al-Marilla's walls are high and strong, and there is always the sea to escape across."

"I thought he blamed you for his defeat at Malaka," said Jorge.

"He did, but it is still a place of refuge. And we do not have to tell him we are there."

"People know you," Thomas said. "Word would spread that Olaf Torvaldsson has come. I would rather put my trust in myself, in you, and a place I know."

"And Muhammed?" asked Jorge. "Do you think he will not hear of your return? He hates you, Thomas, you know he does. I believe he wants you dead. What you did to spark such hatred in him I don't know, but you can't deny it's there."

Usaden appeared like a spirit. He had been tracking to one side of the roadway and popped up now as if from behind a curtain. He stood a little apart, keeping his own council, but Thomas knew he would have taken in what they said. Had probably been listening the whole time.

"We could always throw ourselves on the mercy of the Spanish Queen," said Jorge. "Isabel left Malaka shortly after its fall, but I'm sure we would find her in Ixbilla, Qurtuba, Alcala de Real or somewhere even further north."

"There will be snow in the north," Thomas said, and Jorge laughed.

"And she will have a great fire burning in whatever hearth she sits before. Spain is safer for us now than al-Andalus."

"You forget that Mandana is Fernando's man," Thomas said. "I don't believe Fernando knows all that is going on here, but I don't altogether trust him either. If it came to a choice between me and Mandana, whose side would he take?" He wanted Lubna to speak inside his head again, but she remained silent, if she had ever been there at all. Thomas missed the old certainties, missed the surety he had once possessed in his own sanity.

"We could go home to Gharnatah, of course," said Jorge.

Thomas smiled. "Yes, I suppose we could."

"You have a fine house on the Albayzin with enough room for all of us, and if not, I also have a fine house. Olaf can send for Fatima, I am sure she misses him. It is the last thing anyone will suspect, and we will be surrounded by people who know you—people who will fight for you."

"I have no wish to put anyone else in danger," Thomas said.

"You already have," said Jorge. He raised a hand to take in their small party, each of them slowly growing more visible as the sky to their backs lightened with the coming of the day. "Can you truly consider us safe? Fleeing from five hundred men, each of whom would love to see us strung up by our heels and used for target practice? It would be even worse for the women."

"I didn't force anyone to come," Thomas said, aware it sounded like petulance even to his own ears.

"You didn't have to. People follow you. They follow you because they love you, and because they trust you." Jorge slapped his chest. "I am the pretty one, but it is you who attracts loyalty. Use their trust wisely. Don't throw away a single life you can save."

Thomas glanced behind, more as a means to allow himself time to think than to any other purpose. The day was coming, and Mandana's distant campfires were now hidden in the growing light, not even smoke to show where the men had spent the night. For all he knew they were on the move already, heading toward Pampaneira. A sudden sense of urgency filled him. Mandana possessed loyal soldiers mounted on fast horses. There was nothing to prevent him sending them after Thomas, who felt the world vibrating around him with the promise of danger.

"You're right," he said, turning back, accepting the inevitable as he knew he must ever since Lubna spoke to him. "There is nowhere else. I have brought us to this. Alone. At risk. Vulnerable. How far to Gharnatah?" He looked toward Olaf, who would know better than anyone else.

"Half a day if it was only us four," said Olaf. "More like a day with all of us."

"Too long."

"I cannot make them walk faster."

"But I can ask," Thomas said. "I was a fool to drag us away from the city."

"No, you were not," said Olaf. "Or do you forget men were sent to kill you? And the rest of us too when they found us together. But Jorge is right. They believe you have fled and will never think for you to return. And it will be good to have Fatima sleeping at my side again."

"It's always good to have a beautiful woman at your side. Or beneath you..." Jorge's voice faded as Thomas went ahead, leaving Will with him. A sense of frustration tightened inside his chest. They had fled Gharnatah only to return to it. Was he a fool to be leading them back there? But the fact they were all of them together again offered some hope. If they had not left Gharnatah then Jamila and the others would still be in Pampaneira, unaware of the danger that was about to engulf the town.

He caught up with the women and encouraged them to move faster, telling everyone to discard what they had brought. There would be food and clothing in Gharnatah, and the lighter they travelled the sooner they would be safe.

Helena complained, which was to be expected. Her feet hurt. Her back hurt. Thomas ignored her, taking Jamila by the arm and drawing her to one side.

"Are you willing to come to Gharnatah with us?" he asked. "You and Aban and Dana?"

"To your house?"

"If it stands. If not, there will be another house. I still have friends who will help us."

"Yes," said Jamila, "I will come. Where else do I have now? Nowhere. None of us do. We have been set adrift and you offer us a haven, so of course we will come."

Olaf came forward with Will on his shoulders and cajoled Helena into stopping her complaints. Jamila organised her small group and everyone doubled their pace, not quite running, not quite walking. Thomas knew none of them could keep the pace up for long—other than Usaden, who was nowhere to be seen once more, no doubt gone to scout their flanks.

Thomas searched out Luis and walked beside him. He took the youth's wrist until they both slowed, allowing the others to move ahead.

"Have you considered what we spoke of?" Thomas asked.

Luis nodded, his face set. "I had considered the idea myself before we spoke. It is a good plan, Thomas."

"So, you agree? It is not without danger. Not without great danger."

"They killed my parents," said Luis, and Thomas released his hold and walked ahead, back to the others.

The land continued to rise along the broad flank of a ridge, and when they crested it the track twisted away below, doubling back on itself over and over as it cut through an almost vertical slope. Beyond, the rich Vega plain surrounding Gharnatah was wreathed in mist, which rose higher in a sinuous line to mark where the Darro river lay hidden. Catching the first rays of the sun the palace of al-Hamra sat like some glittering jewel, tiny and perfect. And then, from behind, came the sound of a horse at full gallop. Thomas spun around, his sword already in his hand. Olaf stood beside him on one side, Jorge on the other, and Thomas wished Usaden was with them too.

A black mount came into view, still not slowing, and Olaf said, "Thomas, I take the horse, you kill the rider."

Thomas nodded. "There will be others close behind." He looked around, wondering if they could create an ambush, but it was too late. He looked to the others, pleased to see they were continuing to move, picking their pace up even more.

The horse came at them, became a giant, and then it clattered to a halt and Usaden leapt from its back. He had a curved sword in one hand, its blade stained red.

"I acquired this from a man who no longer had need of it. Put the women and children on the horse, as many as will go." He glanced back. "There are others if you want me to fetch them."

Olaf laughed and clapped Usaden on the back. The blow would have felled Thomas, but Usaden barely moved. Thomas sent Aban back with the horse and instructions— told him to return with Luis and the others.

"How many?" he asked.

"A score. Outriders, nothing more. One of them

stopped for a piss." He raised a shoulder. "I let him finish before I killed him. It was the least I could do."

"He'll be missed."

"He will, but not immediately. Which is why you need to send those who can't fight ahead while we stop the others."

Thomas looked around. Four, plus Luis and Aban. Six against twenty, and he didn't know how the youths would fight, or even if Aban was willing. And Jorge was never much more than a threat. So three against twenty.

"I don't like the odds," he said.

"I don't suppose the odds care much one way or the other," said Olaf. "They are what they are, and we are who we are." He thumped his chest. "Olaf Torvaldsson, *Hvirfla!* I will kill them all." He looked at each of them. "And we have the dog, of course."

Thomas laughed, a cold settling through him. The world took on a brittle sharpness he had not experienced since Lubna had been taken from him. It was the Thomas of old, and he welcomed the once familiar power— accepting it as a sign he was beginning a return to the man he had once been.

"Leave some for the rest of us," he said. He saw Luis and Aban jogging toward them. Beyond, Helena, Dana and the children rode atop the captured horse while Jamila led it at a run, holding on to the pommel so her toes barely touched the ground. He turned back to Olaf. "How do you want to do this? Do we hide or set an ambush?"

Olaf paced forward until he stood at a spot where a large rock had crashed down from the hillside to form a barrier on one side, the land rising steeply on the other.

"We form a line here. They will have to come through us, not around. Three abreast at most, so we won't have to kill them all at once." He nodded. "Yes, this is as good a place to die as any."

Thomas wondered if he meant the men who were coming, or themselves. He knew Olaf never questioned his own mortality. Thomas wondered what *Hvirfla* meant. He would ask Will to tell him, for he spoke the language of the north almost as well as he did Arabic. If they lived that long.

He glanced at Jorge, who stood tall, sword in hand. Anyone who didn't know him might be afraid, which was good enough for the moment. Luis's face had taken on a grimace, while Aban was pale, and Thomas wondered if he had ever faced trained soldiers before instead of hiding from them. There might have been a better time to find out the answer, but that time was not now. He leaned close to Luis and whispered in his ear, "Make them believe in you."

Luis nodded, just as the first of the riders appeared. Their leader saw the six of them standing across the track and grinned, spurring his horse forward.

CHAPTER TWENTY-SIX

Olaf took the centre, his axe swinging softly from the leather thong tied at his wrist, as if he had forgotten it was even there. Thomas stood to Olaf's left, Usaden on the right and a little further out so Olaf had room to swing. Both held a sword in each hand. Jorge was on Thomas's left and behind, with Aban beyond him, while Luis was to the right of Usaden. Thomas didn't know how these others would fight, but they added numbers if not skill, and he knew it would be the three of them standing at the heart of the line who would do the most damage. It didn't occur to him he hadn't fought in half a year and was weaker than he had been. He was filled one again with the ice of battle he believed he had lost after Lubna's death, and with its return he knew he was invulnerable.

Thomas took in the look of the men, judging if they were professional soldiers or new recruits, and saw they fell into the former camp. It would make the coming fight all the more interesting.

"Do you think the tall one in the middle is their leader?" asked Olaf.

"More than likely. He has the best horse and a chain-mail vest."

"Then I will kill him first."

Thomas smiled. "You do that. I'll take the stocky one on my side, he looks like he knows what he's doing." He glanced at Olaf. "Do you think we'll have to kill them all?"

"I do hope so."

Thomas heard a retching sound and turned to see Aban throwing up on the side of the path. When he looked in Luis's direction the young man stood firm, his face set. Beside him, Usaden appeared bored with the waiting.

"Let them attack us," Thomas said.

"Of course," said Olaf. He moved his arm, the axe hanging from it forming a wider arc as he readied himself for what he had been born to do—kill his enemies.

The leader came on several paces before slowing. Thomas started to count the numbers behind, then stopped. There was little point. They would be less once Olaf and Usaden began.

The leader drew his horse to a halt, taking his time to study the six men confronting him.

"Which of you is Thomas Berrington?"

Nobody spoke.

The leader shifted in his saddle to the soft creaking of leather.

"None of you? If that is so, you may continue your journey. We are looking for Berrington only."

"It is him."

Thomas turned his head fast at the sound of Luis's voice. The youth held his arm out, pointing directly at him.

"He is the one you seek, but you will have to kill the others as well. They are stupidly loyal." Luis began to walk toward the mounted man. "I recognise you, do you remember me?"

221

The leader narrowed his eyes and stared at Luis for a long time.

"This is growing dull," said Olaf, his voice so low so it only carried to Thomas and Usaden.

"Yes, I know you," said the leader. "I heard you ran like a coward."

"I had a job to do, that is all. And now I have brought Thomas Berrington here so you can kill him."

Usaden took three paces toward Luis and raised his sword.

"Leave him," Thomas ordered. "You've seen what they do with deserters." Usaden nodded and stepped back.

The mounted soldier waved a sword at Luis to get behind him, but Luis stayed where he was, turning slowly to face Thomas and the others.

Foolish and brave, Thomas thought. *Young and headstrong, just like I once was.*

He sighed. "Well, we'd better start killing them before it's time for lunch."

Olaf grinned. "We wait for them. They are almost ready. Some men ignore the prospect of death, others have to push it from their minds."

As if he had heard the whispered conversation the leader of the troop bellowed an order, encouraging his horse into a gallop.

Thomas, Olaf and Usaden waited in line. Aban turned and ran. Jorge took a single step back, his sword shaking, but he stayed firm.

"Dance for them!" Thomas shouted. He ducked beneath a wild swing a moment before he heard the leader's horse scream as Olaf's whirling axe took it in the chest. The animal toppled like a felled oak, spilling its rider to the ground. Thomas stepped in and took him under the arm, hearing the screams of agony and rage around him but ignoring them. They meant nothing—they were the music of battle, and he hoped Jorge danced to it as he did. Others came at them to die, most to Olaf's axe, but Usaden was as sharp as the blades he wielded, and fast, unbelievably fast.

Thomas felt the breath burn in his lungs—felt his arm grow tired, his legs turn to lead. He killed a man who came at him from the left, pushed him away, barely able to gather the strength to do so. He glimpsed Jorge deflecting a blade and then striking back, pulling his blow at the last moment so it didn't kill, merely maim, but the attacker fell back, clutching at his shoulder.

The soldiers had been thinned by half, the remainder hanging back, unwilling to sacrifice themselves now their leader had been killed. Then Luis swung into the saddle of a spare horse and urged it into a gallop. He came directly at Thomas, sword held above his head in a stupid show of bravado. Thomas pricked the horse's flank and leapt backward, avoiding Luis's swinging blow with ease. He stumbled into someone, pushed against them, then felt a punch to his back and staggered forward. He swung around to face a frightened man who was already backing away, and then someone else crashed into him and he fell to his knees. He managed to turn in time to deflect a lazy swing of Luis's sword. He struck back in return, careful not to injure the youth. His strength was fading, flowing from him like a damaged vessel, and he risked a glance down as he staggered to his feet, afraid the blow had been a sword thrust, but he saw no wound, no blood. He shook his head, trying to regain his senses, then made a fast attack against Luis. The boy was good, skilled, but Thomas had honed his own skills over decades and knew he could vanquish him anytime he wanted. Except again someone grabbed at him and he swung around, almost taking Olaf's hand off at the wrist if his axe had not stopped the blow. Olaf glanced down, gave a small shrug and stepped past Thomas, his eyes on

Luis, who had changed direction and was approaching Aban.

"Go check on Jorge," said Olaf, "I think he's hurt. I'll take care of this one."

"Leave him. Let him live." Thomas stepped back six paces, trying to pull more air into his lungs than they would take. Usaden stood in the centre of a ring of dead and injured men. His sword hung loose at his side as he waited for the others to decide if they wanted to risk his wrath or not, but already men were shuffling backwards, looking away, looking to where their companions waited. Luis backed off from Olaf and joined the others now he had proven himself.

The fight was over.

Thomas turned to find Jorge on one knee, his hand clasped to his side. Blood ran between his fingers to pool on the ground.

"I need to dance better," said Jorge, his voice remarkably calm.

"Or learn to fight better." Thomas went to both knees and drew Jorge's hand away from the wound. Blood pulsed and he rose, grabbed Jorge beneath his arms and dragged him to the side of the track and propped him against a rock. He unlaced the leather vest that had failed to offer enough protection, then tore Jorge's shirt to reveal the wound. Low down, a single sword thrust. Thomas turned Jorge over and found a smaller wound in his back where the blade had gone all the way through. Less blood flowed from the rear puncture, so he turned him back around.

"I think I killed two men," said Jorge. "How many did you get?"

"Be quiet."

Jorge smiled. "So not as many as me, then."

"That's not being quiet. Do you want to live or not?"

"Live," said Jorge. "If there is a choice. Yes, live. Can you fix me, Thomas?"

"Shut up."

Thomas tried to remember how many he had killed and couldn't, their number fading into the distance along with all the other men he had stolen the breath from. Too many men. Too much fighting. He was getting too old for such exploits.

He fashioned a rough bandage by tearing Jorge's shirt into strips. He padded the wound with a square of leather cut from the vest, using the edge of his own sword to fashion it, then wrapped the bandage as tight as he could. He sat on his heels, a hand up to stop Jorge moving, and watched. A little blood seeped beneath the binding, but not as much as there had been.

"How are you feeling? Dizzy?"

Jorge shook his head. "But it hurts. Hurts so much, Thomas."

"It will until we get to Gharnatah. I have herbs and potions that will help, but we need to get you there first. Stay here. Don't move."

Thomas picked up his sword and rose, his body aching, but he knew the fighting hadn't finished yet. He heard Olaf's roar as he worked, the clatter of sword and axe and knife, the screams of the dying, the whinny of horses. When he turned, he saw Olaf standing over a felled man. Usaden was walking slowly toward him. The remaining attackers had fallen back again, trying to regain a semblance of order. A few glanced at their fallen comrades, then mounted theirs horses and rode away.

Thomas looked among the bodies for Aban but didn't see him. Luis, he knew, had fled with their attackers.

"They'll be back once they get reinforcements," said Olaf.

"How far do you think?" Thomas asked.

"The others will be in Pampaneira, so not long. A few hours, no more—sooner if they ride hard. And there will be more of them next time. Perhaps too many for the three of us."

Usaden came toward them. He had gathered four horses and led them, docile now. Thomas looked them over and wondered if Jorge was capable of riding. He glanced around once more, puzzled by where Aban had gone, afraid he had been injured and hidden himself away somewhere. He asked Usaden if he had seen him, knowing the Gomeres mercenary missed little.

"He switched sides," said Usaden. "He joined his friend, the one called Luis. They mounted the same horse and rode off with the others."

"The boy is a fool," Thomas said, knowing who he meant even if the others didn't.

"Is Jorge badly hurt?" asked Usaden

"He may be. I need to get him to Gharnatah so I can treat him."

"Can he ride?"

"I don't think so."

Usaden nodded and released the reins of one of the horses, which wandered away with no destination in mind. Usaden swung into the saddle of another in a single lithe motion. Olaf had been cleaning his axe as they spoke, examining the blade and touching one or two nicks with his fingertip.

Thomas took one of the horses and led it toward where Jorge lay. His skin had paled, and when Thomas saw the colour of his lips he felt a moment of fear he hadn't during the fight. Olaf helped him lift Jorge into the saddle, then Thomas climbed behind. He gripped the reins, his arms pressed tight to hold Jorge in place, then urged the horse into a walk, waiting to see how Jorge fared. He swung from side to side and Thomas had to hold him upright. He saw

Olaf mount the largest of the beasts and follow. Usaden hung back, looking over the fallen men, then he smiled and followed.

"How many?" Thomas asked as he joined them.

"Over a dozen. Olaf killed almost half their number." Usaden made no claim for himself, but Thomas knew he would not have been far behind. Which meant he had not killed as many as he had thought—not if Jorge claimed two —but Usaden said, "I saw you send three to their God, whoever that might be."

Not that it mattered, Thomas thought. Battle wasn't a competition for most men, at least not those who wanted to live long. He caught Jorge as he began to slip sideways and pulled him straight before urging the horse into a canter. Speed was more important than comfort, and he was concerned for his friend. Jorge had come to rescue him, to save his life, and he hoped the gift could be repaid.

CHAPTER TWENTY-SEVEN

Thomas knew they should have taken more care entering Gharnatah, but there was not enough time. The light was starting to fade as he rode through the eastern gate and he hoped that would offer at least a little cover, though Olaf was a difficult figure to miss. They left the stolen horses in al-Hatabin square, a gift for whoever found them, and climbed the remainder of the way on foot. Olaf cradled Jorge in his arms as though he weighed nothing. Thomas remembered how, less than a year before, Olaf himself had been the one close to death. Now there was no sign of the injuries he had sustained in the battle that had sent al-Zagal scurrying east to al-Marilla.

Thomas was unsure what to expect when he approached the entrance to his house. Had Muhammed's soldiers destroyed the place, even burned it to the ground? From the outside it looked unchanged, though he saw most of the expensive glass panes had been smashed, the shattered shards still on the flagstones. Olaf turned side-ways to enter the house without having to put Jorge down.

"No, bring him through here."

Thomas went into his workshop, anger flaring when he

saw what Guerrero's men had done. Almost every jar had been dashed from the shelves to break on the stone floor. A bare few remained intact, but the rest had their contents mixed together, making them useless. Books that Thomas had acquired over years, and his notes, were piled in one corner. Someone had tried to strike a light against them, but for some fortunate reason it had not caught properly and only a few sheets were curled and blackened.

"Put him on here." Thomas patted the worktable, which acted as a makeshift bed for patients. He went to a cabinet and opened a drawer, relieved to discover the instruments within lay undisturbed. He selected what he needed, then searched through the bottles that remained intact, but couldn't find what he was looking for.

Jorge began to moan. He had been quiet on the journey, only half-conscious, but now with some physical relief the awareness of his pain grew in intensity.

Thomas turned to Olaf, who continued to stand in the doorway. "Go fetch Belia," he said, and then as the big man started to turn away, "and Helena. I need them both."

Thomas tore a strip of linen and tied it around Jorge's wrist.

"What are you doing?" Jorge's eyes remained closed, and his voice was barely audible.

"I don't want you thrashing about. How much pain is there?"

"How much do you think!" Jorge's shortness was answer enough.

"There's going to be more. If I don't tie you down I can't work."

"What happens if you leave the wound as it is?"

Thomas stared at Jorge's pale face, his clammy skin, the sweat standing out on his forehead. "If you think it hurts now wait three days. And if you think it hurts then, wait another three. Two more days and the pain will be gone."

"Well, then."

"Because you'll be dead." Thomas turned at the sound of footsteps. Belia entered first. She glanced at Jorge, and Thomas saw she wanted to go to him and stepped aside to allow her. She crossed quickly, took Jorge's hand and held it between her breasts. Helena remained in the doorway, avoiding looking anywhere in the room.

Thomas went to her first, knowing his request for her was the simpler. "Do you remember where Da'ud lives?" he asked, referring to the physician he used to work with, but not for some time now.

"Of course I do."

"Go there and tell him I need hashish and poppy liquor —he will have both. Bring them back as soon as you can."

Helena stared at Thomas for a moment. He half expected her to refuse, for no reason other than she could, but once again she showed how much she had changed, or how much Muhammed had changed her. She nodded, turned and left without a word.

"Will he live?" asked Belia.

"If he lets me work on him."

Belia looked back at Jorge. "Then do it, my love." She kissed his knuckles where they were bruised from the fight, then turned to Thomas. "What can I do?"

"I need honey and egg-white for the infection. It's the best we have for now. Is there anything left in the garden?"

Belia shook her head. "Nothing that's not been dug up, and they killed all the chickens and left them, but there are a few eggs we can use. I saved what I could. There is a little willow bark. They ignored the crab-apple tree, and I think I can use the fennel and plantain. They are drying in the kitchen and we can get other herbs from the market in the morning if we need them. There are also a few lotions in the cellar they didn't smash."

"I need something now. We'll have to manage with

what we have." Thomas wondered if he should have gone to Da'ud al-Baitar instead of sending Helena. Da'ud might have some of the herbs he needed, but he would know well enough what was required and provide it if he could.

Once Belia had gone to start preparing her herbs Thomas returned to Jorge, who lay without protest as his wrists and ankles were tied, lengths of soft linen binding them to each of the four legs of the table.

"Perhaps I should get Belia to do this to me occasionally. Once I am well, of course."

"This is going to hurt." Thomas leaned close, almost kneeling, and cut away the makeshift bandages that were by now stuck to Jorge's wound. Thomas continued cutting, then used water and a cloth to wash away more of the mess so he could see clearly.

He used the tips of his fingers to press lightly against the flesh around the entry wound, which was starting to bruise and continued to leak blood. He glanced up to see Jorge's face set against the pain.

Thomas leaned close, then pressed sharply so the break in Jorge's skin opened a little, and before he could pull away placed his nose close and breathed deep. He cursed at the message the smell told him.

"I'm going to untie you on this side for a moment."

"Are we finished?"

Thomas said nothing, fingers working on the knots so recently tied.

"Why tie me up only to untie me? You are teasing, aren't you? You lust for my body and this is the only way you can get it. Well, I have told you often enough–"

"You have told me more than enough." Thomas pushed hard and Jorge cried out as he rolled onto his side. Thomas held him there with one hand as he cleaned the exit wound and sniffed again. Nothing this time, which was good, but he would still need to open Jorge's body to clean within.

He was sure the bowel had been cut. With luck it would be no more than a nick. Without luck it would be damaged beyond repair, but even a tiny cut could be dangerous. The wound and surrounding area would need cleaning fully and Belia's herbs applied.

He let Jorge flop onto his back again and stood, straightening and trying to ease the deep ache in his body he knew only time and a soft bed would cure, only one of which was available. When he twisted he caught sight of a slight figure standing in the doorway.

"How long have you been there?"

"Only a little while," said Dana. "Is he going to live?"

"He will if I have anything to do with it."

"Good. I like Jorge."

"Most women do."

"I'm still here," said Jorge. "You can come and hold my hand if you want to offer comfort to an injured hero."

Dana offered a shy smile but stayed where she was, which Thomas considered for the best. Jorge didn't need beautiful women close to him at the moment.

"What are the others doing?" Thomas asked, not particularly interested. He would prefer the girl gone, but was unwilling to eject her without reason.

"Jamila is cooking, as usual. The men are talking."

"About what?"

"Fighting, I expect. That is what you all do, isn't it?" She cocked her head to one side. "Do you know what you are doing with Jorge? Should you not be sending for a physician?"

"I am a physician," Thomas said, and heard Jorge make a sound suspiciously like a laugh.

Dana's face remained expressionless. It was clear she didn't believe him.

"I thought Aban or Luis might be in here," she said.

"They didn't come back with us."

Dana stared at him as her face paled. "Are they dead? You can tell me if they are." She worried at her lip on one side.

"Not dead, but they … decided to stay out there." He saw the look of fear in Dana's eyes. "It is not what you think. I'll explain to everyone later."

"We love each other," said Dana. "I know what we share is not usual, especially in this land—a woman with two men—but it is what we are. It is what we do." She placed a hand over her belly which showed nothing, but both Thomas and she knew what lay within. "The child I carry could have been set by either of them, but it doesn't matter which. We will always be together." She cocked her head and looked at Thomas. "Do I shock you?"

"Thomas is shocked at everything," said Jorge from behind him. "But you do not shock me. Do they love you as much as you love them?"

Dana nodded.

"Then all will be well. If they come back, all will be well."

Thomas recalled the drawing Luis had made of her and wondered what others he would have found if he had taken the time to study the other books. For now, he had a job for Dana. He picked up the bucket of water he had used to clean Jorge's wound and held it out. "Take this and throw the contents away, then go see if you can find me more—but hot this time."

Dana looked at the bucket, and for a time Thomas was sure she would refuse, then she started to come toward him.

"No, stop!" Thomas shouted, and Dana came to an abrupt halt. He closed the gap between them, aware her feet were bare and the floor was covered in shards of broken pot and glass. He handed the bucket to her and she took it, having to use both hands. She turned and padded away into the dark courtyard.

Thomas found more oil lamps and lit them so the table and Jorge were bathed in light.

"She likes me," said Jorge, "but I think she is both afraid and drawn to you in equal measure."

"Wait until you begin to scream."

Jorge stared at Thomas. "Will there be a great deal of pain?"

"Only if Da'ud has no poppy, and I've never known him be without. I don't Dana likes me anymore. Should I be concerned, do you think?"

"You?" Jorge relaxed against the table as if it was the most comfortable feather-stuffed mattress. "When have you ever cared what people think of you? What are you going to do, Thomas, after you inflict all this pain on me?"

"Olaf and Usaden are making plans, so I need to wait to see what they come up with. It's you I'm concerned with for now, nothing else."

Jorge smiled. "And I love you too, my brother, but you know neither Guerrero nor Mandana are going to rest until they have killed you."

"Tried to kill me, you mean."

"Of course. And all those who have aided you." Jorge let his breath go in a show of frustration. "We are four. What can we do against a hundred times that number? Not even Olaf can triumph against such odds."

"He will think of something."

"Something like running far and fast from this place. That sounds a sensible idea to me."

"When was the last time I did what was sensible?"

Da'ud al-Baitar came in spite of not being invited. He

234

looked older than Thomas remembered, but strong enough for what was needed. He mixed a potent liquor of poppy, hashish and alcohol, then helped Thomas force it into Jorge, who looked at first as if he might eject it all immediately. But he settled after a short time, his eyes turning glassy as Thomas busied himself with a small brazier and charcoal. He used bellows until the coals glowed white, then let them settle for a time. He pushed three iron rods into the coals—each tipped with a scorched wooden handle, each ranging in size, each for a specific purpose.

"Did the blade go clean through?" asked Da'ud, standing beside Thomas to study Jorge.

"Almost. His gut is damaged, I can smell it. I need to open the wound and clean it before I can repair the wound."

Da'ud stared at Thomas. "If anyone else said they could save him I wouldn't believe them. How bad is the damage inside?"

"I won't know until I open him up." Thomas pulled at the linen straps, ensuring each bound Jorge tight. He brought the brazier close, then laid his instruments on the side of the table ready for use.

"Go to the other side and use your weight to hold him down," Thomas said. "I dare not use more poppy, and there will be a great deal of pain."

As soon as Da'ud was in position Thomas used a small blade to widen the wound in Jorge's side. He pulled the tissue back, and as soon as he did a rank stench filled the air.

"How bad?" gasped Da'ud, using his weight to hold Jorge, who had not woken but still his body fought against what was being inflicted on him.

"I can't see yet."

Thomas brought a lamp closer, tilting it so light fell

into Jorge's body cavity. There was too much blood to see anything, so he put the lamp down and wetted a cloth with warm water. Gently he dabbed into the opening, cleaning what he could until he saw where the stink was coming from and sighed.

"I think I can fix it," he said.

"And clean it?"

"It will take time, but yes, I believe so."

Da'ud shook his head but said nothing.

Thomas continued to work, dabbing, pouring water inside the wound and then wiping it away. Slowly the stench lessened, but only because he was clearing the leakage from the perforated bowel. The wound itself would have to be closed if Jorge was to live.

Thomas brought the lamp closer again so he could examine the cut in the bowel wall. The edge of the sword had sliced through one side only. Jorge was fortunate. Not as fortunate as to be uninjured, but fortunate enough to live, Thomas hoped. He glanced at Da'ud.

"Gut or fire—which would you use?"

"I wouldn't use either. I couldn't do what you are doing, Thomas, you know I couldn't."

"Gut then, I think. Fire might do more damage, and the gut will rot away within a few months, which means we can close him tonight." Thomas went to his cabinets and began to search for what he needed, cursed when he couldn't find it. For a moment he scanned the floor, then shook his head. Even if he found a length of gut, he wouldn't be able to use it.

"In my bag," said Da'ud. "I thought you might need some."

Thomas opened Da'ud's leather satchel and rummaged inside, came out with a small wrap of oilcloth and opened it, withdrawing a length of damp, coiled gut. He used the brazier to bring a needle to white heat, then waited for it to cool before threading the gut. It was of good quality, as he would expect from Da'ud—fashioned from the sinew of a bull, he judged. He used a long forceps in his left hand to press the edges of Jorge's bowel together, another in his right to push the needle through and out the other side. It was slow work, and for a brief moment Thomas had a vision of how Lubna would do this far better than he was capable of, and a wave of grief almost made him swoon. He hesitated, breathing deep, knowing Da'ud's eyes were on him—knowing if he didn't continue Jorge would die. He started to work again, pushing all other thoughts aside.

CHAPTER TWENTY-EIGHT

Olaf and Usaden sat on opposite sides of the table, their heads close together as if they were plotting something, though what it might be Thomas was too tired to care about. He felt defeated. Jorge's wounding had weakened him. They were bound too tightly together, each passing year binding them ever closer. Thomas had considered them both invulnerable, despite Jorge's lack of fighting skill. Thomas had always assumed he could save him from whatever threat came.

He went to Belia, who stood beside Jamila at the open cooking fire and touched her shoulder, amazed as always at her strange beauty when she turned to him.

"I have done what I can for now. You can go and sit with him if you want, but he's sleeping. Tomorrow you must get everything you need and prepare salves."

She stared into his eyes, a look he could not turn away from, captured, implicit in her love for Jorge.

"Will he live?"

"If you and I have anything to do with it. But it will take time. The wound damaged him inside and I had to repair it. Da'ud is with him until you go there, so finish here if you want."

Belia shook her head and walked from the room. Thomas had expected her to do nothing else.

He walked through the big ground floor room to the staircase, barely taking in anything. He ignored the rich scent of good food, the smell of wine, and began to climb steps still familiar after almost two years away from the house. He stopped in the doorway of the room he considered his and Lubna's. Dana lay on her side, small on the wide bed, hair spread about her head like a dark flame. Thomas wondered whether if Luis and Aban were here they would all three be sharing this bed, and knew the answer.

He backed away, thinking he should have asked what the accommodation arrangements were. The women had arrived first and obviously chosen what to them were logical rooms. Thomas continued along the corridor to the end, ducked through a low doorway into the extension Britto had built for him and continued on to the room that had been added for Lubna when she had been no more than a servant. Except, for Thomas, she had always been more than a servant.

There was a narrow cot waiting for him there. He had walked past other, larger rooms, knowing this small space was where he wanted to sleep. This is where Lubna had lain her head each night for more than a year after she first came to his house. He had shared his bed with her sister Helena then. This is the room Lubna had remained in when Thomas went with Jorge to attend Queen Isabel's son in Qurtuba. Where he had clashed with Abbot Mandana for the first time.

Thomas lay on the bed. It was hard, too narrow, but for months he had slept on rock and moss and it felt like the most comfortable bed he had ever lain in. He closed his eyes, intending to rest for a short while only and then to go down and talk with Olaf about what they should do next. Instead, sleep invaded him like a dark cloud, tumbling him into senselessness.

The dream, when it came, was almost welcome.

Lubna sat astride him like she had never done in this room, only later coming to his bed. Thomas reached for her, touched her breasts, her belly slimmer than he remembered because she had been carrying their child a year before. He was hard inside her, knowing he cried tears because even as the dream enveloped him he was aware it wasn't real. He would never lie with Lubna again. Never feel her heat enclosing him. Never smell the perfumed scent of her, hear the mumbled words of lust…

Thomas came awake in an instant with a cry of alarm.

He expected the room to be empty, but instead of Lubna, Helena sat astride him, one sister instead of the other. She was as resplendently naked as he remembered, her movement against him interrupted by his cry.

Thomas put his hands on her waist and threw her aside.

"What are you doing?"

Helena sprawled on the cold floor, slowly pulling herself into a sitting position. If she was upset or disappointed at his reaction she didn't show it.

"Even you must know what we were doing, Thomas, or have you forgotten the feel of me so soon?"

"Not we, you. Why?"

"You have to ask?"

Helena stood, reached for her discarded robe but held it in one hand instead of putting it on. Tall, slim, her exquisite beauty was something most men would pull onto their beds, not toss aside.

"There is no longer anything between us." Thomas sat up, pulling the single coarse blanket to cover himself

240

where Helena had revealed him, uncomfortably aware that the arousal she had sparked remained.

"Then why did you rescue me?"

"You are Will's mother. Did you think I would leave you to be beaten by that man?"

"If I mean nothing to you then you would have."

"You must be thinking of someone with less sense of duty," Thomas said.

"You have no softness in your heart, only calculation and logic."

Thomas considered getting off the bed and throwing Helena through the door, but there was no lock and he doubted she would stay outside.

"What is it you want of me?"

Helena smirked. "I thought it was fairly clear what I wanted. A few more moments and I would have brought you to a peak." She tilted her head to one side so white hair fell to cover part of her face. "How long has it been since you emptied into a woman?" And then she saw his face and took a step back, held up a hand. "I am sorry. I forget myself."

"You *forget*? She was your *sister*—how could you forget?" Even as he spoke, Thomas knew Helena had never considered Lubna to be a true sister. She had been born to Olaf's second wife, Fatima, a Moor. Lubna looked nothing like her elder sisters, which for Thomas was something to be admired and preferred, but he knew he was not like other men. "And I am still waiting for you to tell me what you want, other than the obvious. I hope you enjoyed what little pleasure you might have taken."

"I always do," said Helena. She took a few paces closer to the bed, halted again. "I have something to tell you, if you will listen. Something important. I forgot about it until today. It came to me as we fled down the hillside."

"Dress yourself first. If it's so important why wait until now?"

"I wanted to tell you when we were alone." Helena raised her arms and the robe slid along her body to cover her nakedness. She looked around as if searching for a chair, but the room contained nothing but the bed. Thomas recalled at one time there had been a small table and stool, but they had been removed when the room fell into disuse. "You can tell the others afterwards, but you need to hear this on your own first."

Thomas gave a shake of his head. "You're making no sense. I keep no secrets from Jorge, you know that."

"But he is sick—"

"Not sick. He is injured."

Helena waved a hand, uninterested in the distinction. "Whatever you say, Thomas, for you are always right. This concerns that man—the Abbot, his son, and Muhammed."

"You already told me they are conspiring to defeat al-Zagal." He leaned into the corner of the wall and crossed his legs. As if he had issued an invitation, Helena moved to the foot of the cot and sat as far away from him as she could. She stared at Thomas for a time and he knew she was waiting for him to throw her off the bed again, but for the moment he allowed her to stay where she was.

"Tell it me then, so I can get some sleep. Alone."

"I told you only some of it before, but not everything."

"Why not?"

"If you hadn't come when you did Muhammed would have killed me before long. He grew more and more violent. I think he hit me because he couldn't hit you." Helena stared at her folded hands for a moment, then lifted her gaze. "I want him dead, and those two talked of killing him."

Thomas started at Helena. "You said they wanted his men alongside them so they could defeat al-Zagal."

"That is what they told Muhammed. When he had gone and I was alone with them they spoke freely, assuming I didn't understand Spanish. But I have been learning the language." There was no need for Helena to explain why. Everyone knew the ability to speak Spanish would soon become essential.

Thomas waited, his eyes tracking Helena's face. He searched for the scar that had first brought her to his house as a tainted gift, but could see no trace of it anymore. He nodded for her to go on.

"I didn't want to tell you everything before because of what they did. I was ashamed. Muhammed offered me to both of them. I think it was his idea of a joke, father and son mounting me at the same time, but Mandana couldn't do anything. His son was a different matter. He was harsh. He enjoyed inflicting pain on a woman. But even when he was inside me he talked about you. He wanted to know what you did to me in bed. He did things to me you would never have dared do, and laughed. And then I was discarded like a soiled cloth." Helena's eyes flickered as she scanned his face. "I couldn't confess what they did to me, so I couldn't tell you everything I heard. Now I can, because you saved me.

"I crawled to the corner because I hadn't been dismissed. I have learned that lesson since being taken captive by Muhammed. I only do what is told to me clearly. I have no mind of my own any more, only orders to be followed.

"After a while they forgot I was there. I think they knew I wasn't expected to live much longer. I'm sure Guerrero hoped he would be allowed to kill me, and the thought chilled me to the core because I knew he would take his time over it. But that's not what you need to know. When they were with Muhammed they talked of defeating al-Zagal, and Muhammed liked their words. He hates his uncle even more now than he did before. But when they were alone they spoke of al-Zagal as a friend. Muhammed hates his uncle, but not half as much as al-Zagal hates his nephew. He will never forget how he sent forces to Malaka and attacked his own soldiers from behind."

Thomas nodded, all his attention on her words, wanting to hear the rest. He knew full well of the enmity between al-Zagal and Muhammed—but was that enough for al-Zagal to switch sides? Did he believe by doing so Muhammed could be defeated, and he would take back the position of Sultan he had once held? Thomas knew Helena spoke the truth as she saw it, but was it the actual truth? What if Guerrero and Mandana knew she was listening, knew she understood their words? This could be another ploy—but against who? Not Thomas himself. Guerrero might hate him, but he was nothing in the scheme of things. He also knew there would be a price to pay for the information Helena revealed.

"They laughed at Muhammed," said Helena. "They consider him a fool, and a weak fool at that. They have no interest in fighting alongside him, only defeating his army and killing him."

"Did Fernando send them to do this?" Thomas asked.

"The Spanish King? Perhaps. They mentioned his name, but I think they are working for themselves. They want Muhammed dead for their own purposes, not for Spain, even if it would draw this war to an end. That would be a good thing, would it not?"

"Tell me exactly what was said." Thomas hoped he might learn something Helena had missed.

"Do you expect me to remember every single word?" For a moment Helena showed some of her old spite before her face softened. "But I can tell you their plan. I can do that." She stared at Thomas, and he knew she was about to state her terms.

He shook his head. "No. I saved your life, be grateful for that. There is no place for you here. Tell me what you know and I will ensure somewhere is found for you. Somewhere safe."

Helena returned his gaze, and Thomas believed it might have been the longest she had ever looked at him.

"We can talk of what I want another time. They asked Muhammed for soldiers. A thousand at least, more if he can send them. They are meant to join those Guerrero and his father already have. Their combined forces will travel east to confront al-Zagal. That is what they told Muhammed, but it is not their intention. They will take the soldiers and then attack them, kill them all. Then they will return to Gharnatah and attack the palace. They spoke of no details, no doubt they are already worked out, but I do know they are sure of victory. They have been inside al-Hamra, been shown its walls and dungeons, been allowed to view its defences. They are confident of defeating Muhammed and whatever guards are left behind."

"I don't believe they are capable of killing a thousand of Muhammed's soldiers. He may be an idiot, but Olaf is not, and it is he who trained them. I have seen Guerrero's forces. He doesn't have enough men to kill a thousand."

Helena waved a dismissive hand. "I'm no soldier, but they were sure the men could be killed. All of them."

Thomas stared into space. Could Guerrero have other forces he hadn't seen? And then it came to him, the answer so obvious he didn't know why he hadn't thought of it before.

Helena tilted her head as if she had seen the realisation on Thomas's face. "They were even more sure of victory now my father could be removed from the hill. You have aided them in that."

"He's not exiled," Thomas said, but he was wondering

how long Guerrero and Mandana had been planning their move. "Have they met with Muhammed before?"

Helena nodded. "For some time. Before I was captured. Even before Malaka fell."

"Fernando's a clever bastard," Thomas said, his voice low, and he wondered if Isabel was also a party to the plot. With Muhammed removed Gharnatah would fall, and with it al-Andalus. This long, expensive war would come to an end, with Spain victorious. At one time such an idea would have terrified him, but now Thomas was no longer sure. It might even be the best solution. It would prevent more years of fighting, more death, and he knew the end was inevitable. Al-Andalus was doomed, even more so since Muhammed had become Sultan and sat on the red hill.

"When?" Thomas said.

"Soon. Not within days, but within a month at most." Helena stared at Thomas. "What are you going to do?"

"What I have always been going to do," Thomas said. "Kill them both."

Helena laughed. "Of course. For a moment I forgot who you are." Helena rose, stood over him, her scent filling the air. "And don't worry, I will not accost you again, not tonight. But if you ever change your mind, know that you only need ask and I will be yours once more. And this time I will bring my heart as well as my body."

She turned and swept from the room. Thomas lay on the cot and closed his eyes, trying to still the thoughts that swirled inside his head.

CHAPTER TWENTY-NINE

Thomas woke after a few brief hours and went to Jorge first, who lay alone in the centre of the bed he always used when in this house. Belia was curled into a corner of the room on a pile of cushions, her head at an uncomfortable angle. Jorge woke when Thomas loosened the bandages around his waist, but said nothing until he had finished washing him, his eyes remaining closed as if he wanted to escape back into sleep.

The wound was raw, red—the stitching, though neat, still ugly. Thomas leaned close and sniffed, trying to sense any hint of corruption but finding none. He was sure he had cleaned the wound fully, around the surface as well, and the honey and egg-white would help, as would Belia's lotions.

"Will I live?"

"More than likely."

"I'm glad you are so sure in your diagnosis."

"I'm a man, not God."

"I've seen little results from God's efforts," said Jorge. "And I know you don't believe, just as I don't." He glanced to the corner of the room. "Belia has her own Gods, but I never ask, and she never volunteers. All I know is they are alien to this land."

"Keeping silent is the best way for such as you and I. Lubna was devout, but never attempted to convert me."

"That's because she knew you were a lost cause." Jorge opened his eyes as Thomas lifted his head and made him sip a little water.

"No solid food for a week. No food at all for three days."

"Are you trying to kill me?" Jorge lay on the pillows again, eyes once more closed. "How long can we stay here, in this house?"

"It depends who knows we have entered Gharnatah. If nobody saw us, then as long as we wish. I'll send Jamila and Dana to the market because they are not known. The rest of us will stay close to the house until you recover."

"You don't have to stay because of me." Jorge's voice had softened as sleep blurred the edges of his mind. "Belia and Da'ud can look after me if you want to leave."

"I stay until you can walk and use a sword."

Jorge offered a half smile. "Then you will stay until eternity."

"Swing a sword, then. A month, no more. We can..." But Thomas saw Jorge had gone to sleep. When he sat up Belia was watching him, alert now. She rose when he did and followed him from the room, stopped in the corridor with a hand on his arm.

"Will he make a full recovery?" Her enigmatic face was turned up to his, a pleading in her eyes.

"The truth, between you and I? I believe so."

She nodded. "Good. I will go to the market and find fresh herbs and make a special lotion."

"Make a list and send it with Jamila. She knows herbs— not as well as you, but well enough—and she won't be recognised."

Belia looked as if she might object, then turned away. No doubt she would ignore him, and Thomas wondered if it mattered. Belia had lived in this house for over a year. Her presence was familiar in the city and meant nothing.

There was no sign of anyone downstairs, but when Thomas went out to the still dark courtyard he found Usaden standing like a statue, staring up at the looming palace atop al-Hamra. Lamplight showed in its many windows, torches burning along the tops of the walls.

"I do not know this Sultan of yours," said Usaden. "I have heard things when you and Jorge talk, Olaf too, but I am curious about what he is like. Is he as bad as you say?"

"Worse. He is weak, fickle, and a bully. You met Yusuf, his brother, in Malaka. They are nothing alike. If he had lived he would be sitting on the hill now, with Muhammed nothing but a sour memory."

"And this Mandana—you have history, do you not?"

Thomas walked to stand beside Usaden and, like him, stared up at the palace. For no reason a dog began to bark, setting off others. Thomas heard the click-click of Kin's claws on the flagstones. The dog crossed to the garden and lifted its leg to piss mightily. Then he came back and lay down beside Thomas, his head resting across his foot. Thomas smiled, pleased the dog had stayed with him rather than go with Luis.

"Yes, we have history. And you know as well as I of the son, Pedro Guerrero." Thomas felt a bubble of grief rise in his throat and swallowed it down. He couldn't allow himself to act on emotion, however strongly he felt it. Only logic could destroy the two of them, though exactly how was only now starting to occur to him after what Helena had revealed. "It was you told me it was Guerrero who killed Lubna. Sometimes I..." Thomas waved a hand, unable for once to express himself clearly.

"Your grief will fade with time," said Usaden. "We never

think it will, but it always does. Killing them both will help." For the first time he turned his head to look at Thomas. "You do want to kill them, don't you?"

Thomas nodded, knowing Usaden would see the movement in the slowly gathering dawn.

"With your own hand?"

Thomas nodded again.

"Then I will help you get close so you can do so," said Usaden, "but the final blow must be yours."

"It must. And I thank you, my friend. When Olaf wakes we will talk, the three of us."

Usaden made a sound that might have been amusement. "Three against a horde. Even for us three that may prove interesting."

"We will find more men," Thomas said.

"We will?"

"Of course. Once I have told Olaf what I know."

Thomas was pleased Usaden didn't ask what it was, because the threads were only beginning to knit together in his own mind, and he was sure his idea would sound stupid if he tried to communicate it before he had the thought straight himself.

Thomas left Olaf to sleep until his impatience grew too strong and he sent Will upstairs to wake his *morfar*. The big Northman came downstairs, wiping a hand across his face as he sat at the table and waited to be served.

Fatima brought him meat, sauce, and flatbread still hot from the griddle. Jamila and Dana had gone in search of Belia's herbs—Belia herself was working in the garden, trying to recover what she could from the chaos Guerrero's soldiers had left. Thomas had looked earlier and saw nothing but wanton destruction, but Belia claimed roots remained beneath the surface and would grow again. In a few months they would be eating their own produce once more. The chickens would not regenerate so she intended to purchase more.

Olaf stopped eating and looked up at Thomas and Usaden.

"What?"

"We need to talk."

"Of course. But can I finish eating first?"

"Can you not do both at the same time?" Thomas asked.

"I am a simple man, but I will try. What does this talk concern? Will it bore me, or does it involve killing?"

"Would I bother you with anything less? Helena came to me last night."

Olaf glanced up from his food again, a piece of flat-bread half-lifted to his mouth dripping sauce onto the table.

"She is a difficult girl, I know, but I would not wish you to kill her," said Olaf. He cocked his head. "Did you lie with her?"

Thomas kept what had happened to himself, unsure if Olaf would approve or not.

"No, I didn't lie with her." Even as he spoke the words Thomas felt a flush rise in his face and hoped Olaf wouldn't see it. In any case he spoke partly the truth, for he had not been a willing participant. "She came to me and told me of something she heard Guerrero and Mandana discussing."

"I thought she already told you what she overheard." The flatbread continued its journey and Olaf chewed, reached for more.

"She was gifted to them both for the night, no doubt some joke by Muhammed. She claims she left some of what she discovered out because she was ashamed of what was done to her." Thomas shifted as Fatima set a bowl of thick sauce between him and Usaden, and a slab of bread.

"Helena felt shame?" Olaf shook his head at the strangeness of such an idea.

"Are you expelled from the hill?" Thomas asked, and Olaf stopped eating once more.

He frowned. "That is a good question. I had assumed so, but..." He raised a shoulder. "Perhaps Muhammed doesn't know of my part in any of this. Not that I want to return there. I have made my choice now."

"I want us to go to him," Thomas said. "The two of us, together."

"What about Jorge? He knows the hill even better than I do. Knows Muhammed, too."

"I want to do it today," Thomas said. "I don't know when Guerrero and Mandana intend to put the plan Helena told me of into action, but I suspect the sooner we go the better."

"I assume this is not about their attack on al-Zagal," said Olaf.

"Mandana is still working for the Spanish, that is what Helena overheard. They want to kill Muhammed. With Yusuf dead, and al-Zagal in exile, there is no-one to take Muhammed's place as Sultan. Gharnatah will fall. This war will be over."

"There are always pretenders." Olaf had stopped eating. Thomas now had his entire attention.

"Al-Rashid and his like, of course, but they are all greedy men. The city will not allow them to sit on the throne. Al-Andalus will come to an end. Spain will be victorious."

"I never thought I would hear you say you wanted Muhammed to remain in power," said Olaf. "You hate him."

"Not as much as I love al-Andalus."

Olaf waved a hand, which still held a tear of bread. "It is

a place. The land will remain, only the name changes, and there are other places. I have often thought of returning north when this war ends. If I am still alive, of course."

"I'm not so sure. The people make the land what it is, and the Spanish are different. They worship a different God. Their first task will be to convert the mosque to a cathedral." Thomas shook his head. "More likely tear it down. They won't repeat the same mistake they did in Qurtuba."

Thomas looked at Olaf, knowing they had drifted away from his main purpose. "I want to go to Muhammed with a plan. If he kills me, so be it. It is not so long since I sought death's oblivion."

"But you no longer do," said Olaf.

"You are right. I have discovered a new purpose. But I will never forget Lubna."

"As it should be, of course. Besides, I would not allow it. So, when do we go? I hope he doesn't execute you on the spot."

"Or have us both beheaded."

Olaf raised a shoulder. "He can try. But as you know, we are both difficult men to kill."

"We are all three difficult men to kill," said Usaden, who had sat silently listening to everything that was said. "Which is why we will all go."

Thomas nodded. "Agreed. The three of us." He began to eat, ravenous. "We go later in the day. I need more sleep first, for I was disturbed last night. My mind must be sharp for the confrontation, and it feels I have barely slept since Lubna died."

CHAPTER THIRTY

Four of them followed alleys down through the Albayzin to the banks of the Darro. Once they had crossed the arched bridge Fatima left them to go to her house beside the barracks. She wanted to fetch a few personal items, unsure if she would ever be allowed on the hill after their meeting.

At the outer gate Olaf's presence gave them entry, but when they reached the third barrier the guards refused to admit them.

"You do know who I am?" asked Olaf.

"Of course, General, but word has been sent you are General no longer. I recognise Thomas as well, but not the short one."

"I request an audience with Muhammed," Thomas said.

The guard who appeared to be in charge laughed. "Where is your pet, the eunuch? He has more chance than you do. Now piss off before I lose my temper."

Thomas glanced at Olaf, half expecting resistance from him, but he only shrugged and turned away.

Once they returned to the Darro Thomas stopped. "Do you know of another way in?"

"I don't," said Olaf. "Not one that will be unguarded. But there is still a chance. Most afternoons Muhammed likes to hunt, and there are no guards beyond the palace."

"He won't be alone though, will he?"

"He usually takes a dozen men, no more. He likes to take credit for the kill."

Thomas glanced at the sky. "We could go there now and find a position to watch from, but it's a big area. How will we know we haven't missed him?"

"Muhammed is a creature of habit. He considers it good luck to always approach along the same route. It is so well worn even Jorge would be able to track him."

"There is cover nearby?"

"Enough. But we want him to see us, don't we?"

"What if he orders his men to attack us?"

"I told you, there will be no more than a dozen. Even Muhammed is not foolish enough to think that is enough to defeat the three of us."

Olaf led them out to the Vega beyond the Malaka gate. Close by, men worked fields of vegetables set along the banks of the Darro where the soil held more moisture. Beyond, dense mulberry bushes ran almost as far as the eye could see, framed behind by rising peaks. Women worked with baskets, moving slowly as they picked silk caterpillars from the leaves.

Olaf waded the Darro at a shallow crossing and led them up a rising slope, which brought them to a spot above the palace. Ochre grasses swayed in the breeze. Elsewhere green undergrowth sprouted, small yellow flowers bobbing in a warm breeze.

"Over there would be good," Thomas said, pointing to a group of rocks which offered a place to hide.

"It would if Muhammed ever came this way. We need to go higher yet."

Thomas glanced at Usaden, who as always said nothing

until he had something to say. Perhaps if Jorge stayed in his company long enough the habit would transfer. At least it could be hoped for.

The sun warmed Thomas's back and he began to sweat. Flies gathered and he swatted them aside. Olaf and Usaden either didn't attract them, or ignored their attentions. Thomas wondered why he had left this city he loved, wondered what he had hoped to achieve by fleeing to the high mountains. Yes, he had found Guerrero and Mandana, but now he knew he could have achieved the same by staying here with what was left of his family. He considered himself a fool.

They reached a stand of trees, a mix of pine, cork oak and neglected olives which had gone so long unpruned some of their branches had touched the ground to root themselves.

"We should have brought food," said Usaden. "How long will we have to wait?"

Olaf glanced at the sky. "Not long." He sat on a bed of pine needles and crossed his ankles, leaning against the bole of a tree. He closed his eyes, then opened them again. "Who is taking watch?"

Usaden nodded and started toward the edge of the tree line.

"Call me as soon as you see anything—anything at all. They will come from the south. A dozen of them." Olaf looked to where Thomas stood. "You might as well rest, too." He closed his eyes again.

Thomas walked to one side, deeper into the copse of trees, his eyes tracking the ground. He saw mushrooms that were edible, others that would bring wild visions that he had partaken of at one time. He saw lines of ants marking trails through the loam. He heard birdsong, a constant background accompaniment. When he saw a gap in the trees he made his way to it, rewarded with a magnificent view across the entire city of Gharnatah and beyond, to the rising jumble of white houses of the Albayzin.

He wondered if he would live to see nightfall, and realised for the first time in many months that he wanted to do so. He feared death more than life, with no idea when, or why, the change had occurred. With the realisation came the first tendrils of fear.

Thomas tried to push them away. Fear was sensible, logical, but in the past he had never allowed it to sway him. One more change, he thought, but whether for the better or not he didn't know.

Movement drew his attention to the hillside. He saw a column of men riding from behind al-Hamra. He didn't bother counting them—near enough a dozen, as Olaf had promised, and they could be no other than Muhammed come to hunt. Thomas turned and walked fast toward Olaf to warn him, but when he got there Usaden had already seen the men, and the two of them stood in the shade of a pine, watching.

There came a burst of noise from their right, shouting voices and at least two drums beating.

"Ah," said Olaf, "I forgot about the others. They drive the birds and game toward Muhammed. It is not sporting, but it does guarantee a kill."

"Will they fight if it comes to it?" Thomas asked.

"I doubt it. Half of them are beggars, paid a copper coin to do the work—others will be low palace servants. But there will be no fighting. Muhammed's guards know me." Olaf glanced at the beaters once more, then stepped out into the late sunshine. After a moment, Thomas and Usaden followed.

They had gone a hundred paces before someone spotted them, not Muhammed but one of his riders, who spurred his horse and came fast, pulling up in a show of bravado.

"General," the man said. "Are you lost?"

Olaf made no reply.

Thomas stepped forward. "We have news for the Sultan," he said. "I believe he is in danger."

The rider looked around. "I see no danger. Unless it comes from you, Thomas Berrington."

Thomas wondered if there were any of the guards who didn't know his name.

"The danger comes not from us, but I will talk of it only to the Sultan."

The man looked between them, ignoring Usaden, which if it came to a fight would be a stupid thing to do.

"Wait here." The man spun his horse around and rode off with as great a show as when he arrived.

Thomas watched as he drew up next to Muhammed, saw his head turn, but the distance was too great to see his expression. Then the rider came back.

"The Sultan needs to know what this danger concerns. He knows of no danger. Besides which, we are all skilled men—the General knows that, for he trained most of us himself."

Thomas considered his response, knowing if he judged wrong Muhammed would simply ride back to the palace, or send his men to kill them.

"Tell him it concerns an Abbot, and betrayal."

The rider stared at Thomas for a while, his face showing nothing, then once more he turned and slapped his horse into a gallop. This time when he received the message, Muhammed turned and began to ride toward them. Half his men came ahead, the others behind, protecting their master. Thomas wondered if it came to a fight where the guards' loyalties would lie—with Muhammed or Olaf?

Muhammed came at a slow pace and remained in the saddle when he arrived, but a nod sent the front guards to either side so nothing stood between him and the three men.

"I was told it was you, Thomas Berrington, but could not believe it. Do you want to die so badly you come to stand in front of me this way?"

Thomas raised a shoulder. "You will have heard of my loss."

Muhammed offered a brief nod, but no sympathy.

"It makes a man consider life and death in a new light. Some things matter less, others more."

"I assume your cryptic message concerns Abbot Mandana?"

Thomas glanced at the soldiers accompanying Muhammed. "If we are to talk honestly you need to send your men away. Not far, just out of earshot."

"So you can kill me? I think not."

"I guarantee your safety, Sultan," said Olaf.

"I believe you are no longer my General."

"That may be true, but I am still loyal, and neither of these men will harm you. Even after what you did to my daughter."

Muhammed leaned forward in his saddle, his face showing the first sign of anger. "I had nothing to do with your daughter's death."

"I was not referring to that one," said Olaf.

"Helena came to me willingly."

"If you say so."

Muhammed examined each of them in turn.

"Why should I believe you?" The question was addressed to Thomas.

"Because in the back of your mind you already wonder what those two want of you," Thomas said. "I know what they have told you, but what is the advantage to them if al-Zagal is banished or killed? He is no danger to you or Spain."

"I sit where he sat. He will always be a danger to me while he lives." It was clear Muhammed's concern extended only as far as himself. It had not occurred to him why Guerrero and Mandana were offering help.

"Your uncle is a broken man," said Olaf. "I was there when he was defeated. He never suffered such a loss before. It changed him."

"Changed or not, he continues to sit in al-Marilla, and continues to pose a threat to me."

"Which is what I want to talk to you about." Thomas saw an opportunity, grateful Muhammed had steered the conversation this way himself.

"About my uncle?"

"And the men who promise to help you defeat him."

Thomas stood easy, arms loose at his sides as he waited for life or death, knowing the decision would come soon. He glanced at Muhammed's men. Good soldiers, there was no doubt of it, for they were his personal guard—but Thomas, Olaf and Usaden had fought harder men, and more of them, and triumphed. So perhaps not death. Not yet.

Then Muhammed came to a decision, and it was the right one. He turned to the three guards closest to him. "Dismount. Give your horses to these men." He turned toward Thomas. "We cannot talk out here. Follow me to the palace." With that he turned and urged his horse into a gallop.

Thomas took the reins from the nearest unmounted guard and swung into the saddle of his horse, ignoring the look on his face. It was a long walk back to the palace. He kicked his heels, knowing the others would be close behind. He expected Usaden to come flying past, but he didn't.

Muhammed was already dismounted and waiting for them when Thomas entered the wide barracks yard that lay alongside the stables. Olaf's living quarters were set on one side, and Thomas wondered if Fatima was still there, and if so whether she would see her husband enter the palace beside the Sultan.

They followed Muhammed, Thomas aware that the deeper they went the more guards lay between them and freedom. He wished Jorge had been well enough to attend this meeting, because he understood persuasion far better than the rest of them.

Muhammed turned into a courtyard flooded with light, the sound of birds a constant backdrop, a whisper of water underlying it. He turned to face them, offering neither refreshment nor comfort. A dozen guards entered and took up places at each exit, swords already drawn. Thomas was sure others stood just beyond. If Muhammed wanted to kill them, now was his opportunity because their weapons had been taken as they entered the palace.

"So, what is this message that is so important you risk your life to bring it to me?" As he spoke, his eyes flickered toward Olaf before returning to Thomas.

"You are talking to Abbot Mandana and his son," Thomas said. With someone else he might have eased into the subject, but he knew Muhammed lacked patience and was likely to eject them before they got to the heart of the matter.

"How would you know such information?" Muhammed smiled. "Ah, I see. Helena. Of course. What if I am? It is no business of yours." His gaze shifted. "Nor of yours, Olaf Torvaldsson. You should be out there training my soldiers, had you not turned your back on me."

"Training them for an attack on your uncle?" Thomas asked.

"Of course an attack on my uncle. I have already told you he is a danger to me, and he has many men. Too many men for me to risk my own troops. I would not have half of them slaughtered unless victory can be assured. And Guerrero can assure that."

"I am glad you care so much for those who were once under my command," said Olaf.

Muhammed's eyes didn't shift from Thomas.

"They offer to bring two thousand well-trained fighters, doubling my forces. How many does my uncle have? Do you know the answer to that, Thomas?" He waited a moment. "No, of course not. But my spies do. He has between one and two thousand, the remnant of those he led from Gharnatah against the Spanish and lacked the skill to use effectively. It is only a shame he did not die alongside the others."

"Whatever he claims, Guerrero doesn't have even a thousand trained men," Thomas said.

"Then my agreement with him will be void. I am not fool enough to take his word for anything without confirmation. I will see his army before I commit my own."

"It may be too late by then. Guerrero and Mandana spoke together when Helena was with them. They–"

"Men do not usually speak much when they are with Helena." A knowing smile showed on Muhammed's face. "It is why I made them a gift of her. It amused me to do so. It amuses me even more that she told you of it. I hope she did not spare you any of the details."

"They didn't know she understood Spanish, and she feigned sleep so they spoke freely. They don't care about al-Zagal, and never have. They have a far richer prize in mind. Gharnatah itself. And your place as its ruler."

"I considered that as well, of course I did. I would have been a fool not to do so. But you have just told me Guerrero has less than a thousand men, not all of them as well-trained as he claims. What danger is he to me?"

"He will take your soldiers toward al-Marilla in the belief they will fight al-Zagal, but Helena told me it is only a distraction. They intend to lure your soldiers away from Gharnatah and then ambush them. It is a bold plan, and not without danger, but the element of surprise will give them an advantage. And then, once your army is destroyed, they will march on Gharnatah."

"Where I will still have other men," said Muhammed, but he sounded less sure than he had.

"Indeed. But another army waits for the signal that your forces have been diminished. You know that Fernando remains in Malaka, together with half his army. Six thousand at the last count. Once word reaches them they will march north and attack Gharnatah from the east."

Muhammed shook his head. "It sounds far too complex to achieve success. Battles are simple things, not won by guile. Ask Olaf, he will agree with me." Muhammed's attention switched to Olaf. "In fact, I would talk with you alone, General, without the distraction of this man." He turned his head. "Guards!"

Six men came forward, as if the move was already pre-arranged.

"Take these two away."

Muhammed turned aside, uninterested. He snapped his fingers, and a slim female servant trotted to him and he leaned close, issuing more commands

A guard took Thomas's arm, another Usaden's, who glanced at Thomas and raised an eyebrow. Thomas shook his head. Now was not the time. He would have to trust in Olaf.

Usaden in turn lifted a shoulder, and Thomas smiled, sure the man was confident they could escape at any time they wanted. It was best to allow him his delusion for the moment.

CHAPTER THIRTY-ONE

Thomas had been held in the palace dungeons several years before, when Muhammed's father had been Sultan. This time it felt different—both better and worse. The dungeon was relatively comfortable in comparison to that first one, which had been dank and cold. This one even contained a pair of cots, and Thomas stretched out on one. He knew the problem now was Muhammed and his capricious decisions. His father, the old Sultan Abu al-Hasan Ali, would either kill a man or spare him, and Thomas had always been confident of being spared. Now, he could no longer be sure. His only hope was that Olaf could persuade Muhammed of the sense of their plan.

Usaden paced the small space for a while, before deciding he too might as well save his energy, though he still didn't sit.

"When they come, I will conceal myself behind the door. I'll pull the first man in, grab his sword, and we fight our way out."

Thomas nodded. "All the way past a hundred guards?"

"I did not see a hundred as we came in. We will deal

with them one at a time, as always. Best not to consider odds, don't you think?"

"Muhammed would love us to fight. It will give him all the excuse he needs to execute us. Execute me. I'm sorry, he doesn't even know who you are, but you will share the same fate."

"So we do nothing?"

Thomas dropped his feet to the floor and leaned his elbows on his knees. "Muhammed is trying to scare us, except he doesn't know you can't be scared."

"He knows you can?"

Thomas smiled. "No, he knows I can't. He might be Sultan now, but I have known him since he was a baby in his mother's arms—or rather, in his wet-nurse's arms. I don't think his mother wanted all that much to do with him until he attained adulthood."

"And Yusuf?" asked Usaden. "I liked Yusuf."

"As did I. He was such a sweet boy, nothing like his brother. But they had different mothers. Aixa—Muhammed's mother —is an evil, scheming bitch. I'm only glad she wasn't in that courtyard or my head would be on a spike already, though no doubt she will hear all about our conversation from her spies."

"How can you live in a place such as this? My life is simple—I sell my sword to whoever will pay, and I kill men in battle."

"Much like Olaf."

"Except he has a loyalty to his master that I lack."

Thomas glanced at Usaden, knowing the man didn't speak entirely honestly. Otherwise, why was he still with them? Something had sparked between them all in Malaka which perhaps Usaden had never experienced before.

As if reading his thoughts, Usaden said, "You pay me well for training your son."

"And if I stop paying you?"

"I like Will," said Usaden, and Thomas knew it was the only answer he would get.

After a time, Thomas rose and stalked the walls, tapping on stones.

"I am trying to sleep," said Usaden, who had finally stretched out on the other cot.

"And I am looking for a way out."

"The door is the way out. We have already agreed a plan. Now we should rest until we can carry it out."

Thomas rapped on another stone, cocked his head. Did it sound a little different to the others, or not?

"Did I ever tell you about the tunnels in the palace?"

Usaden sighed and sat up. "No. But I expect you are going to."

"Most of them will have been filled in by now, but I know at least some remain. We used one to get Helena out." He tapped the stone again and shook his head. No, the sound was the same as all the others. Tunnels might remain, but if so none of them offered a means of escape from the dungeon.

"The last time I was locked in the palace a friend opened a tunnel and spirited us away." He smiled. "You would have liked her."

"Was she pretty, like Helena?"

"No, not like Helena. No-one is like Helena—but pretty, yes, though too young for you." A sadness washed through Thomas. "Though she would be old enough by now if she had lived. She would be..." He calculated in his head, surprised at how many years had passed since he had crept through dark tunnels beside the girl. "Prea would have twenty years now."

"She is dead?"

Thomas nodded. "And it was my doing."

"You killed her?"

"As good as. I didn't listen to her, didn't warn her well

enough, and she was killed by the man we sought." Thomas sat on the bed again, a sense of despair filling him. There had been so many deaths over the years, both before and after Prea—too many to count anymore—and he had lost too many people he liked, and some he loved. Just as he had lost Lubna. At the thought of her his despair deepened, so that when the door opened without warning he barely noticed Usaden rise, but by then it was too late to do anything.

Six guards entered, each with a sword drawn. They motioned Thomas and Usaden to follow them from the cell. Outside, another six waited.

Thomas glanced at Usaden, saw a tension in him that was well hidden, and gave a shake of the head. No sense trying anything until they knew what Muhammed's intentions were.

He was surprised when the guards led them through the palace to the outer gate, handed them their weapons, and allowed them to walk free.

"Does this mean Olaf was more persuasive than you were?" asked Usaden.

"Or Muhammed trusts him more than he does me. We are men who follow different paths. Muhammed has never taken to me, not even when I repaired him after battle and allowed him to fight again."

"You have fixed many men over the years, have you not?"

"And lost a great many as well. Battle is a poor place for a physician to work, but it is work that must be done."

"You do it well. I have seen you at work, and if I am ever injured I hope you are beside me."

Thomas laughed, the sound surprising him, an indication that something had changed inside, something he was unsure whether to welcome or not if it meant he would forget Lubna. Except he knew that could never happen. In his grief he had turned his back on life, but life still had much to offer—even if he had less time left than he had already lived. Maybe far less if the plan he proposed ended in disaster. He knew that neither Guerrero nor Mandana would hesitate even a moment if they had the chance to kill him. Nor he them.

When they reached Thomas's house on the Albayzin the day was tipping into night. The big main room was filled with talk and the rich smell of cooking. Will rose from playing with Kin and ran to Thomas, who lifted him against his chest while he walked to the table.

"How long have you been here?" he asked Olaf.

"Several hours. Have you only now been released?"

"Muhammed," Thomas said, shaking his head. "He was always one for petty punishments. What did you talk of?"

"You have persuaded him." Olaf reached out to take Amal from Belia. Thomas's seven-month-old daughter had woken in a bad mood and Olaf always seemed able to comfort her when others could not. Perhaps it was his strength. His love.

"It didn't feel as if we had." Thomas accepted a mug of wine from Jamila and emptied half of it in one long swallow. "I have no doubt you helped him make his decision."

"You know how he is," said Olaf. "Too afraid to act, too afraid not to. Today, for once, he made the right decision. But who knows—come morning he might have changed his mind again."

"Is there a plan?"

"The one you hinted at. I am to lead a cohort of five hundred rather than the thousand asked for, supposedly to add to Guerrero's number, but as soon as we are close we turn on them."

It didn't surprise Thomas that Muhammed was sending only half the promised men. He only hoped it would be enough to achieve victory.

"When?"

"Not anytime soon. Guerrero claims not to be ready yet, and Muhammed is happy to sit on his hands until the end of time if it means he doesn't have to act."

"Was Aixa there after we left?" Thomas was interested to know if Muhammed's mother had made an appearance, for he was sure it was she who ruled on the hill rather than her son.

"No, but she will hear of what happened soon enough."

"Will she approve? It will be she who decides, after all."

"She approves of whatever presents Muhammed in a good light, and this would do so. They can pretend they launched an attack against a band of Spanish renegades and defeated them."

"Can we defeat them?"

"How many of this Guerrero's claimed thousand are real soldiers?"

Thomas shook his head, sat up as Jamila placed food on the table. She said nothing, her expression sour, and Thomas was sure she blamed him for Aban's loss.

"About half, but I can't say for sure. I'm hoping some of the others, the captured men, will help when the attack starts. Have you any idea how long Guerrero will allow us to be among them before turning on us?"

"It will be difficult. My own men will have to be told they are putting themselves in danger if they are to respond fast enough when the time comes. But they cannot, must not, let any of that show. Guerrero has to believe we have no idea of his plan. As for when ... that I do not know."

"What if it was you?" Thomas reached out and tore a strip of meat from a capon.

"I would never stoop to such subterfuge."

"I am aware of that. But pretend you could—what would you do?"

"I would attack on the first night our armies come together. The longer we are there the better chance they might discover all is not as it seems. I trust my own men to keep a secret, but can Guerrero say the same? And there are those he stole away from their homes. Forced men do not love their captors." Olaf tapped a finger on the table as something occurred to him. "It is a shame we do not have one or two men among them to spread dissent, to spread the word so that when the time comes at least a few will fight with, rather than against, us."

"Yes," Thomas said. "It is a pity, isn't it?"

Olaf stared at him.

Thomas withstood the attention as long as he could, hoping Olaf would ask, but when he didn't Thomas knew he had to respond.

"Luis has returned to them, but as our man on the inside. I have been planning it since he first escaped but didn't know if he would agree. He confirmed it in Pampaneira. His aggression during the attack was all for show, so they would believe him. Did you notice he attacked only me?"

"And Aban?"

Thomas glanced toward Jamila, but she was busy at the fire. He lowered his voice in case she might overhear. "He wasn't meant to go. Did you see what happened to him?"

"I was too busy." Olaf glanced at Usaden. "What about you?"

"I saw him sneaking away to one side and hiding behind a boulder. I believed him a coward, but now..." Usaden glanced at Thomas and offered a nod. "Perhaps he and Luis discussed the matter and he wanted to prove himself. It is a good plan if it works. Those two are close."

"Closer than you might think," Thomas said.

Usaden did as Thomas had and glanced to where Jamila was busy at the fire and lowered his voice in turn. "His mother keeps him too close. A boy cannot become a man if he is tied to his mother's skirts all the time. If they are as close as you claim he might believe Luis can protect him, vouch for him."

"I understand why Jamila does it," Thomas said. "She has lost too much already and doesn't want to lose him as well."

"And now she has," said Usaden. He turned away, making it clear the matter was ended as far as he was concerned.

Thomas considered pressing the argument further but knew there was little point. Luis had been willing enough to undertake the task he had been set. Had Aban been equally willing, or taken prisoner? If what Dana had revealed to him was true he could imagine the two youths hatching a plan between them. He knew he should talk to Jorge as soon as he was well enough. Would their relationship be defined by the two men plus Dana, or all three of them together? Thomas needed distraction before he lost himself in the endless tunnel of his own thoughts. He turned to Olaf, who had listened to the conversation without expression.

"Guerrero and Mandana will return when Muhammed doesn't send the promised soldiers, demanding he give what was offered. When they come do you have a plan?"

"I have an idea, and would like for you to help me put it into action."

"Me?"

Olaf nodded. "Both of you, if you are willing. Usaden?"

"To plan mayhem? Of course."

Thomas wondered why the Gomeres mercenary remained with them. He claimed it was because Thomas continued to pay him to train Will, but that was an excuse, not a reason. He hoped perhaps Usaden was becoming part of the extended family that had gathered around them. If so, he was welcome. Thomas liked the man's quiet certainty, not to mention his other-worldly skill with weapons. He could have found no-one better to train Will if he had searched for a score of years.

"It will have to be a good plan," Thomas said. "We all saw what Guerrero and Mandana's men are capable of when they fought in Malaka. They were demons, offering mercy to no-one: man, woman or child. They are creatures of the worst kind."

Thomas saw Usaden's mouth quirk in what might have been the start of a smile, both aware the same description could apply equally to him.

"We will talk of the plan tomorrow, test it out between us," Olaf said. "Tonight, we eat and drink and celebrate our freedom. You, Thomas, if we are to succeed, need to regain your strength. You fought well enough, but not like I know you can."

"Muhammed knows where I am now. What if he still wants to kill me?"

"He could have killed you in the dungeon if he wanted. He gave me his word he would not harm you."

"And you believe him?"

"Of course not—which is why tonight, and every night we are here, we set a guard."

Thomas was about to say they were still vulnerable but was interrupted by Belia, who came running down the stairs.

"Thomas, you must come at once. I think Jorge is dying."

CHAPTER THIRTY-TWO

Jorge lay on his back, arms spread, eyes closed. His chest rose and fell in shallow gasps and sweat stained the single sheet that lay across him.

"How long has he been this way?" Thomas went to the bed and pulled back the sheet to reveal Jorge's naked body, looking for signs of mottling beneath his skin, relieved to see none.

"He was better at noon, he even managed to swallow a little broth. Then he said he was tired and slept again. I left him, thinking it was for the best. When I came up just now he was like this." She looked toward Thomas. "He is dying, isn't he?"

"He has a fever, certainly, but he's not dying yet—not if I have anything to do with it. Or you. I need you to prepare something for his fever." Thomas knew if anyone could conjure some magic to help Jorge it would be Belia, and the work would distract her.

"I looked in your workshop, but there is little left anymore. Willow is a start, but this is no ordinary fever, is it?"

"No." Thomas knew he didn't need to offer false hope.

Belia was as wise in the ways of the body as he was, as wise as Lubna had been. They had been a formidable team, the three of them working side by side, and he pushed aside his grief before it had a chance to gain hold.

"Will you need to open the wound again?"

Thomas nodded. "First we have to bring his fever down, so go into the city and get whatever you can. Willow bark to start with, wort, lemons. You know better than me what you need. And get Helena to take you to Da'ud's house, he'll have everything you might need. I'll stay with Jorge." As Belia started for the door Thomas said, "Don't say anything to the others. Not yet."

When she had gone, Thomas cut away the bandages around Jorge's waist, grimacing when he saw the raised inflammation around the wound, experiencing a sense of despair when he smelled corruption. His fingers twitched with the need to act but he knew he had to wait for Belia's return. In the meantime, he wiped Jorge's body with cold water, cleaning as much as he could. It was a body Thomas knew almost as well as his own. A body he had mistreated when Jorge was barely more than a boy, unmanning him at the request of a Sultan—not Muhammed, not even his father, but a Sultan four times removed from the present one. Jorge had been barely thirteen years of age, Thomas only a little more than twice that, but he had been strong enough to resist the call to create a eunuch using the old methods—methods which involved much cutting and hot coals. Instead, he had rendered the boy almost comatose and cut only what needed to be removed to ensure Jorge could never father children. His manhood remained, which Jorge claimed worked no less well than that of other men. In fact, he boasted his worked better than that of most men, and from the sounds Thomas overhead when he and Belia made love he had no cause to doubt it.

He stared at the smooth skin between Jorge's thighs, at

his flaccid prick that lay to one side, and wondered if he regretted never being able to father children. He suspected he did. Thomas recalled when Jorge had asked if he would lie with Belia to set a seed in her belly and he had refused, even though Lubna had offered her blessing. Now, he determined that if the request came again he would agree. Jorge would make a good father, even if he was unlike other men. More so perhaps because he was unlike other men.

Jorge was Thomas's closest friend. His companion. He would not let him die. If he couldn't save him then he knew nobody could.

Thomas laid two fingers against Jorge's belly, pressing lightly. Jorge stirred but didn't wake, and Thomas eased the pressure. He wondered if it was possible to save this man he loved more than any other, and had no answer. He rose and went downstairs to the workshop, opening and closing drawers that had been repaired and replaced. Britto was coming in the morning to examine the other damage to the house and let Thomas know what could be done. Friendships, Thomas thought, amazed he seemed to be capable of forming them, even more amazed he was able to maintain them.

He set aside a few items on the workbench that might prove useful, then went out to the garden that ran down the slope beyond the courtyard. Belia had replanted what was not dead, but the few things growing looked sparse in comparison to what had been there before. Thomas looked up at the looming palace and wondered how much Muhammed could be trusted. If his men had not done the damage here, then others were allowed to do so. The man had taken Helena prisoner, subjected her to beatings and worse, and handed her over to Guerrero like some delicacy on a plate. Thomas shivered despite the warmth of the evening, then heard the door from the street open. When he turned he saw Belia had returned. He pushed aside all thought of failure and followed her back to the room where Jorge lay awaiting their skills.

When Thomas re-opened the wound he saw what the cause of Jorge's fever was. Two stitches had pulled loose, and fresh matter oozed out. Thomas ignored the stink, as he had always been able to, knowing it would not concern Belia either. Between them they washed and wiped and washed some more.

"I'm going to leave the wound open for a day or two," Thomas said when they were finished. He had re-stitched the cut to Jorge's bowel and packed the space around it with more egg-white mixed with honey, and Belia had prepared a tincture only she knew the ingredients of. She applied it to the stitches, re-applying it twice an hour as they waited. Fatima brought them food and took away the tainted cloths to burn, averting her gaze from the cavity on display.

They had forced liquor of willow bark and poppy into Jorge and he slept more peacefully. Thomas knew he would have to keep him sedated until the wound was closed, but was unwilling to do so until he knew the internal stitches were going to stay in place this time.

The night passed in fitful bursts of sleep.

Dawn brought a cold light, which Thomas used to examine Jorge's wound. The stitches were holding, but he knew it was still too soon to hope. A week might not be long enough, but another day, two at the most, would allow him to close the flesh on Jorge's belly.

"His scar will be worse," Thomas said to Belia, who leaned against him, her exhaustion matching his own.

"It will worry him, but not me. A man should possess a few scars." She smiled. "Like you."

Thomas thought of how Will liked to touch them and ask where each had been acquired. How Lubna's fingers would trace them lovingly, using each as an excuse to lead her fingers elsewhere. The memory of Lubna hurt, but not as much as it had, and Thomas didn't know if that was progress, or the loss of something he didn't want to lose.

After a while he roused himself from what might have been sleep to hear the clash of metal on metal, and rose to look through the narrow window.

Usaden was training Will, and as he watched Thomas saw how much his son had improved in half a year. He was too young to fight, but sometimes being too young didn't prevent the fight coming to you. As it had come to Thomas. Older than Will, certainly, but not by so many years. He had lived thirteen of those years on earth when his father John Berrington had accompanied John Talbot, Earl of Shrewsbury, across the sea. They were meant to teach the French a lesson. Except this time, it had been the other way around—a battle to end a war which had gone on far too long, with the English expelled from a region of France they had ruled for centuries.

John Berrington had survived the first hours of the fighting, but late in the afternoon a French knight had spilled him from his horse, which toppled across him to crush his legs. The knight had ridden on in search of more glory. Thomas hadn't found his father for several hours, by which time he was delirious with agony. There was nothing could be done, other than one final mercy—a mercy Thomas had administered himself. Recalling that day, he realised it was perhaps the first time his father had ever smiled at him, in that final moment of rationality, his hand clasped around Thomas's, which in turn held a knife. He had pushed it into his father's chest, closing his own eyes as he did so. When he opened them his father stared sightlessly at a grey sky, all life fled. Thomas closed his father's eyes, then struggled to pull his boots off. He took them, together with a chain mail vest, but nothing else. He had felt no emotion, not even pleasure. He had hated his father with every fibre of his being, and knew his father hated him in turn for not being more like his elder brother, another John, who had died in their manor house in Lemster, alongside their mother. She, at least, had loved Thomas. And then he was alone. For a long time he had been alone.

He turned to look at Jorge.

No longer alone.

There were people who loved him, and people he loved in return. The ice that had held his heart in an iron grip for half a year began to loosen its grip.

Life staggered into motion again.

Thomas let his breath go so loudly Belia turned to see what was wrong.

He shook his head and wiped at the tears that filled his eyes. Nothing was wrong. The memories reminded him of all the people close to him who had died, and when they were gone he had carried on. He had done much since that battlefield, and knew he would do more if he could only grasp the reins of life once again.

He crossed the room and sat beside Belia, took her hand and kissed the palm. She frowned at him, but Thomas said nothing, and after a moment her frown turned to a smile and her fingers twined through his. She leaned against him, as if she was privy to all the secret thoughts that filled his head.

Three days later Thomas closed the wound in Jorge's side.

A week passed before Jorge managed to stand for the first time since being carried to the bedroom.

Within two days he could manage the stairs and descend unaided to eat with them, small meals to begin with, but the stitches in his side had already healed and Thomas was sure those within had healed too.

There was no return of the fever.

It was time to talk about the future. Olaf had been patient, but Thomas could see he wanted to finish things, or at the very least start them.

They went to Muhammed.

And then they went to war.

CHAPTER THIRTY-THREE

Thomas was dressed as an ordinary foot soldier, surrounded by almost five hundred others. Like him, few of these men had been born in al-Andalus. They were a mix of North Africans, of French and German, Italian and English, still others from more distant eastern lands, yet more from the north, like Olaf, who sat astride a tall white stallion at the head of their company. Thomas wished he could ride beside him but knew such was impossible. Guerrero and Mandana were expecting Olaf. They would not be expecting Thomas, and if they saw him would instantly recognise the betrayal. So Thomas put up with the binding of the leather jerkin he wore and tried not to complain too much to Usaden, who walked beside him as though their march was nothing more than an early morning stroll. Kin remained close to Thomas. He had wanted to leave the dog at home with Jamila until Olaf told him other men would have brought their dogs. He was glad he was at his side. Kin's unquestioning loyalty was a mystery Thomas welcomed.

Muhammed had come to watch them leave Gharnatah,

but there was never a chance he was going to accompany the soldiers. Instead he sat astride a tall horse and watched the column pass. Even before the last man left the city walls, Muhammed had returned to the palace, no doubt to fill his hours with worry over his action. Thomas only hoped the man wouldn't back down and send a message to Guerrero telling him what had been done.

An hour after leaving Gharnatah, a small group of riders appeared ahead in a pass that led into the foothills of the Sholayr. Ten riders, no more. They waited while the eight-wide column of men climbed the slope. A quarter mile away, Olaf rode ahead and spoke with them. Thomas assumed at least one of the men had Arabic, because Olaf's grasp of Spanish was truly awful.

The ten riders moved aside as the first men reached them. Olaf took up the lead once more.

"Do you think they are suspicious?" Usaden asked, not the least out of breath even though Thomas was, despite a month gaining strength. There was no need to keep their voices low because the sound of so many feet prevented their words carrying.

"A welcoming party, nothing more," Thomas said, saving his breath for when he had something important to say. He didn't know if he spoke the truth or not, only that if Guerrero wanted to attack them, he would have sent more than ten men.

They stopped a little after noon where a small river cut their path. Thomas was tempted to remove his boots and bathe his feet, but noticed no-one else was doing so. They drank water, ate the meagre supplies they had brought, and within an hour were forming up and making their way once more.

The afternoon would have brought heat and flies, except they moved through a deep valley into which sunlight couldn't reach. Instead it glimmered along the precipitous slopes above. The roadway rose, climbed through a pass, then fell in a series of twisting switchbacks. Thomas drifted back through the ranks of men until he was at the tail of the convoy. From here he could see above the heads of the others to what lay ahead.

Guerrero and Mandana's camp looked as if it had lain in the valley floor for months. Piles of detritus lay around the edges, and even in daylight feral dogs, wolves and foxes came down to snatch at the scatter of food and human waste that filled the air with its stink. Three large tents were erected on a raised plateau to one side, obviously where Mandana and Guerrero made their headquarters, no doubt with one or more of their generals. Thomas had seen Mandana's men—a mix of priests and soldiers—often enough over the years to recognise some of them. Loyal men, devout to their notion of God in their own misguided way, even more loyal to Mandana. Thomas wondered if Guerrero had such men of his own but doubted it. Guerrero was the undoubted leader here, young and charismatic, but Thomas wondered which of them made the decisions when the two spoke together alone. He recalled his first encounter with Guerrero the year before in Malaka, carrying his already dying wife in his arms. Guerrero had been sent to spy on the city's defences but had blamed Thomas for not saving his wife, even though he and Lubna had managed to save the baby she carried. That hatred had festered in Guerrero's soul until it led to Lubna's death. No doubt that fire still burned, Guerrero feeding the embers so they never grew cold. Mandana would add the coals of his own hatred, Thomas was sure.

He knew he would either kill or be killed by one of those two men before his plan came to an end. Mandana or his son. He wanted to destroy both for what they had done to him. What they had taken from him. And if he couldn't succeed, and it was they who destroyed him, at least Thomas knew his pain would come to an end at last. Two months before he wouldn't have cared what happened to him. Now the cold and ice that had held him fast was melting. He wanted his life to continue. Wanted to watch Will and Amal grow into adults. Wanted to discover how Jorge and Belia would forge their lives into something new and strange.

He stumbled on a rock, and would have fallen had Usaden not reached out a hand to steady him.

"There," he said, pointing to the far side of the valley.

Thomas had been so lost in his own thoughts he had barely noticed they had arrived. Olaf's troops stayed back, waiting until they were told what to do. Olaf dismounted and walked through the ranks of Guerrero's men toward the tents. Before he reached them the canvas was pulled aside and Mandana emerged. A moment later Guerrero came out behind him. Both wore pristine white robes, freshly washed. Mandana's body was more stooped than the last time Thomas had seen him close to, and he wondered how the stump of the hand he had lost to wolves five years before fared—infected and painful, he hoped. But even wounded, perhaps more so wounded, Mandana was not a man to underestimate. As for Guerrero, Thomas already knew the son was worse than the father. He had killed Lubna deliberately and, according to Usaden, with his own blade. Guerrero would be the last to die, Thomas promised himself, alone and begging for a mercy that would never be granted.

As Olaf approached them Mandana came to greet him while his son hung back. The old Abbot embraced Olaf, almost his equal in height, nowhere equal in strength but more so in guile. Thomas wondered how Olaf fared, discussing tactics with the two of them when one had murdered his daughter. Guerrero might not be aware of that fact, but Mandana certainly was. Did they consider Olaf weak for coming to them on Muhammed's orders?

A man stood to one side, translating back and forth. Thomas itched to be there, to know what was being said, to know how much was lost in translation through either ignorance or deliberation. Without conscious thought he found himself drifting through the ranks of soldiers toward the small gathering. He knew he couldn't approach too closely, for if he came within twenty paces Mandana would recognise him in an instant.

Thomas glanced around as he made his way through the men, passing smoking fires, blankets laid on the ground, small collections of food: meat, bread, vegetables—nothing fancy, but enough to live on for a while. It was clear to him which were the conscripted men and which those who had been with Guerrero and Mandana for longer. The conscripts avoided his gaze, knowing he was part of the new army that had come to join them, ashamed at their weakness in being captured and forced to fight. Thomas wanted to kneel and speak to some of them—ask where their families were, ask how they were themselves—but knew he couldn't draw attention to himself by doing such a thing. Instead he passed through, trying to ignore their misery. His eyes scanned their number, searching for Luis or Aban and failing to find either.

He stopped well back, still too far away to hear what was being said. There appeared to be no argument. Several times Guerrero turned and pointed to indicate positions he wanted Olaf to take up. After a while, both Guerrero and Mandana turned away. Thomas expected Olaf to return, but instead he followed them into the tent.

Thomas again resisted the urge to approach closer. He reached down to touch the soft fur and hard bone of Kin's head. A half dozen stone-faced men stood near the tents, their eyes constantly moving, and Thomas realised Mandana was afraid of the men he had captured, even if his son was not. They needed them to bolster their numbers, but it was clear they were not to be trusted.

Thomas drifted back to where Olaf's troops were setting out their camp a bare few feet from the others. A few feet it might be but there was a clear difference between the two forces. Olaf's men arranged themselves automatically into cadres of a dozen, set their blankets around a small cleared area and went in search of kindling and firewood. Thomas knew they would have to travel some distance to find any and wondered what would happen if they asked for help from the others. It would prove a good test of their intentions, but nobody did, perhaps deliberately so, keeping themselves apart until they knew exactly what those intentions were.

"If it was you," Thomas asked Usaden, who had stayed at a short distance from the others, as if he didn't want to be associated with either group, "how long would you wait before attacking?"

"The sensible move would be for them to fall on us in the small hours of the night."

"This night?"

Usaden offered a nod. "Before we are fully settled, when we are tired from our march."

"But we will set guards, won't we?"

"Of course. But guards grow tired. You know what it is like, that dark hour before the first glimmer of dawn. Men drift between this life and dreams."

"Not if they are warned."

Usaden smiled. "Even then. You know I am right."

Thomas did.

"Perhaps they will not come tonight," Usaden said.

"Perhaps they mean to merge our forces as they spoke of and there is no subterfuge here."

"Except you don't believe that, do you?" Thomas said.

"Of course not."

"You said to attack tonight is the sensible choice, but it's not what you would do, is it?"

"No, because they will have some respect for us and know we will expect it."

"Only if we don't believe their story."

"Two armies who are natural enemies? Both will be wary."

"So what would your plan be?" Thomas asked.

"Attack now, immediately, before we can settle. Or attack as we gather to travel east toward al-Marilla. That will be soon. Either tomorrow or the day after. The day after would be best, when we have grown comfortable and lowered our guard."

"Despite what they told Muhammed, they have no intention of going to al-Marilla, do they?" Thomas said.

"Agreed."

"Will Olaf think the same as you?"

"Of course. He is a good general. He is alive, as are you. Do you not agree with me, Thomas?"

"I do."

"So why have we wasted all this time in idle chatter?"

"Not wasted," Thomas said. "They are watching us. You have seen them, as have I. Here and there men are set to study what we do." He sighed and shook his head. "And they will have noted us standing here talking. We are marked men now, because they are wondering what we have been talking about. When Olaf returns we should attack them immediately."

"What about your spy?" asked Usaden. "Do you think Luis has managed to sow dissent, or even hope, among the captured men?" He turned and looked over the gathered troops, and Thomas noted Usaden's attention was noted in turn. "How many real soldiers does Mandana have? There are indeed close to a thousand men here, but how many are willing to fight? More importantly, how many are willing to kill?"

Thomas scanned the heads. Men from a score of lands. Dark-skinned, light-skinned and all shades between. Tall and short, fat and thin. The difference between the fighting men and those stolen from their families was clear to see, as was the organisation of both sides. Each group of ten or twelve conscripts was accompanied by four hard-faced soldiers. Any hint of rebellion would be instantly punished. Thomas knew the punishment had been ingrained into the captives' souls. He had seen it being meted out for all to see. He saw that the ratio of hardened troops to captured was consistent throughout the camp—three times more conscripts than soldiers.

"They have no more than four hundred trained men," Thomas said.

Usaden nodded. "Agreed. And we have five hundred." He grinned. "A fair fight, for once." His grin broadened. "Which will make it an unfair fight, of course."

"Don't underestimate them. They've been fighting with Mandana for years against skilled opposition. I would judge it an even match."

"Except there is me, and Olaf." Usaden glanced at Thomas. "And you, of course."

Thomas knew he was offering false flattery but made no comment.

"You should try to find Luis," said Usaden. "Find out what he knows, what orders have been issued. The more we know the more we will be ready."

"What about you?"

"Me? I thought I would lay my blanket here beside my

new friends and get some sleep. If I am to be attacked in the dark hours I need to be fully rested."

Thomas turned away, amused but not wanting Usaden to see he was. Besides, it was a good suggestion. He would find Luis, and Aban too if he could, and warn them both trouble was coming.

CHAPTER THIRTY-FOUR

Thomas wandered through the camped men, their presence wrapping around him, together with the chatter of conversation, an occasional argument quickly dealt with, the smell of sweat and unwashed clothes, the stink of latrine pits, the sweet scent of woodsmoke coming from a hundred campfires. It was all of it familiar, sparking memories that spanned his entire lifetime. He saw Olaf's men returning with firewood, some of them carrying the carcasses of rabbits, one with an ibex slung over his shoulders, which meant someone would eat well tonight.

Sunlight picked out the highest peaks, but shadows spread between groups of men, the flames of their fires more intense as the day began to draw to a close. Thomas walked among them, eyes searching, aware of other eyes on him. Now and again he nodded to one or another as though in recognition, even receiving a few acknowledgements.

He didn't see Luis or Aban, unsure if Jamila's son was still alive. After what Dana had told him of their extended relationship, he had no doubt Luis would have told Aban all about the plan. He wouldn't be surprised if they had changed sides together, Aban loyal to his friend … or his lover?

Thomas shook his head. Whatever the reason, this is where he would expect them to be. He hadn't intended to go far, wanting to return to hear what Olaf had learned from his talk with Guerrero and Mandana, but he had still been inside the tent when Thomas started his slow search. When he found himself on the far side of the camp he followed a small river that wound along the valley floor, twisting from one side to the other. Boulders brought down during spates made the ground treacherous under-foot. Kin roamed ahead, poking his long nose into every nook and cranny. Slowly the presence of men faded, and Thomas listened to the soothing rustle of water over stone, watched as small fish darted away from his presence, smiled as bright vermillion frogs leapt yards when Kin pounced at them. Their croaking grew louder around the deeper pools, faded as he moved away. Thomas followed a rough track made by men in search of wood or game. It rose on the northern flank and he let it guide his feet, no destination in mind as memories surrounded him. The men he had fought … countries crossed … fiends made … women loved, and lessons learned.

He had stopped looking for Luis and Aban when Kin barked twice, drawing his attention to a small clearing on the left. He saw two figures, knowing he would have missed them had the dog not drawn his attention. As he took in what lay in the clearing a cry escaped him. He had found Luis and Aban both.

Luis was both tied and nailed to a cross—well-made, sturdy, set in a deep hole and held vertical with rocks. A second cross stood beside the first, but it was empty. Aban crouched in front of Luis's body, arms wrapped around himself as if wanting to stop his body shattering into a thousand pieces. Kin lay on the ground at his master's feet, a thin whine coming from him.

Thomas looked around.

Why here? Why not in front of the other men? Then he saw how the hard ground had been disturbed by many feet. There had been witnesses. This was another of Guerrero and Mandana's lessons.

"Tell me what happened." Thomas went to one knee beside Aban. When his hand touched the boy's shoulder he flinched, but didn't shift his gaze from what lay in front of him.

"He found out." Aban's voice came out barely a whisper.

"Mandana?"

"No, the Warrior."

"Luis talked to the wrong man?"

Aban shook his head like he might never stop. "No. I did. Luis asked me to help, but I was stupid. I'm always stupid. And a coward. The Warrior called me a coward and his father laughed at me. I was sure they would put me on the other cross, but they didn't. They beat me, but not enough to kill me. They left me here at Luis's feet as my punishment … as if they knew. I kept expecting someone to come back so I hid, but when they didn't, I came out to watch over him. To keep the birds off." He glanced at Thomas. "They came for his eyes and I threw stones to keep them away. I am so tired now. I haven't been able to sleep for over a day."

Thomas walked to Luis's body, examined the nails holding him to the board. He had to be released. Thomas pulled his dagger, reached high and prised at one of the nails, working it loose. He said nothing, but after a moment Aban came and started to help. They carried Luis's body to a flat area beside a narrow stream.

"Bury him," Thomas said. "And when you're done, say

whatever prayers you know and then go to your family. Dana will need someone to care for her."

"She doesn't need a coward."

Thomas tried not to lose his temper. "You stayed with him. That wasn't the action of a coward. A time will come when you need to fight for those you love, and when it does you will find the courage. Remember Luis's love and hold it in your heart so he never leaves either of you."

Aban began to scrape at the loose soil with his hands. Thomas watched for a while then turned away. Aban would become a man, with or without him. The decision was his … and perhaps Dana's.

Thomas began to walk faster as night began to steal across the land. After a while Kin caught up with him, and he realised the dog was his now and felt none the worse for the responsibility. He stumbled across boulders, followed the river until he staggered into camp, knocking into a man who turned on him, but Thomas felled him with a single blow, ignoring his companions who came after him, following him all the way until he found Usaden.

"Where's Olaf?" Thomas asked.

"Still with them. You do know there are men behind you looking for a fight, don't you?"

"Ignore them."

Usaden raised a shoulder. "If you say so, but perhaps you should tell them."

"Olaf's been gone too long." Thomas pushed past Usaden, heard him catch up, heard the men following him come as well. He considered gathering more of Olaf's men around him but knew it would only trigger a conflict that would come soon enough. Better it came at a time of their own choosing.

"What happened?" asked Usaden, Thomas's agitation finally making him aware something was badly wrong.

"Luis is dead."

"You knew it was a risk."

"He was crucified."

"What about the other one? Dead too?"

"Alive, but they made him watch." Thomas glanced at Usaden. "They were lovers. All three are lovers."

Usaden showed no reaction. Instead he stopped and turned to look at the men who continued to follow. "We're going to have to teach this bunch a lesson."

Thomas glanced behind. Six men, three of them holding weapons. The last time he had looked their hands were empty. His ignoring of them had made them bold.

He glanced around. They stood in clear ground between the leaders' tents and the edge of the camp, but Guerrero's army remained close. Too close.

Thomas turned to Usaden and threw a punch. It caught Usaden on the cheek and rocked his head back, then he was throwing his own punches, except each landed without any power, and Thomas pretended to fight back, relieved Usaden had gleaned his purpose so quickly. He wrapped his arms around Usaden and lifted him from his feet, turned and threw him away. Usaden staggered backward, threw out an arm as if to steady himself, except there was a flash of silver and one of the men following them clutched at his neck and fell to the ground. Usaden spun around as Thomas ran at him, moved at the last moment and Thomas took another man. And then it was over. Six of Mandana's men lay on the ground, dead or dying, and barely a sound had been raised.

"I don't believe they could have captured Olaf without anyone hearing something," said Usaden, breathing normally. "He's not an easy man to subdue."

"Mandana drugged both Jorge and me once. We almost died—should have died. I'm sure he's not forgotten such skills. But if Olaf remains alive he is in their tent. They couldn't risk carrying him out and our men seeing what they have done."

"How many guards went in with them? No more than ten as I recall, so they must have used some kind of drug to subdue him."

"We go in the front way, no subterfuge. I'm relying on you to kill as many as you can while I find Olaf."

"And Guerrero and Mandana?"

"Both are mine. You can wound them, but they must remain alive. Their deaths are mine."

Usaden slowed, stopped, his hand grasping Thomas's sleeve. "It is impossible for the two of us."

"Ten men, plus Guerrero and Mandana? I think not."

"There will be noise. Guerrero's men will come, and everything ends then."

Thomas stared at Usaden. "We have to do something. If Olaf remains alive he may not be so in an hour."

"Agreed." Usaden looked around. He offered a cold smile. "This is it, Thomas. This moment. We cannot wait for them to attack us in the night. It is sooner than I would have liked, but if they have Olaf, now is our only chance to free him."

"You want us to attack them now?"

"The men, yes. You and I will do as you said and free Olaf. We will take a few others with us; we'll need them to carry him out if he's been drugged." Usaden began to run back the way they had come.

Thomas caught up to him where the knot of men they had killed lay and passed by without a glance. Usaden knew Olaf's commander, another Northman by the name of Buri Bolverkesson, who might have been Olaf's twin if he wasn't a third his age. Usaden allowed Thomas to explain the situation.

Thomas expected Buri to raise objections, but none came.

"I had myself begun to worry," he said, his accent even stronger than Olaf's so it made his Arabic near incomprehensible. "Tell me, what is your plan?"

"Mine?"

Buri nodded. "Of course yours. Olaf told me if anything happened to him I was to consider you in command, not me. He says you are clever, and he knows I am not. Though if they have harmed him not a man of them will live."

Thomas glanced at Usaden, who nodded agreement to the silent question.

He told Buri what he wanted.

Thomas and Usaden crouched forty feet from the entrance to Guerrero's tent. Behind them, a dozen of Olaf's best soldiers waited in silence. None of them spoke, waiting for what had been agreed.

From the gathering darkness behind came a shout, sudden and loud, followed by the scream a man makes when a knife is thrust into his belly. It was the signal.

Thomas rose and ran to the tent. There were no guards outside, but as soon as he entered he found two standing within. His sword took the one on his right and he ran on, knowing Usaden would deal with the other. From across the scattered campground came the clashing of swords, the shouts of men. It had started—both the distraction and the final battle.

Thomas pushed through another layer of canvas into a second empty room. He went on, wondering where the other guards were. The sight he witnessed in the third chamber brought him to a halt.

Olaf Torvaldsson lay naked, tied to a wooden frame. Long trails of rope led from his wrists and ankles—the same kind of bindings Thomas had seen on the man dragged behind a horse.

"Keep watch." Thomas moved to the table. He took his knife and sawed through the bindings, but when he was free to do so Olaf didn't move.

Thomas laid a hand on the big man's chest, forcing himself to wait, wait…

He felt Olaf's heartbeat. Felt his chest rise and fall. The man was alive, but still drugged.

Thomas gripped Olaf's jaw and squeezed hard, rocking his head from side to side. Still Olaf showed no sign he felt anything.

"Fetch the others," Thomas said, and Usaden ran from the chamber.

Thomas slapped Olaf across the face, pricked his arm with the tip of his knife, and then he froze as he heard a laugh from behind.

"I knew you would come." Abbot Mandana stood beside his son. Both held swords, Guerrero with a knife in his other hand—the one his father lacked.

"The others will be back soon. A lot of men."

"Oh, I am sorry, Thomas," said Mandana. "I dispatched some of my own to take care of them." He glanced at his son beside him. Thomas wondered how long the two had been working side by side against both al-Andalus and Spain, for he knew that was the truth of it. Mandana had never been taken back into the fold of Fernando's protection, he had only allowed the king to believe so.

From beyond the canvas walls Thomas heard the clash of sword on sword, the bellow of men fighting for their lives. He smiled, knowing Usaden was out there, inflicting mayhem.

Mandana mirrored Thomas's smile, misinterpreting it.

"You have given me fine sport over the years, Thomas Berrington, but it is time for it to end. We have bigger plans now." He glanced at his son. "Hold him, Pedro, while I finish this."

Guerrero grinned and moved forward, light on his feet, all his attention on Thomas, who stepped back. He knew, despite six weeks of good food and hard practice, he was not yet as strong as he had once been.

Guerrero jabbed with his sword, laughing when Thomas jerked away.

"Shall I tell you how your pretty wife squealed when I stuck her? How she called your name? But you were not there to protect her, were you? You abandoned her." Guerrero threw his head back and emitted a piercing scream that turned into raw laughter. "She squealed, just like that. But the laughter was mine, as I am sure you must know."

As Thomas stepped back another pace Lubna's voice came to him, as clear as it had on each rare occasion before.

He lies, she said. *Now, avenge me.*

Something settled through him—a certainty, a calmness, the coldness he had once welcomed in battle and believed lost for good. The cold strength he had always relied upon, for it had never let him down.

Thomas leaned forward, his eyes on Guerrero, who felt the change of power. All at once the man was no longer sure, as if he too had heard Lubna's voice, and if he had it would have been screaming obscenities at him, for Thomas knew she possessed a great many, kept for moments of great danger or great passion. This moment would be passion. Blood-red passion.

He leapt at Guerrero, striking down, planning to cut into his neck, but the man twisted away faster than Thomas expected and his raised sword deflected the blow. He swung around in a vicious response that Thomas barely managed to block.

Thomas stepped back, aware of each ragged breath sharp in his chest.

Guerrero was young, fit, and strong. Perhaps this was the time Thomas would not triumph against another man.

Guerrero came at him, a blow low to the waist, which was easily parried, but the knife in his left hand came in hard and Thomas felt a sharp punch to his side and staggered away to discover Mandana beside him.

He glanced to where Olaf lay, no longer comatose, his hand reaching out, and Thomas shouted, "No—he is mine!"

Guerrero darted to one side, turning to protect himself from behind.

Thomas turned to Mandana as Olaf closed a hand around Guerrero's wrist, stopping his escape. Guerrero slashed out with the knife in his other hand, but only succeeded in allowing Olaf to clasp his other wrist.

Olaf turned his head, shaking the remnants of confusion from it.

"Kill him, and be quick about it."

Thomas didn't know which of them he meant, the decision taken from him as Mandana came at him.

He jerked to one side, the sword missing him by a finger-width. Mandana came again, as relentless as he had always been. But he was older now, sicker, and Thomas spun around and his knife took him in the neck.

Mandana went to his knees, the stump of his lost hand rising to the spray of blood. Thomas put his foot on his chest and pushed him backward, stood over him, watching as the man died. Mandana's eyes remained open, and Thomas left them that way. Let him gaze on the fires of hell, for that is what he was bound for.

Thomas let out a bellow of anger and frustration. *This was not enough!*

He felt no sense of vengeance, no sense of justice. How

could he? This man had stalked his life for years. His son had killed Lubna, the one who could never be replaced. There should be more to his death than this sense of emptiness.

"I see you're getting back your old skill." Olaf tried to sit up and failed, falling back to the table. As he did so Guerrero broke free of his grip.

Thomas advanced, but Guerrero held his sword across Olaf's neck, drawing a narrow line of blood, and Thomas stopped. They stared at each other with raw hatred. Thomas knew if he attacked now, Olaf would die. Guerrero knew if he killed Olaf, Thomas would kill him in turn. Thomas wondered which of them would triumph. Guerrero was not old like his father. He was young, strong, and vicious.

The decision was taken from him when Usaden burst into the chamber. In an instant, Guerrero turned and ran. Thomas started after, but Olaf gripped his wrist as he had gripped Guerrero's and used the contact to raise himself up.

"Let him run, we will find him again. Find me an axe, or a sword—there is a battle raging out there, and it needs to be finished."

CHAPTER THIRTY-FIVE

"How many men did we lose?" Thomas had found a stool from somewhere and perched on it, unsure he was capable of standing. He had helped Olaf from the slab he had been tied to, the big general regaining his wits rapidly. Outside, Olaf had found a sword and waded into the battle, still not fully recovered, but even a weakened Olaf was more than a match for any other man. It was a bizarre sight, because he had not bothered to dress, but no doubt this worked to his advantage. He strode naked into battle, a vision enough to weaken any opponent—even more so as his body turned red with the blood of his enemies.

Now he sat cross-legged beside Thomas, dressed once more. He looked tired.

"A hundred," he said.

"Too many."

"Their men fought better than I expected, but every one of mine came willingly. They were good men." Olaf scrubbed a hand across his face, but it did nothing to clear the blood spatter. He raised his gaze to meet Thomas's. "This is what I do, Thomas. What men do. We fight. Some live. Others die."

"Even for a master you don't respect?" He was talking of Muhammed, and Olaf would know it.

Olaf stared at him, and after a while Thomas looked away, unable to hold his gaze. Olaf's loyalty remained unshakeable, as permanent as the mountains that surrounded them. It defined him, and always would. Even an undeserving master such as Muhammed was offered all his allegiance. Just as he gave the same to Thomas, more a son to him than he had ever been to his own father.

Around them prisoners were being corralled into groups, archers standing guard alongside swordsmen. Most of the captives were those taken from their homes, their spirit broken first by Guerrero and Mandana, then again by the battle they had endured. Many had been slain, Olaf's men unable to differentiate between enemies in the wild fighting. Some of the survivors had requested leave to return to their families. Each was questioned to ensure they were not merely Guerrero's men pretending to be something else, then corralled into a guarded group. Not that Guerrero's soldiers could ever pretend to be these broken souls. They differed in every way possible, their arrogance visible through each lie they told. Exactly what would happen to them Thomas didn't know. Gharnatah wasn't able to hold hundreds of prisoners. He knew their fate was up to Muhammed—which meant every man would be executed as a lesson to discourage others. A lesson to who was less clear, but Thomas had no argument because he knew if the men were returned to Spain they would have to be fought again in the future. A future pushed a little further away by this battle, but still the threat remained. Had Guerrero and Mandana succeeded, then Muhammed would be captive or dead, and Gharnatah would have fallen to Spain. This small battle might offer al-Andalus another year, perhaps two, but the end could not be avoided.

"You will go after him?" Olaf asked, and Thomas turned back to him.

"Of course."

"And kill him." It wasn't a question.

"As slowly as I can."

"Good. Take Usaden with you. I can spare a few other men if you want, but I need to keep most to deal with these maniacs I have on my hands."

"Use the captives," Thomas said. "Use the men taken from their homes. Arm them and let them guard the prisoners." Thomas glanced across the battlefield. "In fact…"

Olaf waited, then said, "In fact what?"

"Leave their fate up to those men. Take your own troops and return to Gharnatah. Leave the fate of those left alive up to those they captured and tortured."

Olaf stared at Thomas. "You do know what that means, don't you?"

"What would they have done to us?"

"It is not chivalrous."

"Fuck chivalry!" Thomas saw Olaf wince, but he did not disagree, not this time. "These are Guerrero's men. You have seen what they are capable of. They are worse than scorpions and can never be trusted. I thank you, but I will go after him alone. You must return to Gharnatah. What becomes of those we leave here is in the hands of the Gods."

Olaf gave a brief smile. "My Gods or yours?"

"I have no Gods, so they had better be yours." Thomas knew Olaf's Gods could be harsh. He rose, tried to stretch the ache from his bones and failed. He knew he should sleep, but every moment he stayed in the valley offered Guerrero more chance of escape.

Thomas offered a hand to Olaf, who took it and allowed him to pretend to help him to his feet. The two embraced. Thomas kissed Olaf on the cheek then turned away. He was passing a group of the captives when he heard a voice call out loudly, "Aban!"

Thomas turned, looking for the youth, saw him walking with his head down.

"Aban, here!" The cry came again, and this time the youth looked up.

Thomas watched as a recognition came to him and he began to run. Thomas started forward as well, seeing one of the guard turn, sword raised.

"Wait, he's with me," Thomas shouted.

Aban stood, breathing hard, a tall man the other side of the guards facing him, and as Thomas watched their similarity sent a jolt through him and he stepped closer.

"Biorn?" The man turned his gaze from Aban to Thomas. "You are husband to Jamila?"

The man frowned. Aban came closer and Thomas caught his arm. He led the youth through the line of guards, most of who knew Thomas, until he stood in front of his father. For a moment nothing happened as both stared at each other, then the older embraced the younger, clutching his head to his shoulder.

Biorn lifted his gaze until his eyes met Thomas's. "You know my wife?" He asked.

"Jamila lives. Take Aban and go to Gharnatah. Ask for the house of Thomas Berrington and someone will tell you the way. You will find your wife there." Thomas turned to the line of guards. "This man can go free." He waited two men moved apart.

Biorn needed no other encouragement. He gripped his son's arm and walked through the space made for them. When he reached Thomas he stopped. "What is my son doing here, and how do you know him?"

"Aban will explain it all. Take him, and may your God be with you."

Biorn nodded, grinned. "Gods. We Northmen have a surfeit of Gods."

As they turned away Thomas called after him. "If you get bored ask for Olaf Torvaldsson. Tell him I sent you." He raised a hand and turned away. He had reached the edge of the battlefield when the sound of raised voices caused him to turn back.

A white stallion rode down the pass they had followed to reach this place, and at first Thomas had the illogical idea it was Muhammed come to witness their victory, except he knew the Sultan would never risk himself in such a way.

Thomas narrowed his eyes, unable to believe who sat astride the horse when he finally made the figure out.

They had left Jorge in the house on the Albayzin. He had recovered, but needed a month or two more rest before he was fully healed. He was told to help the women, to protect them even though they all knew it was no more than a pretence at work. And now here he was, dressed as only Jorge could in flowing silks, sitting tall in the saddle, a sword sheathed at his side.

He watched as Jorge reached Olaf and leaned down to talk. When he looked up, Thomas saw his eyes scan the chaos of men in search of him. For a moment Thomas stayed stock still, resisting the urge to raise his arm, unsure why he wanted to remain hidden in the crowd. Then he smiled and started back the way he had come, knowing he could not turn his back on Jorge, of all men. Were they not brothers, after all? Were they not more than brothers?

Usaden came with them in the end, because neither Thomas nor Jorge were trackers. It was one more skill Usaden possessed, among a myriad of others. Thomas believed Olaf wanted to accompany them too, but duty forced him to remain with his men. He had finally agreed to Thomas's suggestion. Guerrero's captured soldiers remained in the valley, together with the remnant of those they had stolen from their homes—two hundred men watched by five hundred. Thomas knew it had been a risky strategy, that if the captives managed to fight and recover their weapons the balance of power would turn in an instant. He also knew those who had been forced into the company needed to achieve some kind of resolution, but as they rode into the foothills of the Sholayr he dismissed them from his mind. There was only one person he wanted to think about: Pedro Guerrero … and his death.

"There are at least eight of them," said Usaden, rising from where he knelt to examine the remnants of a small fire. "About six hours ahead, and they think they are safe. Why else would they have camped and made a fire?" He grasped the pommel of his horse's saddle and pulled himself up.

"Which direction?" Thomas asked.

Usaden encouraged his horse into a walk and circled the place Guerrero and his men had made camp. He stopped at the far side, not bothering with any words. When he started to move off, Thomas urged his own mount after him. Kin ran ahead, passing both of them, head to the ground as he tracked a memory of scent.

"What are you going to do when you catch them?" asked Jorge.

Thomas suspected the journey must be taking a toll after his injury, but if it was Jorge refused to show it. Thomas thought it was a pleasant change not to have him complaining all the time, but didn't expect it to last.

"Kill him, of course." Thomas barely acknowledged there would be others with Guerrero. They would have to

305

be killed too, of course, but he gave them less thought than a fly that buzzed around his head.

"So you will be judge and executioner both?"

"The judgement is already made, you know that. Now I am merely executioner."

"How will you do it?"

Thomas smiled. Jorge had accepted the decision and moved on. It seemed they were all changing.

"Mandana died too quickly. I will not make the same mistake again."

"You may have to if he puts up a fight. The heat of battle, all that manly pride ... He's not old like his father. The man can fight."

"As can I. I will cut him piece by piece. I, of all men, know how to cut a man and still keep him alive. I will kill him in the end, but he must suffer first, in payment for his sins ... his *sin*."

"Remind me never to cross you," said Jorge.

"I would never kill you," Thomas said. "Or if I had to, I would do it quickly."

"I'm glad to see you still love me."

Thomas urged his horse into a canter, wanting to avoid further conversation. He knew Jorge was trying to soften his resolve, to restore some measure of humanity in him, and he didn't welcome such. Later, when the deed was done and Guerrero was dead, he would let Jorge soften him as much as he wanted, but not yet. Later, he would allow himself to feel again. He would embrace his pain and grief, not run from it as he had done after Malaka. Thomas knew he had never truly grieved for Lubna. Her death had driven him into these mountains, but all he had done was run from the grief, and he knew he needed to embrace it. He wanted to remember the Lubna he would always love in a way she deserved.

He caught up with Usaden as they crested a low rise,

and both pulled their horses to a stop. A mile distant, on the far side of a steep valley, nine men on horseback followed a twisting track up a hillside clearly lit by the rays of the setting sun. Guerrero was plain to see even over the distance, his white robes now dusty and stained, but still unmistakable.

Thomas glanced at the sky, trying to judge how many hours of daylight remained, and was disappointed.

"They won't make camp tonight," said Usaden. "They can see us as well as we can see them. I suspect they have known we are coming for a while."

"Then we follow through the night," said Thomas. He knew there would be no moon, only stars to light their way. He had travelled in such darkness before, and no doubt would do so again if he lived. "We should ride hard and catch them as soon as we can."

"I would be better to let them draw ahead, to believe they are losing us. Approach too fast and they'll turn and fight. Better we make them run and tire."

"Nine against us? Nine against you?"

"Guerrero will have only the best with him. I saw how the others fought— the ones he had trained, the ones loyal to him. Nine against you and I would normally cause me no concern, but this will be a hard fight."

"Nine against three," said Jorge, who had caught up with them and overheard the conversation.

"That is what I meant, of course," said Usaden, but a glance at Thomas told otherwise.

Thomas wished Jorge wasn't here for this. Not for what had to come next. Even so he took comfort in his presence, in the friendship that had brought him here to be at his side.

He sat and watched the figures across the valley. They didn't stop, didn't slow—always climbing, trying to flee from a danger they must know couldn't be escaped. He

307

saw Guerrero slow and turn, his figure tiny, unrecognisable other than by his robes. The man sat, raised a hand to shield his eyes and looked back at them. To Thomas, it was as if a connection was forged across the distance, linking them.

He raised an arm in salute, pleased when Guerrero turned and bullied his horse into motion.

Soon, Thomas promised himself.

They descended into the valley, crossed a dry riverbed and began to climb the far side. Guerrero and his men had disappeared some time ago, and already the deep valley was falling into an early dusk. The snow-capped peaks of the Sholayr drew the last rays of the sun, but soon they too would fall into darkness.

When it came the ambush was unexpected and sudden. Kin was first to show any sign danger was close as he gave a sharp bark that caused Usaden to pull his horse up short. He kicked with his heels, making the animal back up just as a boulder came crashing down from the right to roll directly over the place he had been a moment before. Thomas put his hand on the hilt of his sword, expecting more rocks. Instead, men came from their left, close already, weapons drawn. They made no sound, not needing to cry or yell like some did. These men were the best of the best, otherwise Guerrero would not have brought them.

Thomas drew his sword and slashed at the nearest man, barely aware of the clash of metal on metal as Usaden set about counter-attacking. Thomas's strike was deflected, and he knew this fight would be vicious, with no certainty of victory. He struck again then dropped from his saddle. The height was not helping him, and he slapped the animal's rump and set it cantering away. He glimpsed Jorge still mounted, his own sword drawn, but hanging back from the growing confusion.

Three men worked together, two coming directly at Thomas, the third from the side. Thomas deflected the blade of the first then twisted away to avoid the second. All was wrapped in shadowed gloom, with only the clash of blade on blade until a man screamed as Usaden struck him.

Ice filled Thomas, the familiar cold whose return he welcomed. He let it flow through him, giving him strength, making him invulnerable. And with it he became a dervish, whirling, striking out. He caught a man high on his face and opened the cheek, and when instinct caused him to raise his hand Thomas thrust a knife into his chest. He turned away, raising his sword to stop a killing blow, then ducked beneath it and slammed the knife in his left hand through ribs to pierce the heart. Kin snarled and barked among the melee, biting at their enemies, avoiding their strikes. Thomas had no idea how Usaden fared, for there was no time to consider anyone else. Thomas had killed two, yet still three men confronted him, and he shook his head as though to clear the confusion. This time all three came at him together, barely any space between them. Thomas struck a fearsome blow, aimed at the man on his right, but it was parried, needing both the man's sword and his companion's to deflect it. The block sent a shock along Thomas's arm, numbing him for a moment, and in that instant the third man thrust his blade forward. Thomas turned, but was too slow. He felt a searing burn in his side, and knew he had been struck.

The three took a moment, their eyes watching to judge his injuries, and Thomas took a breath as he tried to work out how bad the wound was. Bad enough, he decided. He wouldn't die of the injury, but it was slowing him, and he knew that three men were too many for him in this condition. Even so, there was nothing he could do but fight or die, so he steeled himself as his mind played through the moves he would make. He stepped forward and struck, the blow parried easily. The man followed up, coming forward fast, and Thomas stepped back, stepped again and crashed into a figure coming the other way. He cried out and tried to use his sword. Jorge came past him, robes dancing around his slim body, his own sword flashing. Jorge danced death upon Thomas's adversaries. He killed one instantly, turned and caught another across the arm, causing him to drop his sword. Thomas followed Jorge, killing the injured man, then they both struck at the last, their swords impaling him at the same moment—one on the right, the other on the left. The soldier's legs went, and he fell in a tangled heap at their feet.

Thomas lowered his head, breathing hard. "Where the hell did you learn to fight like that?"

"I thought you looked as if you needed some help. Usaden taught me a few tricks when he was training Will."

At mention of the name, Thomas turned to see Usaden drawing his sword from the body of the last man. Four men lay at his feet, arms and legs tangled together, so keen had they been to kill Usaden.

"Where is he?" Thomas said. "I told you he is mine!"

"He's not here." Usaden used his foot to push at one of the men to reveal a face, did the same to another. Thomas could see Guerrero wasn't among the fallen.

He looked along the slope, but everything was darkness. His enemy might be a hundred paces away or a thousand, and he would never know.

He pressed against his side, cursing the pain. When he drew his hand away it was wet with blood, black in the darkness. And then the darkness came closer and Thomas fell to the ground before Jorge could reach him.

CHAPTER THIRTY-SIX

The sky was dark when Thomas woke, but a fire sent flickering light dancing across the surrounding boulders. Thomas rolled his head to one side and saw nothing, rolled it to the other and found Jorge sitting beside Usaden. Both were leaning toward the fire where an arrangement of sticks held a rabbit, which looked close to being ready. Kin lay near the fire, watching the cooking meat.

Thomas tried to sit up but collapsed back in pain, his groan bringing Usaden across. He placed a hand on Thomas's chest and pushed him to the ground.

"The wound is not serious, but you need to rest. I will bring you food when it is ready. Jorge bound your wound. He says he learned how by watching you do the same for him."

"Who judged it not serious, you or Jorge?"

Usaden almost smiled. "I did."

Thomas nodded, satisfied. He lay on the bed of grasses and fine branches that had been fashioned for him, knowing it would also have been Usaden who built the bed. He watched him return to the fire, saw Jorge lift his eyes to look at him, but his expression was unusually serious. Killing a man could do that, but Thomas knew without Jorge's intervention it would be he who was dead. Thomas closed his eyes, trying to ignore the other fire—the one that burned in his side. It was only pain, and he was used to such.

He woke when Usaden came to bring him the best cut of meat from the rabbit. Thomas tried to sit up and failed, then Jorge arrived. He sat behind and wrapped strong arms around his chest. As Thomas sat upright Jorge wriggled closer, his legs gripping his waist, arms providing more support. Thomas leaned against the warmth of the man holding him and accepted the meat that Usaden fed to him, piece by piece. When it was done Jorge eased him down once more, but instead of leaving he lay close, once more his arms about Thomas to protect him from the cold. After a while Kin came and lay on his other side, the rank smell of his coat a comfort.

"Guerrero?" Thomas asked as he lay cocooned.

"Gone ahead. Usaden says he can pick up his trail, and that dog of yours has been running off and coming back whining—I'm convinced he knows where the devil is. Don't worry, he won't escape. He will be yours to kill as soon as you are recovered."

"That will take too long."

"Then I will kill him for you," said Usaden.

"No."

Usaden watched, waiting. "I loved Lubna too," he said eventually. "Not as you loved her, but I loved her in my own way. As did everyone who knew her."

"Not everyone."

"No, you are right. But know you do not have to do this on your own. Guerrero will be just as dead by your sword or mine."

"It must be mine," Thomas said, and Usaden nodded, the matter settled.

It was two days before Thomas could sit unaided, three before he could stand, four before he managed to pull himself astride his horse. Each day Usaden had roamed wide, Kin at his side, until one day he came back to their camp in the evening to say he had located Guerrero. The man was on foot now, climbing ever higher, as if the mountains might protect him.

"Why isn't he heading for Spanish land?" asked Jorge.

"He knows he wouldn't be safe there either." Thomas said, "Not after what they have done. He thinks if he can cross the Sholayr I might die in my pursuit."

"So he flees ever higher," said Usaden. "What will you do if he crosses the highest peaks?"

"He won't make it that far. There is deep snow, ice chasms—it is impossible for a man to climb so high. Even him." Thomas shifted, easing the ache in his side, but it was an ache now rather than a flame, and he knew he was almost healed enough for what he had to do. "Tomorrow, Jorge and I will pursue him. I want you to return to Gharnatah and protect the household." Thomas met Usaden's eyes. "It is your household too now, is it not?"

"If it will have me."

"Of course it will have you." Thomas smiled. "Besides, you have trained my son too well already. If I try to eject you I believe he would fight me, and probably win."

"Eight more years and yes, he will be good enough," said Usaden.

Thomas expected more resistance, but in the cold dawn Usaden embraced each of them, taking care not to apply pressure to Thomas's wound, mounted his horse and rode away without a backward glance.

"Maybe we should be taking him with us. Guerrero is dangerous."

Thomas shook his head. "You and me, as it should be.

The two men Lubna loved most, and who loved her in return."

"Don't mention that to Belia, even if it is true."

"She already knows." Thomas kicked his heels and the horse started a slow walk, which was fast enough for now —even the steady swaying pulled at the healing skin in his side. Kin loped from side to side of the track, never leaving their sight.

Late in the afternoon Jorge said, "I know this place."

Thomas looked around. They were on a shallow slope, trees to their right, rocks ahead, and beyond lay the looming bulk of the Sholayr.

"How can you tell? It doesn't look any different to a dozen places we have ridden through already."

"I passed here when I was searching for you." Jorge pointed to one side. "Jamila's village lies that way, half a day's ride. It is where I bought the bread we ate."

"Stale bread."

"Well I'm sorry. Next time you can bake your own."

"There will be no next time."

An hour later, just as the last light of the sun was fading, they came across the remains of a small fire. Thomas dismounted and ran his fingers across the charcoal traces. They were cold, but dry.

"He camped here last night," he said. "I thought we might be in danger of losing him but he's fleeing in a straight line, directly toward the mountains." He glanced up at Jorge, still astride his own horse. "How do you feel about riding through the night?"

"I'm looking forward to the adventure. Is there going to be moonlight?"

"You tell me. Was there last night?"

"I was asleep last night."

"There will be a new moon, but it won't rise for a few hours yet. We will travel as far as we can while there remains light in the sky, then rest until it rises." Thomas felt an excitement, a sense of resolution building. Until this moment catching Guerrero had been little more than a dream. Now it was becoming reality. He climbed to his feet and pulled himself into the saddle, grimacing at the pain in his side.

As they started climbing once more, he began to consider how he would take Guerrero's life.

When Jorge's horse stumbled in the darkness, almost tipping him onto jagged rocks, Thomas called a halt until the moon rose. He eased himself to the ground and looked around for somewhere comfortable to rest while they waited. Looking upward toward the high peaks, a glimmer of something caught at the edge of his vision, visible only because the night had become so dark. Thomas narrowed his eyes and stared at the spot, but the longer he looked the less sure he was that he had seen anything at all. He looked east, but although a faint illumination showed where the moon would rise it offered no help yet.

"I think someone has a fire up there," said Jorge, pointing. "I thought I was mistaken, but if you don't look directly you can see it."

"Someone?" Thomas said.

Jorge's teeth showed white in the dark. "Guerrero, then. There can be no other idiots out here but you and me and him. You know where he has gone, don't you?"

"How would I know that? I don't even know where we are."

"You must have come this way before."

"Must I?"

"That sorry excuse for a farmhouse you were living in

when I found you is close to here. He's made his camp there, just as you did."

Thomas looked around, back to where a tiny flicker of red showed now he knew where to look, and laughed. "Well, at least he'll be good and cold. Perhaps he'll freeze to death and deny me satisfaction."

"You lived through being here—the Gods know how, but you did. You're a hard man to kill, Thomas Berrington."

"Not as hard as I once was."

When the moon rose Thomas made the decision to stay where they were. He had an idea in mind. He also wanted to draw out the moment before he encountered Guerrero. It would make the killing of him all the sweeter.

When they reached the hut the following morning, Guerrero was no longer sheltering there, but his fire remained warm. A fresh dusting of snow showed the direction he had fled in.

"You found me here once," Thomas said to Jorge. "Could you do it again, do you think?"

"Why would I want to do such a stupid thing?"

"But you know the way."

Jorge seemed to think about it for a moment before nodding. "I expect so."

"Good. So you can find your way home. Take Kin with you if he will follow. I go on from here on my own."

Jorge shook his head. "You said the two of us."

"I did, but I've changed my mind. This is between me and Guerrero, nobody else. And as much as I love you, I want you back in Gharnatah lying beside your beautiful woman, where you will be safe."

The argument lasted an hour. All the while Thomas was aware Guerrero was moving further and further away. He believed Jorge only agreed in the end because he, too, didn't want the man to escape justice.

Thomas watched him pick his way down the hillside, a second horse held loosely beside the one he was mounted on. Kin loped beside him but kept stopping to look back. The land rose precipitously from here and Thomas knew he would have to go the rest of the way on foot.

He waited until Jorge disappeared from sight. One last turn, one last wave, and then he was gone. Thomas drew a deep breath, the icy air sharp in his lungs. Then he turned and started to climb after Pedro Guerrero.

CHAPTER THIRTY-SEVEN

The entire world was white. An almost constant cloud hid all but the ground directly ahead. When it occasionally parted, Thomas made out the highest peaks, some jagged, others broad. It was a world of ice. A world of pain. Pedro Guerrero's footprints showed clearly. He had abandoned his horse the day before, finally aware it was slowing him. His footsteps wandered from side to side. In one spot there was a flattened area where he had fallen, or simply collapsed.

The air was thin. Cold. Thomas had come to these high places at one time to die, but now he welcomed the cold as a friend.

The snow lay unfathomably deep, and at times Thomas knew he was walking where the wind had fashioned it into curling ledges, where nothing lay beneath but a thousand feet of clear air. There was nowhere else he could go, for Guerrero's trail led him onward.

He reached the man on the third day after leaving the hut, the third day after sending Jorge and Kin to the warmth of lower ground—except the dog had returned, staying close to him now.

Guerrero sat awkwardly, his robe pulled tight around him, the hood almost obscuring his face.

"I thought you would reach me sooner than this," he said.

"I was enjoying the journey too much to rush."

"Will we fight?"

"That depends on you."

"Oh, I am more than happy to kill you."

Thomas laughed. "Fight it will be, then." His fingers twitched, but he forced them to remain at his side. He looked around and then sat, wriggling to fashion a surprisingly comfortable seat in the snow. "Can I ask you something?"

Guerrero smiled, but there was nothing of humanity in it. "If you must. As long as you expect no answer."

"When did you learn Mandana was your father? I have known him several years now, and he never mentioned a son."

Guerrero stared out into space, into the thin air where snow swirled and blew, revealing an occasional glimpse of the distant sea and its warmth. Thomas had reconciled himself to killing the man without an answer when he spoke.

"We are to talk like civilized men, are we? Very well, then. My father was an Abbot, as you know—a man of God, like myself. He was not meant to lie with a woman."

"But you had a wife." Thomas saw the curl of anger cross Guerrero's face and knew he still blamed Thomas for her death.

"I am no Abbot."

"And your mother?"

A shake of the head. "I don't know—no-one. Some woman he lay with and set a seed inside." Guerrero's breath plumed, drifted slowly around his head. "I didn't know my father until I had thirteen years."

You found your father at the same age I lost my own, Thomas thought. He knew Guerrero wanted to tell his story, and that he wanted to hear it. Wanted to hear what had brought him to this place, this time, to die. For die he would.

"And before?"

"I was in the care of nuns at first, then later, monks. Not much difference between them—except the nuns beat me more often and the monks beat me harder."

"Your mother?"

"I told you, I don't know, but I suspect she was most likely a nun too."

"And your father didn't know who she was?"

Guerrero's gaze returned from the swirling snow. "He must have, because he told me he placed me with those who were meant to care for me and didn't, but he never told me who she was. I used to dream she was some Duquessa fallen to a man who ravished her. I used to dream they might be true lovers, their love thwarted. But I expect the truth was far more mundane." A smile touched his lips, gone almost as soon as it came. "The kind of dreams a boy has. It must have been someone close for him to know she was with child, but it could have been anyone."

"What happened at thirteen?"

"He came for me. Oh, he was magnificent then, at the height of his powers, before he fell from favour."

"Except Fernando took him back," Thomas said.

"Then Fernando is a fool."

"You have no argument from me. Did you love him, your father?"

"What do you think? Do you love yours?"

Thomas gave a brief shake of his head. He wondered how long he would let the conversation continue. He didn't want to begin to feel sorry for Guerrero, and it was starting to feel as if he might.

"No, of course not," said Guerrero. "Mine was a harsh master. He sent me to fight, told me it would make a man of me. In France at first, and then later for Spain—but never alongside him, no matter how many times I asked. Not until Malaga did he allow me close." Guerrero smiled, a genuine smile this time, and a cunning settled in his eyes. "And you know how that ended, don't you."

Thomas struck out. Not a killing blow, the tip of his knife opening Guerrero's cheek. The man reacted in an instant, his own weapon flashing from beneath his robe. Thomas had thought him exhausted, but it had been nothing but a ploy. Guerrero leaped at him, and they went rolling through the snow together. Kin barked and tried to bite Guerrero, but they were too tangled together.

Thomas kicked out, landed a lucky blow, and Guerrero rolled away toward the edge of the snow ledge. Thomas watched, waiting for it to give way, but Guerrero came to a halt too soon and rose to his feet.

"So, we fight to the death, do we?"

"It was always going to be thus," Thomas said, and Guerrero nodded.

"I should have fucked her before I gutted her," he said. "Let her find out what a real man was like between her legs before she died."

Thomas let the taunt flow past him—beyond anger, at one with the ice. He glanced at the jagged peaks, black between banks of snow, and waited. There was nowhere for Guerrero to go. Behind lay an endless drop. Ahead stood Thomas. He knew if it was him, he would choose the drop.

Guerrero was not him. He attacked, hands a blur, sword and knife flashing.

Thomas stepped aside, the world seen in perfect clarity,

the other man moving as if through water, and Thomas picked a spot and thrust his arm out.

Guerrero stopped and looked down, confusion on his face.

"You can't," he said.

"I did."

"Nobody has ever bested me." Guerrero sank to his knees, his blood already colouring the snow around him.

"There is always someone. One day I will be bested, but not today—and not here." Thomas cocked his head to one side. "Does it hurt?"

Guerrero appeared to need a moment to think about it before shaking his head.

"That is a shame. But one I can remedy."

Thomas walked toward Guerrero, the human anatomy held in his mind—the nerve points, the soft places—and then he stopped, because Lubna spoke to him for the very last time, though he did not know that then.

No, my love—do not become like him.

Guerrero rested his brow against the snow.

Kin came and stood beside Thomas, who started to shiver hard.

Guerrero surged to his feet, bellowing, launching himself at Thomas. Who met him with his sword. He held him up as he felt the life leave him, then lay him in the snow and walked away.

It was not enough.

He screamed at the sky, only to hear his cries echo back over and over as the mountain caught and returned them.

Not nearly enough.

He walked, not knowing in which direction, not knowing if he was going home or going to his death. He walked until his legs gave out and he fell on his face. He would have stayed there, smothering in the snow, if not for Kin, who nipped at his shoulder.

Thomas rolled onto his back.

He pulled his robe tight around himself, then loosened it and made a noise with his tongue. Kin came and lay against him, and Thomas wrapped the robe around them both and closed his eyes.

He waited for Lubna to come for him.

When Jorge passed a body half-buried in snow he thought at first it must be Thomas and knelt, scraping snow off the face until he recognised Guerrero.

When he did find Thomas he believed him equally as dead, his body wrapped in a grey cloak, the hood covering his face. Snow had fallen so it almost obscured the fact a man lay there at all. Only when Jorge knelt and shook Thomas, then shook him harder still, did a curse emerge from beneath the robe, followed a moment later by a growl as Kin's head emerged, and Jorge laughed and sat hard in the cold snow.

HISTORICAL NOTE

This will be short.

Although events continued in the rest of Spain, the period after the fall of Malaga was one of recovery and rebuilding for the Spanish monarchs following the unexpected resistance encountered in taking that city. Instead of advancing on Granada, as had perhaps been originally planned, they took some time to consider their next move.

This story is less about the history of 1488 and more about Thomas's revenge. As such most of the events related in these pages are entirely fictional. They did not happen ... but they could have.

Abu-Abdullah, Muhammed XIII (Boabdil to the Spanish), knew he was vulnerable, but is claimed to have made a pact with Spain years before when he was captured and held for almost a year. In many accounts it is considered that for most of his short rule he was working for the Spanish, not al-Andalus. This pact influences the central section of The Promise of Pain, and explains Guerrero and his father Mandana's plotting.

Two more Thomas Berrington novels remain before

the fall of Granada on January 1st 1492, and there is a great deal of history to cover in those books.

If you have enjoyed the adventures of Thomas and Jorge fear not. The fall of Granada will not see the end of their tale, but there will be a short hiatus before they return to England in the company of Catherine of Aragon. Just imagine—Jorge in the English Shires. Oh my...

ABOUT THE AUTHOR

David Penny is the author of the Thomas Berrington Historical Mysteries set in Moorish Spain at the end of the 15th Century. He is currently working on the next book in the series.

Find out more about David Penny
www.davidpennywriting.com

Printed in Great Britain
by Amazon